ILLUSIONS OF DEATH

ALEXA ASTON

OLIVER
HEBER
BOOKS

PUBLISHER'S NOTE: This is a work of fiction. Names, characters, places, and incidents either are the product of the author's imagination or are used fictitiously. Any resemblance to actual persons, living or dead, business establishments, events, or locales is entirely coincidental.

COPYRIGHT © Alexa Aston

Published by Oliver-Heber Books

0 9 8 7 6 5 4 3 2 1

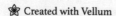 Created with Vellum

PROLOGUE

He placed the last of the wet dirt on top of the second grave. Smoothed it with the back of the shovel. Reached for the collection of branches and rocks and leaves that he'd gathered before he began digging. He tossed them haphazardly over his handiwork and stepped back to survey the ground. Perfect. Anyone venturing off the Appalachian Trail this far would have no idea what rested beneath the soil.

If only people knew how much he'd accomplished in his killing time.

He took pride in his handiwork. Years of honing his skill had made him a master of death. He'd started years ago in his teens, picking up hitchhikers. Perfecting the art of torture. Perfecting his knife skills. Dismembering the specimens. Learning how to dispose of body parts.

Other hunts followed. Sometimes, a single specimen. Sometimes, a group. He'd especially enjoyed seeing Atlanta frantic during his series of child abductions and murders. He thought it pure genius to focus on the little ones of public servants. He'd taken the kids of a fireman. A city council member. The school superintendent's daughter. A cop's twins. And the pièce de résistance? The mayor's grandson.

His latest specimen gathering consisted of high-end prostitutes. The Chattahoochee National Forest had provided cover for this most recent hunt. Its miles of wilderness proved the ideal disposal area. He'd witnessed the arrival of spring as the area greened up. Watched it blossom into its summer loveliness. Seen the explosion of fall colors come vividly to life as he buried his precious specimens.

But he was at the end of this cycle of murders. He refused to tramp through isolated areas during winter snow. Last night's kill would be the final in this series.

He chuckled to himself. Plus, the unexpected bonus.

The lone hiker appeared just before dusk settled. He'd already made camp. Set up his tent. The specimen, bound and gagged, waited for him inside. The Rohypnol's effects had faded. She would know everything that happened from this point on.

Then the kid arrived, sporting a backpack almost bigger than he was. Made himself at home. Admitted he was lost.

They chatted over bottled water and protein bars. The teen spilled that he was traipsing around during Thanksgiving break in hopes of having some majestic, eye-opening experience that would be good enough to write about in his upcoming college admission essay. Everyone these days had come from another country and had to learn English, only to land at the top of their graduating class. Or they'd come from divorced parents and had to live out of a car when the custodial parent was laid off and couldn't find work. Or they volunteered from everything to food banks to homeless shelters and were homecoming queen and Most Likely to Succeed.

All his classmates had a story to write about. Except for him. He came from a middle-class family that had never struggled. The boy had decent grades. Had made National

Honor Society. Was vice president of the chess club. That was his undistinguished resume. He was looking for something life-changing that he could write about.

He'd certainly experienced it. Of course, the kid changed from the living into the dead. Over many hours. As had the whore.

At least the kid wouldn't be put through the agony of writing that essay. Or being rejected by his top choices and settling for community college and a mundane life. If you thought about it, he'd actually done the teen a favor.

He returned to the campsite as the rain slacked off to a drizzle. Packed up. He pulled his keys from his pocket. Noticed the rain had stopped. The sky lightened.

And then he saw it. A rainbow in the sky.

Of course. That was it.

Just as God placed the rainbow in the sky as a promise to Noah that He would never flood the earth again, He'd generously gifted him with a new idea.

His next mission would be served as The Rainbow Killer.

Thoughts raced in his head as he planned a new series of murders to commit. The specimens would share nothing in common, making him impossible to catch. But every murder would end in spectacular colors. In hues of the rainbow.

Confidence pulsated through him. This could be his claim to fame. A lasting legacy.

He couldn't wait to begin.

1

Karlyn Campbell entered her publisher's New York office building in high spirits. She'd finished her sixth Matt Collins book and considered it the best of the series. She couldn't wait to hand the flash drive to her agent.

On top of that, she'd come up with a terrific idea for another stand-alone suspense novel while jogging this morning in Central Park. She raced home and captured as much as she could before showering in time to make her appointment with Alicia.

All while wondering when Mario would turn up.

He hadn't come home last night—or the past two nights. She'd forgiven one slip-up six months after their honeymoon. Then brushed aside another. And another. But she refused to turn a blind eye anymore. If Mario couldn't keep it zipped up, the marriage was over. She already carried them financially and couldn't keep doing it alone emotionally. At least she could always find escape in her writing. Killing people on the page released real-life demons.

Karlyn pressed the button for twelve and The Lindon Agency. She remembered her first ride up over ten years ago, thrilled that she'd connected with an agent who believed she had talent. Over time, Alicia Lindon had grown into a close friend as well as her representative in the publishing world. She'd pushed Karlyn after three years from romance into romantic suspense, wanting her client to stretch her creative muscle.

The move paid off. Her novels regularly debuted in top ten lists. The increase in sales gave Karlyn the boost she needed to try her hand at straight suspense—thus the birth of Matt Collins and his sidekicks. Part Bond, part Bourne—and all charm—Matt was bright, hot as hell, and walked on the wild side more often than not. He bent the law at times, but he was loyal, funny, and oozed charisma.

And he always got the bad guy.

The elevator chimed. Karlyn stepped out and headed through the frosted double doors.

"Hi, Karlyn." Her agent's long-time assistant, Candi, greeted her with a bright smile. "Can I get you anything before you head in?"

She held up her Starbucks cup. "I made a vanilla latté run on my way over."

Candi came around the desk. "Please tell me you've finished up the next Matt."

Karlyn grinned and slipped the flash drive from her purse, handing it to Candi. "Waiting for your approval."

She had actually given Candi the very first Matt manuscript before she let Alicia read it. She was unsure trying something that new and Candi had been a fan from the beginning of Karlyn's career. Twenty pages into it, the assistant called and declared Matt a winner.

"I'll start printing out a copy for Alicia."

"And maybe read a few pages as they come off the printer?" Karlyn teased.

Candi shrugged. "What can I say? Matt's fast with a gun and even faster with a smooth line. He's my fantasy man—and I'm all about the fantasy."

"Hope you enjoy this latest effort. I'm off to Alicia's office."

She walked down the corridor, waving at agents as she passed their offices. Karlyn had seen The Lindon Agency grow in the decade she'd been a client and was happy to be a part of its success.

She tapped lightly on Alicia's open door. Her friend was on the phone but motioned her in.

"Thanks, Frank. I'll Fed Ex the contracts to you. Let's do lunch Thursday. *Ciao.*"

Alicia hung up and crossed to wrap Karlyn in a bear hug. Though Karlyn clocked in at five feet and seven inches, she still felt dwarfed by her agent's height of six feet. Of course, a good four inches of that came from her Jimmy Choo heels.

"How are you, darling? Your text said that Matt's finished. That's terrific."

Alicia led them to her sofa and plopped, slipping off her stilettos. She cocked her head, studying Karlyn.

"Your smile tells me that you have another idea already."

Karlyn nodded and briefly outlined what she'd knocked out this morning after her run.

"Sounds fantastic. I'm glad it's not Matt again. I love that sexy man and what he's done for both our bank accounts. But it's better to dole him out in small portions. We have to make the public crave more and not oversaturate them."

"Candi's printing out the manuscript now."

"I can't wait to curl up in bed tonight with Matt

and a stiff vodka tonic. Random House has been on my ass, wanting you to produce more quickly. As if you could. Shall I tie this new novel in to your upcoming deal with them? Publish the next three Matt Collins, along with another three standalone novels?"

Karlyn shook her head. "That's the business end, Alicia. I won't say I don't care but that's why I have you to make those decisions. I want to write and have fun while I'm doing it."

Alicia crossed her long legs and Karlyn watched the corners of her mouth turn up in a Cheshire cat grin.

"You have news."

"Do I?" The agent stretched like a feline. "I suppose I had you come in today for a tiny bit of news. I'm ecstatic you brought the finished manuscript along ahead of schedule. And even happier you're ready to go to work again so quickly on something new."

"But?"

"I do have something to spring on you."

"Foreign rights in China finally?"

"No."

"Step-backs in the paperback versions of my Matt hard covers?"

Alicia shook her head. "Not even close."

Karlyn sat back, arms crossed, her wheels turning as she studied her agent. Suddenly, it came to her.

"A movie deal for Matt."

Alicia sighed. "You are no fun, Karlyn. That logical little brain of yours can solve any kind of puzzle."

She jumped to her feet. "Are you kidding me? I guessed it? Matt is going to the movies?"

Alicia nodded. Karlyn pulled her friend to her feet and locked her in a tight hug.

A knock sounded on the door. Candi poked her head in.

"Guess you told her, boss." The assistant entered with a bucket of champagne on ice and two crystal flutes.

Candi placed the items on the coffee table and smiled. "It took everything in my power not to scream the news when you came in."

Karlyn hugged Candi. "You were great. I didn't have any indication."

Candi nodded sagely. "I did some acting back in the day. Off-off-*off* Broadway. But I was pretty good."

"Hmm." Karlyn thought a moment. "Executive assistant and former actress. Knows a big secret about her boss but has the acting skills to keep it under wraps. He doesn't even know she knows. And then he's killed."

She paused, her thoughts racing. "What if—"

"Not now, darling," Alicia chided. "You've already got a fabulous new plot to work on. Plus, a movie contract to celebrate."

Candi poured the champagne and discreetly left. Karlyn sat back on the sofa as it hit her.

"So, my sexy, wonderful, amazing Matt will be a movie star. He'll actually come to life. I wonder which actor will be cast in the role."

Alicia sipped from the crystal flute and almost purred her satisfaction. "We can't control that. The deal is for all the rights to the character, the titles, the plots for the first book in the series—and the possibility of you writing the screenplay."

She sat up. "Me? I've never tried one before. I don't know if I could do it. I'm so green, all I know is that one page of script equals one minute of film."

"I said possibility, my dear. If we sign as it reads,

you will have first crack at the screenplay. You may work alone, or the studio will assign a seasoned writer to work with you. But if the studio execs don't like your draft, they can pass and move on to another screenwriter of their choosing."

Karlyn chewed on that a moment. "Wait. You said rights to the character. Does that mean they would own Matt Collins? They could write any old storyline for him? Beyond my novels?"

"That's correct."

She frowned. "I don't like that, Alicia. Not at all. I can see selling the title and first book. Possibly, the two following books. And having a shot at the screenplay would be an interesting challenge. But I don't want them to put Matt in some piece of shit twenty years down the road." She shook her head. "No, I want to retain rights to the character. Period."

Alicia finished her champagne and poured herself another glass, topping off Karlyn's at the same time.

"I figured as much without having to ask. I countered their offer. We're discussing the possibilities now." Her eyes twinkled. "But it looks good, Karlyn. I think we'll be able to keep the rights to the character. If we come down in price on the rest."

"Do it. I won't give away the story rights, but I'd rather have creative control over the character. If they could put Matt in any story, it could even hurt my future book sales."

"We could make more in the long run if they bought titles one at a time, as well." Alicia thought a moment. "I may pitch them the first book and allow them an option on the next two. Do you want the chance at tackling the screenplay to remain part of the deal?"

"Why not?" Karlyn clinked her glass with Alicia's and drank the bubbly in one gulp.

Alicia patted her hand. "Then let me work a little more of my magic. I'll get back to you soon."

Karlyn laughed. "Your magic? I've seen you at the negotiating table. You're like a pit bull locked onto the butcher's best bone. If you ever went to law school, you could make a killing as a divorce attorney."

Alicia grinned.

Karlyn stood. "I don't want to keep you. You have other clients' needs to deal with. Besides, I won't make it to the elevator before you're manipulating this movie deal to your liking."

Her agent shrugged. "All in a good day's work." She kissed Karlyn's cheek. "Take care, darling. Go home. Write the afternoon away."

She said goodbye and returned to the reception area. Candi was on the phone, so Karlyn waved at her and left the office.

Now all she had to do was share the good news with Mario.

Dread flooded Karlyn.

2
_____

Logan Warner reached to silence his phone's alarm before it went off. He couldn't remember the last time it had buzzed to awaken him.

He didn't sleep much. Not since Carson Miller turned his life upside down. Whether he was bored, sad, lonely, or depressed, he simply put in more hours at work.

Cops usually did.

He tossed back the covers and headed to the shower, letting the hot water clear the headache pounding behind his right eye. At least they'd closed the string of B&E's late yesterday. Two teenagers with too much time on their hands and plenty of creativity.

He shaved and scrounged around for clean underwear, finding he was down to his last pair. His mom had pestered him for more than a week to come for dinner. Maybe he would tonight and take his laundry. How pathetic. In his mid-thirties and still bringing home dirty clothes for his mama to wash.

Logan decided he'd buy a new package of Hanes before he would play frat boy and cart home smelly laundry. Dinner, however, he could get up for. His mom would be glad to see him. She'd pile up tons of leftovers for him to take home—even though home was a three-room flat above the local diner.

He picked up his cell and dialed his parents' number.

"Good morning, son. Off to work?"

Mitchell Warner's warm voice reached out to him. Always calm and mellow, the doctor who soothed everyone around him.

"Hey, Dad. I wondered if you and Mom will be home tonight."

"On a Thursday? Let me see."

Logan waited while his father checked the calendar. The sun wouldn't dare shine unless Resa Warner marked it on her calendar.

"You're in luck. No bridge. No choir practice."

"Can I stop by for dinner?"

"Don't see why not. That means I'll actually get a home-cooked meal. About time."

"What, Mom's starving you?"

"With her sewing circle and Bible study and bunko nights, I'm lucky she feeds me at all. With you expected for dinner, we'll get something decent, like lasagna or beef stew. You coming after your shift?"

"I'll be there no later than six. Unless someone gets himself killed."

"Hah! Last time that happened in the Springs was three years ago. Jim Marshall got drunk after his wife left him and ran smack into that old oak."

Logan thought about the violent deaths he'd seen in Atlanta every day, especially once he joined the homicide department. "Let Mom know I'm coming."

"I'll have her dust off her apron and cook up a feast. I've got to get going. Bridget Marley thinks her kid has the chicken pox. I'm heading over there now."

"Bye, Dad."

Logan hung up, feeling better hearing his down-to-earth father's voice.

He grabbed his gun and holstered it, tucked wallet and keys into his pockets, and headed down to the diner. He plopped on his favorite stool and coffee instantly appeared before him.

"Thanks, Mandy."

"What can I get you, Logan?" The brunette server leaned on the counter to give him a better shot of her ample cleavage.

"Two eggs and strips, hash browns, toast, and a tall OJ. That'll do it."

"You got it."

Mandy sashayed away as Logan doctored his coffee.

"Morning, Logan." Mayor Joe Vick perched his heavy frame on the stool next to him.

"Good morning, Mayor. You're out and about early this morning."

"Coffee to go, Mandy," Vick barked at the server.

She grabbed a Styrofoam cup and filled it to the brim, placing it and a top in front of him.

"Thanks, hon." Vick waited for her to leave before he turned to Logan.

"You hear anything about Bobby retiring?"

Logan shrugged. He and Chief Risedale had actually discussed it two days ago, but Logan didn't know if that conversation had gone beyond them.

"He's mentioned it a few times. I don't know if he's serious. Louise probably wouldn't put up with him being underfoot day in and day out."

Vick leaned in. "Bobby wants you to run as chief in the next general election."

So Risedale had let the cat out of the bag, after all. He'd approached Logan with the idea. Logan told his boss he would think about it. Now that Joe Vick knew, everyone else in town would by noon. Sooner if he'd already been down to the gas station and talked to Casey Attaway, the best gossip in the county. All news in the Springs filtered through the mayor or Casey. Twitter had nothing on the pair's social network.

"I'll have to think about it, Mr. Mayor."

Vick held up a hand. "Think fast, boy. May's around the corner. You're a hometown football hero. Won the athletic scholarship to University of Georgia. You have big city experience on the mean streets of Atlanta. Now, you're home. You've put in time on the force. People trust you. All in all, you would make an excellent candidate for the position."

He stood and slapped Logan on the back. "Keep me posted on your decision." Vick slipped the top onto his to go cup, threw a dollar on the countertop, and waltzed out.

Mandy set Logan's breakfast in front of him. He sensed her assessing him as he buttered his toast. He bit into the toast and looked up innocently.

"If you hadn't thought about it before, you should," Mandy said. "Seth Berger will run if you don't. No one wants that pissy little weasel as police chief in the Springs."

"Seth?"

That bit of information surprised him. Berger was in his late forties, thin as a rail, and didn't seem the ambitious or political type. Logan worked his way through breakfast and thought about how little he'd like to answer to Seth Berger if he became police chief in Walton Springs.

"Hey, buddy. Hey, Mandy. Can I get a coffee to go, sweetie? Little cream and a whole lotta sugar."

Logan's partner, Brad Patterson, sat next to him.

"Stool's still warm. Who're you keeping company with? I saw Mayor Vick leaving as I came in."

Brad rocked back and forth. "Yep, the whole surface is warm. Had to be Joe Vick's ass here. You know, Vick's about the size William Howard Taft was. Taft weighed over three hundred pounds. They installed a new bathtub in the White House just so he'd fit." He sighed. "Definitely Joe Vick's ass. Probably bigger than Taft's."

"Brilliant deduction, Patterson," Logan said between bites. "Maybe they should make you a detective."

His partner flashed Mandy a smile as she returned with his coffee. "I believe they already did, Warner. Thanks, babe." Brad slipped her a five and slid off the stool.

Logan stood and placed a couple of bills on the counter. His room rent included any meal he wanted from the diner, but he always made sure he left a tip. Felicity waited tables when they were in college, and he remembered how important each gratuity had been to a newly-married couple living on a shoestring.

He nodded to Mandy and stopped at the register. Nelda Vanderley smiled at him and laid down her pen.

"Heard you and Brad cleared those B&E's yesterday."

"Yes, ma'am."

"I knew that Jones boy was up to no good. Glad you busted him before it got any worse. Say, I'm planning the menus for the next couple of nights. Anything special you want?"

"I'm eating with the folks tonight so fix anything but meatloaf. You know that's my favorite. And don't ever tell Mom—but you make it better than she does."

Nelda laughed. "Considering I've told your mother everything I know since first grade, secret or not, she's probably figured that out. But I'll be sure meatloaf won't appear until tomorrow night at the earliest." She made a note of it.

Logan kissed her cheek. "You're one in a million, Nelda."

"If only a man twenty years older than you would tell me that, I'd be sold on him. I'd take him bald, pot-bellied, bow-legged—you name it."

Brad appeared at his elbow. "You know I'd take you, Mrs. Vanderley."

"Oh, pish-posh, Brad Patterson. You might be good-looking for a man approaching forty but you're lazy as the day is long. I don't know how Logan puts up with you and all that charm you ooze."

"I'm the brains of the team, ma'am. Logan's just the brawn. He scares most of the bad guys away, while I outthink them."

Nelda's eyebrows arched a good two inches. "Is that so?"

Logan nudged Brad. "We better get going. I'll tell Mom you said hi, Nelda."

He walked outside, following his partner to the police-issued sedan parked on the square. Brad tossed him the keys and Logan climbed into the driver's seat.

"You're up early this morning."

Brad sipped his coffee. "Couldn't sleep. Figured I'd catch up with you at the diner. Thought we could ride in together."

Logan turned west on Elm. He waved to a woman pushing a stroller with twins. She'd been a few years behind him in school. A lump formed in his throat. He missed his own twins with a fierce longing that actually brought a physical pain. He ran a hand through his hair and took a deep breath, pushing away the memory of Ashley and Alex.

And what Carson Miller had done to them.

Up ahead, he spotted Broderick Campbell crossing the street. Something seemed off about the old man's gait. Logan slowed the car and pulled over to the curb.

"Something's up with Mr. Campbell," he told Brad.

He got out of the car and hurried to Campbell's side. The man weaved in a crooked line. It was if he knew where he wanted to go but his body wouldn't take him there.

Campbell turned to look at him. Logan saw panic in the man's green eyes.

"Hurts," Campbell croaked before he collapsed in the street.

"Get a bus. Fast," he hollered. Brad picked up the radio and called it in.

Taking off his jacket, he folded it and slipped it under Campbell's head. The older man twitched and spasmed suddenly, then went totally limp.

Logan took his hand. "You're fine, Mr. Campbell. The ambulance is on its way. It'll be here any minute."

The most famous author in America looked up at him with sad eyes and a crooked mouth.

"Stroke," he moaned.

Logan saw the downward turn in Campbell's face on the right side. His grandfather had been a stroke victim during Logan's teens. He recognized the same slack expression appearing on Broderick Campbell's face.

"Call . . . Karlyn."

Logan nodded. He knew Campbell's wife was named Martha. It hit him that Campbell must mean Karlyn Campbell, the best-selling suspense author. He had no idea the two writers were even related.

"We will call Karlyn, sir," he assured him. "And your wife."

Logan continued talking in soothing tones until he heard the wail of the ambulance in the distance. Campbell must have, too. The man closed his eyes and sighed.

The attendants quickly loaded their patient into the emergency vehicle, with Logan describing what he'd seen and what Campbell had said. He figured maybe the writer had had a previous stroke when he self-diagnosed himself.

Logan promised to contact the wife as the paramedics pulled away. He got back in the car and told Brad, who radioed in their next destination since they were now officially on the clock.

The Campbell house sat three blocks away on Magnolia Lane. It was by far the nicest house on the street, a red-brick Colonial with a large, wide porch and tall, elegant, white columns.

The two detectives walked up the front sidewalk and rang the doorbell. Moments later, a petite blonde answered. She was probably in her mid-fifties but could pass for a decade or so younger, thanks to artfully applied make-up.

"Mrs. Campbell?"

"Yes? How may I help you?"

"I'm Detective Logan Warner. This is my partner, Detective Brad Patterson." He flashed his credentials and saw the concern cross her face.

"We spotted your husband having trouble walking and got out to assist him as he collapsed."

"Oh, dear. Is Broderick all right?" She glanced around them to see if might be sitting in their car.

"The ambulance came. He's been taken to Our Lady of Mercy in Lexington. It looks like it might have been a stroke. May we take you to the hospital?"

Tears welled in her eyes. "Yes, of course. Let me get my purse."

She returned after a minute and seemed to go limp all at once. Logan supported her as they walked to the car.

As they pulled away from the curb, he leaned over and said, "Your husband wanted us to call Karlyn. Is that your daughter, ma'am?"

Her eyes misted over. "Yes. Karlyn is our only child. Strange that Broderick said that."

"Why is that, Mrs. Campbell?"

Martha Campbell shook her head. "Because they haven't spoken to each other in almost four years."

3

K arlyn climbed out of the cab. The brisk March wind almost knocked her over. She headed for the revolving glass doors. Once inside, she proceeded straight for the ladies' room.

As she glanced in the mirror, smoothing her wind-blown hair, her stomach twisted violently. She ran into a stall and leaned over, knowing she had nothing to lose. She'd never been a breakfast eater and hadn't been able to get lunch down, either. Especially not on a day like this.

The day she would officially be known as a failure. A statistic. A party to the "one in two marriages fail" rule.

She fell on the failed side.

A few dry heaves later, Karlyn forced herself to stand. She exited the stall and rinsed her mouth with water before popping a breath mint. She touched up her lip-gloss. But the inevitable couldn't be delayed any longer.

Arriving upstairs at Benton, Lawler, she found herself being led down a lengthy corridor of hardwood floors and dark paneling to a windowless conference room.

She wasn't the first to arrive.

Seated with his whippet-thin attorney was her soon-to-be ex, Mario Taylor. Both looked up as she entered. The lawyer offered a brief nod. Mario did not. He sat with a sullen expression, his hooded eyes like slits, studying her silently.

What had she seen in this man?

Other than physical beauty, that is. Mario was a dark angel, with thick black hair, brooding brown eyes, and a body that rocked her world in the beginning.

What he'd hidden—or what she'd refused to see during their whirlwind courtship—was his artist's temperament, coupled with alcohol abuse. Karlyn had suffered long nights of her husband's anger, quick to erupt. The shouting. The insults. His immense jealousy of her success grew swiftly as his own star dimmed in the art world.

Finally, the constant betrayal of their marriage vows, the last time with a woman she had considered a good friend. It ripped her life apart like a jagged lightning bolt in its speed and damage.

That affair had been the final straw that led her to file for divorce.

"Good afternoon, Karlyn."

Her patrician attorney, Archibald Benton, swept into the room and led her to a seat at the conference table. He greeted the pair across from them and busied himself pulling out various papers from his briefcase, setting them in separate stacks before him.

"I believe we're ready to reach a settlement in this matter, Barbara."

Barbara McCarthy, cool and ash-blonde, gave him her best *Go to hell* look. Karlyn had decided that Barbara would be a character in her next book. She hadn't decided how to kill her yet. She would never write Mario into anything. Murdering his lawyer would be the next best literary revenge.

The attorney raised her pencil-thin brows. "I don't see how we can agree to any of this rubbish."

Benton raised his own shaggy white brows and glared back. Karlyn noted her lawyer's look trumped McCarthy's by a mile.

"I don't see what the problem is, Barbara. Mr. Taylor may keep any profits from his paintings since the marriage began, as well as any future earnings on paintings already in progress. My client will adhere to the same, retaining her income from her novels. The condo and all furniture within will be sold, with the money divided equally between the two. There are no children and no pets to consider. What objection could Mr. Taylor have?"

Barbara splayed her hands flat on the table. "It's grossly unfair. It will leave my client destitute until the sale of the property goes through. He is accustomed to living in a manner suited to—"

"Don't go there," Benton warned. "Your client has sponged off Miss Campbell for years. He earns a decent living from his art and can support himself. He will neither be homeless, nor will he starve."

"But he—"

"He can have the condo. And everything in it. I want this to be over."

Karlyn's interruption brought the argument to a halt.

"Karlyn, I would advise you—"

"I know, Archibald. We've had this discussion. Several times. And more than anything, I want to be free of this monster and his trail of tramps."

Mario leapt to his feet. "You would call *me* a monster, you little whore? Writing crap that the public gobbles up like candy?"

"Sit down," Barbara cautioned her client through gritted teeth.

Mario spread his arms wide. "Why should I? This little slut spread lies about me to her friends. Our relationship and its problems have been fodder for every tabloid and TV entertainment program. The gossip has ruined my career. I'll be lucky if I ever have a showing again in New York."

Mario sat, his eyes smoldering hate as he eyed Karlyn.

Benton flipped through a few papers and withdrew one. He turned it around and pushed it across the table.

"This is the private investigator's report that details multiple incidents of extramarital conduct on Mr. Taylor's part." He reached for an envelope and dumped out dozens of pictures on the table. "And here are the photos to back up the report."

Barbara placed a warning hand on Mario's forearm to ensure his silence.

"Yes, the tabloids have speculated about the marriage and my client's filing for divorce. The *paparazzi* have sold numerous pictures of Mr. Taylor with other women, both during the marriage and the separation. But my client has never made any of this public. In fact, she doesn't comment about anything in her private life—and that includes her soon-to-be ex-husband."

Benton shook his head. "None of this is news to you, Counselor. And now my client has generously offered all proceeds from the sale of an approximately three-million-dollar condo *and* its contents to go to

Mr. Taylor. Or he may choose to continue to be a resident thereof. The choice is his but the free ride on my client's coattails is over."

Mario said through gritted teeth, "You give me no choice. I cannot afford to live there."

Benton sat back, folding his hands in his lap. "Then sell the property, Mr. Taylor. It should net a healthy profit. You will have a tidy sum in your pocket and be free to pursue your art—and love of women— to your heart's desire."

Mario pushed back his chair and stood, his anger obvious. "I will sign," he spat out. "Anything to be rid of ... her." He began pacing the room.

Benton reached for a different stack, and she knew the legalese would include Mario receiving the condo and its contents.

"Here are the papers drawn up as you requested, Karlyn. Let me get my notary." The attorney reached for the phone and pressed a few numbers. "Yes, now, please."

Moments later, a young redhead entered with her registry and stamp. Karlyn noticed Mario's eyes light up with interest as he assessed the woman. In less than five minutes, all the paperwork had been completed and would be filed with the court. Karlyn watched her ex-husband walk out of the room and her life. For good.

Benton turned to her. "That was expensive, Karlyn. You were rash to give him so much. Especially when he didn't deserve a dime."

She shrugged. "He'll squander it and then find some rich, older matron to keep him in Prada and Armani. He's a fair artist with gigolo looks and a flamboyant personality. I don't think any rumors about what went wrong in our marriage have hurt his career. It steamrolled downhill long before that."

"Enough about Mario Taylor. What will you be doing now? I know writing is your salvation."

She laughed. "After months of negotiation, I'm starting work on my first screenplay and trying to finish writing a new novel at the same time." She paused. "I'll need to find somewhere to live. I've been staying at Alicia's apartment."

Karlyn patted Archibald's hand. "I know you think me foolish, but I needed to quickly cut the old ties and usher in my new life."

"Well, let me know where to send my bill." Benton chuckled. "And you promised me a signed copy of your next Matt Collins book." The lawyer's face lit up in pleasure thinking about it. "I think every man wants to be Matt Collins."

"And every woman wants to sleep with him," she quipped. She kissed his cheek. "Thank you for everything, Archibald."

Karlyn left, her step lighter with the burden of her marriage over. She turned the corner and spotted a Starbucks and decided to grab a coffee.

She walked in and ordered a grande mocha with a light whip and moved to the side to await her drink.

Suddenly, someone invaded her personal space.

Mario.

She forced herself to stay calm as she looked into his eyes.

"You are a bitch, Karlyn Campbell," he ground out. "You write commercial shit. You are not an artist as I am. You crank out worthless drivel. I think so. Your father thinks so. You know we are right. You have no talent."

She remained silent. She wouldn't give in to tears. She wouldn't let Mario get to her. Ever again.

Nor her father.

"Grande mocha, light whip," called out the barista.

Karlyn stepped around Mario and picked up her drink. Without a backward glance she left the coffeehouse, gripping the cup tightly.

She flagged a cab and climbed in. "Drive. Anywhere. I need to think."

Fortunately, the cabby remained silent as the buildings went by. Tears gathered in her eyes. She kept them at bay as she sipped the hot brew, hoping it would dispel the chill running through her.

What if her novels were popular with the public? What was wrong with that? Both Broderick Campbell and Mario Taylor seemed to think it was a crime to make money through her writing. Both denigrated her with cutting words and looks.

She didn't care. She loved getting lost in her world of characters. Stories poured from her, and she published two to three novels a year. She didn't care that she hadn't won a Pulitzer Prize or National Book Review Award, as her father had on multiple occasions. She didn't strive to compete with his career. She was a respected author in her own right. She took pride in the work she'd done and the stories and characters she'd created.

Her cell rang. She pulled it out reluctantly and stared at the Caller ID as it continued to ring.

Why would her mother be calling her?

"Hello?" she said cautiously.

"Oh, Karlyn. I'm so glad I reached you."

"Mother? You sound odd."

"Oh, honey. I don't know where to begin. But your father wanted me to call you."

Karlyn froze in disbelief. "Is he there? Are you all right? What's going on?"

"He's asked for you, dear. He's had a stroke. You need to get here as soon as you can."

4

He looked at the bald, strapping man lying helplessly on the dirty linoleum floor. His wrists and ankles duct taped to restrain him. More duct tape over his mouth. His eyes wide now in panic realizing that his new drinking buddy wasn't much of a buddy to him at all.

He flipped through the wallet. A couple of gas cards. A VISA and MasterCard. A Costco card. Eleven bucks in cash. He pulled out the driver's license and held it close to the man's face, comparing the picture with his specimen on the floor.

"Randolph? Hmm. Your mama and daddy stuck you with a pretty pretentious name for such a happy-go-lucky guy. No wonder you introduced yourself to me as Randy."

Randy whimpered behind the tape.

He returned the license to its slot and tossed the wallet aside. He wasn't a thief. He didn't need the money.

What he needed was the kill.

He looked back at his specimen and smiled. "Well, Randy. I'm happy to share with you that you're Number Eight. I've worked my way through all seven colors of the rainbow."

Randy's began blubbering behind the duct tape, his eyes wild.

"*Oh, I see you're familiar with my work. I'm sorry I didn't clue you in from the beginning. They're calling me Roy. Roy G. Biv—for the colors of the rainbow.*"

Randy started this funny-as-all-get-out scoot. Wiggling his fat ass and trying to push his heels in. Trying to get away. From what lay ahead.

"*Oh, come on, big boy. You're going to be famous.*" *He smiled at the truck driver.* "*I have become quite the news story in Atlanta.*" *He raised both arms and air-quoted,* "*Rainbow Killer Strikes Again.*" *And laughed.*

Randy kept scooting.

"*I've had the time of my life on this spree, my new friend. An Asian hooker. A gay white architect. A retired teacher.*" *He thought a moment.* "*She was a black widow.*" *Laughed at his own little pun. Thought a moment.* "*Who was next? Hmm. I know. The Hispanic plumber with five kids and one on the way. Oh, then another gay. Atlanta's full of 'em these days. He was a Black bookstore owner. Then it was the white accountant. Divorced. Cried for his kids in the end.*

"*And I finished up with the white immigration lawyer last week. No, she was married to an immigration lawyer. I think she did tax law. Anyway, she was a handful, let me tell you. Talked dirty—and fought dirty when the time came. She was an awesome specimen.*"

Randy had run out of crawling room. He'd hit a line of cabinets that formed an L. Backed into nowhere.

He took a step forward and watched the fright dance in Randy's eyes. God, he loved his job!

That's what he thought about killing. It was his job. His calling. His raison d'être. He couldn't imagine anything more enjoyable or more satisfying.

"*I thought that would be the end. That I'd move on to something else. I'd gone through the entire cycle of colors. But I'm really enjoying this, Randy. This time, I've gotten more press than ever before."* He chuckled. *"I suppose I've become addicted to the fame."*

He took out his knife. And the piano wire.

"But you know what comes next. If you've been listening to the news. Or reading the papers. Or trolling the Internet."

Randy moaned behind the tape, tears leaking from his bloodshot drinker's eyes.

He crouched next to his specimen. Ran the knife's blade against his temple. Watched the thin red line of blood appear.

"I'm just sorry that brown isn't one of the colors of the rainbow. You know—painting you brown. How appropriate that would've been for a UPS guy."

He drank in the terror. Let it wash over him like a balm.

And then got to the business at hand.

5

Logan glanced at his watch and logged off his work computer as he turned to his partner.

"I'm outta here."

Brad flipped another page of *Sports Illustrated*. "Got a hot date?"

He snorted. "Yeah. Cruising down to Peachtree Plaza to rendezvous with Mila Kunis. We'll pick her up a little slinky something at Victoria's Secret before grabbing drinks. Then we'll head over to the *W Hotel* and crash in a suite where we'll have wild animal sex all night long."

Brad tossed the magazine into his lower desk drawer. "I love it when you talk dirty, Partner." He paused. "But that sounds like one of *my* nights, Choir Boy. Not yours."

Logan stood. "I'm going to my parents for a home-cooked meal."

"Whoa. And break up Mahjongg night? Or is it pinochle?"

Logan flashed a grin. "Hey, we'll be old, too, some-day. That's probably all the action we'll be able to handle."

Brad shook his head. "Not me. Never gonna get

married. Just like James Buchanan, our only bachelor president. In fact, never gonna fall in love. Or play board games. The only cards I'll ever pick up will be for strip poker." He stood. "Besides, I'm the one who plans to zip down to the city and catch some action tonight."

Logan shook his head. "Just keep tomorrow's hangover to yourself, okay?"

"Right, Mr. Boy Scout. Will do."

They both pulled their suit jackets from the back of their chairs and slid into them as they walked out of the station. Logan watched as Brad climbed into his year-old Corvette, midnight blue and as fast as the devil. He figured Brad had family money, based upon how frequently he traded in expensive sport cars, as well as his fashionable wardrobe. No way could he look like he did on a small-town cop's salary.

He never asked, though. Brad was all smiles and charm, but he didn't advertise his personal life. Logan understood because he kept most of his bottled up. That made them a perfect team.

He started up his modest sedan and pulled out of the parking lot, turning onto Franklin. Within five minutes he'd arrived at his parents' ranch-style house. Violet and white pansies bloomed in the flowerbeds. The paint job he and his dad did last fall still looked crisp and fresh.

Logan rang the doorbell. His mother answered, drinking him in as if she hadn't seen him in months.

"Oh, sweetie, how are you?" She wrapped her arms around him. "I made lasagna. Hope that's okay."

"Sounds good, Mom. I'll be sure and take any left-overs off your hands if Dad'll let me." He followed her into the kitchen, where the table was set for three.

Mitchell Warner tossed a salad. "Hey, son. Thanks

again for coming." He lifted his nose in the air and breathed deeply. "Smells delicious."

"Oh, Mitch, you act as if I starve you." Resa swatted her husband's butt with a dishtowel. "Tell Logan the truth. After forty-two years, you're tired of my cooking. You'd rather eat out or zap a microwave pizza or Hot Pocket."

"Whatever you say, honeybun. Why don't you check the sourdough? Should be warmed by now. Logan, open that wine, please."

They gathered around the table, the food rapidly vanishing as the conversation flowed.

"So you closed those B&E's. Anything else new?"

"Broderick Campbell collapsed today in the middle of the road."

Resa gasped. "My goodness, is he all right?"

"We called an ambulance. It might've been a stroke."

Mitchell Warner perked up. "Stroke, you say? Did he go to Our Lady?"

He nodded. "Brad and I went to his house and drove Mrs. Campbell to the hospital. I haven't heard how he is."

His mother sighed. "My book club wanted Martha Campbell to join when she first moved here. She expressed no interest, which I found odd for an author's wife. She does come in every eight weeks for a color and cut but she doesn't say much."

Resa shook her head. "Quiet, that one. Haven't gotten to know her in all the time she's come to the salon. She's thoughtful, though. Brings me a little Christmas treat each year, like a candle or a box of Godiva chocolates. Nice lady. I sure hope her husband will be all right."

"I see him out walking every morning when I head to work," Mitchell Warner volunteered.

"Maybe he walks and thinks about his books," Logan suggested. "He's written enough of them. I remember junior year we read *Time Marches On*. Symbolism out the wazzoo. Mrs. Donovan raved about it, but I thought it was worse than Faulkner. Way over my head."

"Yeah, dumb jocks like you don't get literature," his dad teased. "But then again, you only minored in English Lit in college."

Logan laughed. "I get Hawthorne and Hemingway. I can even jazz up a conversation about symbolism in *The Waste Land*. But Broderick Campbell remains over my head."

Resa patted his hand. "That's why he's so famous, dear. No one can understand him. Everyone buys him but I doubt anyone ever finished one of his books." She grinned. "Even Mrs. Donovan."

"Sounds like a scam to me," Mitchell proclaimed as he glanced toward the island. "How about some hot peach cobbler?"

They dished up cobbler and vanilla ice cream and sipped on decaf coffee for the next few minutes, gossiping about what was going on in the Springs.

Then his father changed the subject.

"I saw where another of those Rainbow Murders happened north of the city. First time outside of Atlanta."

Logan grew somber. "People expect crime in a big city. Not in a small town like Mortonville. Especially with it being just a few towns over from the Springs."

"I hope it never happens here," his mother said. "I couldn't stand you being involved in something so sordid, Logan."

His mom had no idea of the horrors he'd witnessed in Atlanta on a daily basis. Aside from the knifings, rapes, and assaults while a patrolman, Logan had seen a slew of murder victims during his time in homicide. Ghastly images haunted him even now.

Especially the last ones of Ashley and Alex.

His dad must have realized where his thoughts had wandered. "More cobbler, son?"

"No. I better hit the road. Thanks for dinner."

His mother slid the remaining lasagna into a Tupperware container and handed it to him. "Your sister will be in town next weekend. Will has a soccer tournament. Try to make a game if you can. Cathy complained that she never sees you."

"I'll try."

His dad walked him out to his car. "Good having you over, Logan. Don't be such a stranger."

He waved as he pulled out. The lasagna now sat like a hard lump in his stomach. He knew he should get over it. Cathy's two boys were great kids, but he found it hard to be around them. All he could think about was Alex and Ashley playing with their cousins. How old they'd be now. What they would be doing. Playing soccer? Taking piano lessons? Wearing braces? Begging for a cell phone?

Five years had done nothing to heal the rip through his heart.

Especially since Carson Miller had never been caught.

6

Karlyn's temples throbbed as she exited the airport in her rental She was a poor flyer and plenty of bumps occurred between La Guardia and Hartsfield. The plane being held on the tarmac for an hour hadn't helped her growing headache. Hertz losing her car reservation iced the cake and brought the pounding to the forefront.

She was driving a sleek BMW convertible that screamed money, which was the last thing she wanted to be seen in as she drove to a place she'd only visited once. Karlyn remained frugal despite her writing success. Driving an ostentatious sports car made her uncomfortable. Unfortunately, it was either the convertible or a monstrosity that resembled a cross between a Hummer and an army tank since that's all the reservations agent had to offer. Since she rarely drove, she decided the BMW would be the lesser of two evils.

She headed north toward Walton Springs and popped another two naproxen tablets before guzzling the remaining half of her bottled water, fortifying herself for what lay ahead.

Ambivalence filled her. The South—and Walton Springs—weren't home. Her parents moved there from the Pacific Heights area in San Francisco while she was away at college. Karlyn made excuses not to come visit—Maymesters, a year of study abroad, a summer internship in Boston and then one in New York that was vital to her degree and career goals.

Besides, why bother? Home never had been home, not in a traditional sense. Home conjured pictures of leisurely family dinners. Doing chores together. Parents putting together bicycles on Christmas Eve so Santa wouldn't disappoint.

All that was as foreign to Karlyn as a homeless orphan from the hills of West Virginia being adopted by a doting billionaire and thrust into life in Beverly Hills.

Dinners in the Campbell home consisted of a tray in her room. Her father was always in his study writing, the unspoken *Do Not Disturb* sign keeping him from family meals. That or book tours and the lecture circuit all added up to no time spent together.

Besides, Martha Campbell didn't cook so Karlyn's dinner usually consisted of a sandwich she made herself.

And vacations? Unheard of. Her classmates went from the Grand Canyon to the Grand Caymans, New York City to Disney World. But Broderick Campbell was too famous to go anywhere. He'd be recognized, which he loathed. He cherished privacy over riding on Space Mountain with his only child.

Whenever she twirled her baton at a football game or danced a ballet solo, no loving adult in the audience cheered her on.

Just like no one cheered on her fast-rising career in publishing.

Her father remained critical of her writing. Karlyn stopped showing him anything she'd written by the time she turned fourteen. When she actually published her first historical romance novel, she flew to Georgia with the first copy off the press, signed and dedicated to her parents. Her father swiped the paperback from her hands, vanished into his study, and emerged three hours later uttering one word.

Rubbish.

Nothing but that one, scathing word of criticism.

At that, something broke inside her. All the hurt and anger built up from childhood crashed. And then the void arose, a black hole as vast as the Bermuda Triangle. Karlyn felt absolutely nothing for the two people that supposedly raised her.

She'd raised herself—and hadn't done a bad job. She graduated from a prestigious Ivy League university. Landed a job within a month of graduation. Published her first novel at twenty-three. Everything seemed to be golden in her life as her writing career took off faster than a Triple Crown winner.

Except when it came to men. Total strikeouts in that area. From unrequited love to broken love affairs and now the huge disaster of divorce. Men were the oil to Karlyn's water. They just didn't mix.

As she cruised down the highway, she spoke aloud a vow she intended to keep.

"I, Karlyn Campbell, do solemnly swear I will not get involved with a man for the next ten years. Minimum. Look briefly at a good ass—maybe—but that's as far as it will go."

She glanced into her rearview mirror and saw the determination on her features. If anything, her stubbornness would allow her to keep the promise to herself.

Then she remembered the one good man in her life.

She added an addendum. "All except the amazing Matt Collins, of course. Plus any other interesting, fictional man I can create and have total control over."

She brusquely nodded for good measure. "I promise I will create good men who will make even better women happy. Furthermore, I swear to kill off any man that is mean, unfaithful, or uninteresting."

Karlyn chuckled at her resolve. She supposed a shrink would say she was killing her father over and over again in her suspense novels. If she were, it was certainly fun. And definitely profitable.

She glimpsed the sign for Our Lady of Mercy Hospital and exited the freeway, following the large signage rather than her mother's vague directions. She parked in a visitor's lot and found the information desk in the lobby.

"Hi. I'm here to visit my father, Broderick Campbell but I don't have the room number." Thanks to her mother, who hadn't bothered with details.

The slender receptionist stared at her open-mouthed. "You're . . . you're . . . Karlyn Campbell! Oh, wow, you're like my favorite author ever. And I saw on *E! News* where Matt Collins is going to be a movie. That is so awesome!" She hesitated. "Uh, can I have your autograph? No one is going to believe I met you. You're like . . . a goddess."

Karlyn smiled and took the offered pen and memo pad. "Only if you give me my father's room number."

"Sorry." The young woman's fingers flew over the keys. She frowned. "He's in ICU. That's the sixth floor. Room 638."

"What's your name?"

"Ava."

Karlyn scribbled a moment and handed over the pen and paper. "Thank you, Ava. I appreciate your kind words. I enjoy meeting my fans."

"Hey, would you use my name in your next book? That would be so cool."

Karlyn pursed her lips and thought a moment. "Ava. Sounds like a woman with a past. And a juicy secret. You're on, Ava. Keep buying my books. You'll see your name one of these days. I can't promise if I'll keep you alive. Dead seems to work better for me."

She walked away as the receptionist squealed. Karlyn pulled out her phone to make a note about it. She did like the name. It was old-fashioned and yet sexy. Maybe Ava could be the heroine in her next romantic suspense. For now, that would have to wait. Completing the screenplay loomed over her, as well as trying to finish the novel she'd begun a few months ago. And now this thing with her father had come up. Karlyn didn't know how long she'd be in Walton Springs, much less why he wanted to see her after so many years of silence.

She made her way to the bank of elevators, gritting her teeth as she stepped inside. She liked being in control of a situation and she had no idea what she was about to walk into.

The doors opened at the sixth floor and a bedraggled Martha Campbell appeared in front of her.

"Oh, Karlyn." Her mother rushed into the elevator and clutched her tightly, her body shaking.

"It's okay, Mother."

"He's going to die, Karlyn, I know it."

The doors started to close.

"Let's get out."

She maneuvered her mother out of the small box and tried to put on a brave face, which was hard because her mother was a mess. Karlyn was used to Martha being the most put-together woman in any room, but she looked as if she'd slept in her clothes. Her hair was flat and most of her make-up had worn off. Martha Campbell without make-up spelled the end of time.

"What do I need to know before I see him?"

Her mother's face crumpled. She dissolved into tears again. Karlyn pulled a tissue from her purse and handed it over. Martha dabbed at her eyes and then blew her nose at a surprisingly loud, unladylike level.

"Let's get some of that bad coffee hospitals are famous for, and you can catch me up," she suggested, hoping that would give her mother time to compose herself and reveal what the doctors actually had said.

She led them down the quiet corridor until they reached a small lounge with vending machines.

"Nothing for me, dear," her mother said. "I've had enough coffee to float to China. I doubt I'll sleep a wink tonight."

Karlyn put some change into the machine and pressed a few buttons. Her coffee with milk and some kind of sweetener appeared. She probably wouldn't drink it, but she needed something to keep her hands busy.

Martha led them over to a couple of empty chairs and they sat. Neither spoke.

Karlyn refused to be the first to continue the conversation. She'd flown in from New York, she'd asked about her father's condition, and her mother had fluttered around and told her nothing.

"He had another stroke, you know. Before this one," Martha finally offered.

That news surprised her. "What? Why didn't you tell me?"

Her mother toyed with the wadded-up tissue. "He didn't want you to know. It was three years ago. He didn't want anyone to know."

Martha Campbell stood. "It was mild. The doctor said if you had to have a stroke, this was the one to have. Broderick bounced back almost immediately. Began walking again in the mornings. It never affected his speech or his coordination. Pretty soon, he was writing as if nothing had happened. He finished his next novel on schedule. Even his agent was none the wiser."

She frowned. "I wish you would've told me."

Martha waved her hands helplessly. "I couldn't go against his wishes. You know how he can be."

Her temper flared. "That's great, Mother. My own father breaks off all contact with me and you go right along with him, punishing me for who knows what."

Karlyn stood and began pacing to hide how upset she was. She should have never come to Georgia in the fragile emotional state she was in. This trip had *mistake* written all over it.

"Well, I do call you when I get a chance. I've never told Broderick. I can't believe I do it, but I need to see how you are every now and then."

"Right now, Mother, I'm not too great. I signed my divorce papers yesterday."

"Oh, no. Poor Mario."

Anger sizzled inside her. "*Poor Mario*? That is the story of my life with you, Mother. You think about anyone but your own daughter, ignoring that I'm burning up with hurt over it all."

Martha looked startled, blinking rapidly several times. "Oh, Karlyn. You've always seemed so self-sufficient. As if you didn't need me or anyone else. I thought you must have initiated the divorce. I felt sorry for Mario losing you. He's such a handsome, sweet boy."

"He's a grown man, Mother and he's no angel." She clammed up, determined not to describe her ex's temper tantrums and affairs. She doubted her mother saw any rumors printed in the tabloids. Her father would expressly keep that kind of trash out of their house. Since she knew her parents had a housekeeper who did their marketing, Martha Campbell never set foot inside a supermarket where she could peruse the screaming headlines while in the check-out line.

Besides, Martha would be in denial about anything concerning Mario. His dark, Spanish looks and impeccable manners had charmed her mother from their first meeting.

"Well, I'm sorry, dear. At least you have that lovely apartment with its wonderful views."

No sense in getting into that. Karlyn waited for her mother to continue.

"I suppose you want to hear about your father's condition. He had the stroke yesterday morning. Two nice policemen found him and called an ambulance and they brought me here."

"So, you've been here since yesterday morning? Have you eaten anything?"

Martha looked blank for a moment. "I don't remember."

"Have you called anyone?"

"No. Broderick wouldn't want anyone to know. Like before." She turned tear-filled eyes to Karlyn. "Except you, dear. One of the detectives said your father specifically asked for you to be called. That's what I did."

"Then let's get this over with." She took her mother's arm and helped her out of the chair.

They moved down the corridor, both pausing a moment when they reached the room. Karlyn could see through the window that her father was hooked up to a couple of machines, his eyes closed.

"You can only go in for the first few minutes at the top of the hour," her mother informed her. "ICU rules."

Karlyn glanced at her watch. "It's five till two. I think we can bend the rules a little and go on in."

Martha put on the brakes. "No. They only let one at a time see him. You go. I'll wait outside." With that, Martha turned and retreated down the hall.

Karlyn steeled herself. She stepped into the dim room and paused. The beeping monitor sounded at regular intervals. The only other sound beyond it was her father's slow, even breathing. That had to be a good sign.

She moved closer and sat in the chair next to the bed. Should she take his hand? She'd never held it before. Never received a hug or a kiss from him, not upon graduation, not even when she left for college three thousand miles away. She had even pushed Mario to elope because she couldn't see herself on her father's arm coming down the aisle on her wedding day. They went to St. Lucia and were married barefoot on the beach instead of in a church with her parents looking on. That is, if they would have come. Karlyn thought of the excuses they'd made at other momentous occasions in her life. Even her wedding wouldn't have guaranteed their attendance.

She leaned closer and studied the great Broderick Campbell. He seemed smaller somehow, not the intimidating giant of her childhood. Reluctantly, Karlyn reached out and placed her hand over his. It was cool to the touch.

His eyes opened. "You ... came."

She noticed the slur in his speech. Awake, she also could see the downward tilt of his mouth. She wondered if he'd suffered any paralysis from the stroke.

"You asked for me." She paused a moment. "I wondered why."

"Tell you ... how proud I am. Of ... you."

Karlyn froze. Her father was a man of few words. And he'd said he was proud of her.

"Is this your idea of a deathbed confession that'll make you look good to God and get you into heaven?"

Broderick Campbell snorted. "Never one ... mince words."

She shrugged. "I guess since I've never received a compliment from you, it's a little hard to buy into it now."

"I ... read ... it all."

Even slurred, she understood the words perfectly.

"You've read all my published works? All the rubbish?"

A pained look crossed his face. "Jealous," he croaked.

They sat in silence a few minutes, her hand still atop his, his words turning in her mind.

Finally, he spoke again. "I like ... Matt. He's tough . .. but ... good. Your plots ... good. Make readers ... think."

His breathing seemed more labored to her. His words became harder to understand.

"Not good father. Never ... wanted. You ... stand on own. Make success. You ... good."

Karlyn squeezed his hand. Words of love might have been what other daughters wanted but for the amazing Broderick Campbell to praise her writing meant more to her than any other declaration.

"I'm glad you like my work, Father."

His eyelids fluttered a few times. "Better . . . me. Take care . . . Martha."

The monitor screeched wildly.

7

Logan awoke to the smells of bacon frying in the diner below. His stomach growled in response. He glanced at the clock and smiled. He'd made it past six-thirty today. That was a good sign. Too many nights over the last few years had been long and sleepless. Cases he worked kept him up all hours of the night, second-guessing who the perp was, what he might be up to, and how to stop him.

Then endless nights came calling when no cases simmered on the front burner. Those nights wore him out. They always involved images of the twins. Or replaying the bitter arguments with Felicity in the months after the funeral.

Logan threw back the covers and hit the shower. He intended to enjoy this off-duty Saturday. Taking his motorcycle out and roaming the countryside topped his agenda.

As he dressed, he wondered how Broderick Campbell had fared. Maybe he would run by the hospital. He chuckled at his mom trying to rope Mrs. Campbell into her book club. Maybe the woman didn't join because the group never read any books. They paid a retired schoolteacher to give book talks once a month on the latest bestsellers so they wouldn't have to read. Instead, after their guest speaker did her thing, the women shared a potluck dinner and gossiped like fish-wives about the thickening plots surrounding the Springs—rumors about possible affairs, cheating businessmen, and disrespectful teens.

His mom and Nelda spilled the beans regarding everything they'd heard at book club, whether real or imagined. And women thought men were bad with their poker nights.

Logan debated on toasting some English muffins and firing up the coffeemaker but decided it would be quicker to eat downstairs. Some mornings he liked privacy and chose to make his own breakfast. Today, he was ready to eat and escape on his bike.

He lifted a leather bomber jacket from the coat rack and slung it over his shoulder as he made his way downstairs. The place only had a handful of customers. He climbed onto a barstool and Nelda poured him a cup of coffee.

"Eggs? Pancakes?"

"I'll take French toast and bacon. Tall OJ with it."

"You got it."

She turned the order in to Leon, the morning fry cook. Leon worked the A.M. shift because he only knew how to cook breakfast foods. He could whip up omelets and hash browns and the finest eggs over-easy around but diner staples such as fried chicken and meatloaf baffled him.

Logan waved at Leon and sweetened his coffee. Suddenly, he felt a tap on his shoulder. He turned. Chief Risedale stood behind him.

"Morning, Chief."

Risedale grabbed a stool. "We gotta talk." His tone was quiet but urgent. The policeman turned to Nelda.

"Two sunny side ups, sausage, biscuits and gravy, please. And coffee."

Risedale made small talk until both men had their meals in front of them.

"Okay, Logan. I'm officially out of the race. If I want to stay married to Louise, I'm not running." He glared at Logan's grin. "And no, I'm not pussy-whupped. I tend to agree with my wife in order to keep the peace. You'll need to declare by the Wednesday after next at noon. Get a petition with a minimum of five hundred registered voter names on it. Once someone signs one, he can't sign for another candidate in the same race."

Logan nodded. "If I decide to run, I can get the names."

Risedale mopped up a bite of biscuit drenched in gravy. "Seth Berger picked up a form yesterday. With today being Saturday, he'll be out in full force. Probably hitting up Little League parents at the park and women doing their shopping at Ralph's."

Logan waved a hand. "It's a few hundred names, Chief. The Springs has over forty thousand here."

"That's not the point. Seth'll get his name out there first. People think about the race—and they'll think Seth Berger." Risedale paused. "I don't want my town to belong to Seth Berger."

Logan frowned, interested that the chief had feelings similar to his regarding the detective. "What do you have against Berger? Besides the fact he resembles a skinny weasel."

Risedale shrugged. "Can't say. Man does his job, but he's always seemed sneaky to me. I've never trusted him." He clapped Logan on the back. "You, I trust. Why, I don't know."

He grinned. "Maybe it was those *For Sale* signs we put in Miss Galaway's yard back in middle school after she gave me a C in math? Or possibly you catching me drinking beer with the Baptist preacher's daughter when I was sixteen? Or could it have been—"

"—the Nekkid Jaybird Race you organized your senior year in high school?" Risedale interrupted. "Seems like you should be the last person in charge of my town, Logan Warner, but you finally grew up. Made something of yourself. You're good people. Folks respect you. I know they'll vote for you."

"But I'll have to put forth some effort."

Risedale stood. "You got that right." He pulled a sheaf of papers from his jacket pocket and handed them to Logan.

"Here's what you get your signatures on, the back pages. The front one is typical name, address, occupation. Get it in before the deadline."

"Chief, I still haven't decided if I want to run."

Risedale's eyes narrowed. "Your thinking about it days are over. Shit or get off the pot." He placed a ten on the counter and walked away without another word.

Logan shook his head. Did he want the bureaucratic problems that came with a job like this one?

No. But he sure didn't want Seth Berger in charge of anything. He had the same sense the chief did of Berger. Something was a little bit off, a little bit untrustworthy.

Logan put his tip on the counter and pulled on the leather jacket. He craved a long ride. He'd let his mind float and see how he felt when he returned home.

❧

KARLYN PUT HER FOOT DOWN.

"Mother, you're going home. Now. Here are the keys to my rental."

"But Karlyn, what if—"

"You're exhausted. You've spent forty-eight hours at this hospital. I don't think you've gotten more than two hours of sleep total. Go home. Get a hot bath. Take a long nap and then come back here for dinner."

From a window, she pointed out the candy-red BMW convertible parked in the third row and promised to notify her mother if any changes occurred before she pressed the elevator button and practically shoved her mother into it.

Back in the waiting room, she noticed she could return to her father's room in another fifteen minutes. She stretched out her legs. Her joints ached from sitting so much the last few days—on the plane, in the car, and now at the hospital.

Broderick had died yesterday afternoon. The crash cart team arrived within half a minute and shooed her out of the room as they worked on him. They got his heart started again and attached a breathing apparatus to him, but the doctor told them that things didn't look good. He refused to give them a timeframe, though. She hoped sending her mother home was the right thing to do under the circumstances, but she didn't want Martha to collapse from exhaustion.

She rubbed her eyes, gritty from her own lack of sleep. When was she supposed to work on the screenplay? The deadline loomed over her. Tackling a new form of writing was exhilarating. At the same time, she didn't know if she had the feel for something this complicated in so short a time. She certainly didn't want to make a mess of things. Matt Collins deserved her best effort.

If she stayed in Walton Springs beyond a few days,

she would call Chris Stevenson. He was an experienced scriptwriter whom the studio had offered to help her if she ran into any roadblocks with the first draft. She'd spoken to him twice on the phone since she'd begun her draft. He'd been helpful, getting her back on track with a few key suggestions. Ironically, he worked from his home in Atlanta. Maybe he could drive up for a few days if she got further behind schedule.

"Miss Campbell?"

Karlyn looked up to see a man in his mid-thirties standing a few feet away. Tall with thick, dark hair and wary green eyes that probably saw more than they should. Instinctively, she pegged him as a cop. A very hot cop. So hot that she was ready to renege on her promise of avoiding men for the next decade. *That* kind of hot.

"Yes?" She rose but she still had to look up a good distance to meet his eyes.

He offered her his hand. "Logan Warner. I'm a detective from Walton Springs. My partner and I came across your dad a couple of days ago."

"You're the ones who called the ambulance? Thanks."

~

LOGAN LOOKED DOWN at the tall, slender blonde. Her tone didn't sound thankful. It was more on the weary side. He guessed she'd been worn to a frazzle spending the last few days at the hospital. But even a tired Karlyn Campbell took his breath away.

Without meaning to, he blurted out, "Your book jackets don't do you justice." He wanted to kick himself, acting like a starstruck fan—and sounding like he was hitting on her. Both were way out of character for him.

She ignored his comment. "If you came by to check, my father is in poor condition. He suffered another stroke yesterday. He hasn't regained consciousness."

"Were you with him when it happened?"

Her emerald, green eyes drilled into him. Logan shuffled self-consciously under her scrutiny.

"I mean, he asked for you. I hope you got to speak with him."

"I did." Her gaze softened. "He said he liked my writing."

Logan chuckled. "Your dad and about a bazillion other fans."

A strange look crossed her face. He didn't know how to interpret it. He read people well, from defenses in college to perps in interrogation rooms, but Karlyn Campbell proved to be an enigma.

He filled the silence. "I enjoy your books. For a civilian, you have police procedure down pat. Your dialogue rings true. Even from a male point of view. I guess you try it out on your husband," but as his words tumbled out, he noticed her finger empty of a wedding band.

He could swear her bio said she lived in New York City with her artist husband. He had an eye for detail, but apparently, that status had changed since he devoured the last Matt Collins book.

She rubbed her ring finger absently and then caught herself doing it. She quickly dropped her hand.

"I do my own research and writing, Detective. No help from anyone. Especially not a spouse or my father."

Jeez, she was prickly. But that only intrigued him. He couldn't say what it was but for the first time in years, a woman held his attention.

She glanced at her watch. "It's time to visit my father." As she turned to go, Logan saw the indecision cross her face.

She turned back, her tone softening. "Since it's intensive care, we can only visit for the first five minutes of the hour." She took a deep breath. "Thank you for coming. I'll tell Mother you stopped by. She bragged on how nice you were to her."

And then Karlyn Campbell walked away. Logan ran a hand through his hair and watched perfection in motion as she moved down the corridor.

What the hell had happened here?

8

Karlyn awoke with that yucky taste. The one that said she'd drunk too much bad coffee and not brushed her teeth in more hours than she cared to remember. She turned and saw her mother curled into a small ball on the rock-hard couch of the hospital waiting room.

All she wanted to do was leave. That hospital smell hung heavily in the air and clung to her skin. She wanted a long, hot shower and a real bed and a piping hot cinnamon dolce latté with as heavy a whip as she could get.

She began pacing the corridor, the subtle beep of machines permeating the quiet. She wondered how much longer Broderick would hold on.

It didn't cause her guilt to think so. Her time of aiming to please him ended too many years ago. He remained a stranger to her. She stayed for her mother, though she had no true bond with the woman who gave birth to her. Her mother always chose her husband before her child, so flagrantly that Karlyn hadn't known how odd that was until she left home.

Death hovered around the corner. She wondered what kind of funeral Broderick had mapped out. He paid meticulous attention to details. Naturally, he would have planned his service, especially after the first stroke.

Karlyn nodded to the night nurse at the station as she passed and returned to the waiting room. Her mother still slept. No others were present. Four families had come and gone since she'd arrived. Two left joyfully for rooms on other floors. The other two departed in tears, off to make funeral arrangements.

It was time again for the hourly visit. She decided not to interrupt her mother's rest and entered her father's room.

Machines dominated the small space. A breathing tube helped him along after the last setback. Karlyn shivered at the Darth Vaderesque noise filling the room. She sat next to the bed. Didn't take his hand. Couldn't. She wasn't the little girl aching for Daddy's approval anymore.

Besides, he gave it to her when they last spoke.

She thought about his precise handwriting that filled pages of legal tablets, with additions captured in the margins and huge passages deleted with a black marker. That's what Graydon Snow, his long-time editor, received—a manuscript next to impossible to read —but anything from the sacred mind of Broderick Campbell was like manna from heaven in the book world. Somehow, Snow crafted it into a readable form and a novel appeared, gracing the top of the bestseller lists before it even shipped.

As an unpublished author, her experience differed wildly. From formatting to grammar to engaging characters and an enticing plot, she'd aimed for perfection with that first manuscript. She realized fortune smiled upon her when her work got pulled from the slush pile.

A small part of her wished she'd chosen a pen name. When her connection to Broderick came out, she downplayed it, repeating in numerous interviews that she wanted to be judged on her own merit. Fortunately, the majority of readers wanted exciting plots, fearless characters, and surprise endings. Karlyn learned how to deliver all three with a bang, no matter what genre.

She looked at her father, the elder sage of the literary world. Sitting here did nothing for either of them. She would insist her mother take the next visit.

Suddenly, the machine screeched, piercing the quiet.

LOGAN HELPED Loretta Cankins from the car. One hand clutched his wrist in a death grip, her eyes wide and frightened.

"It's all right, Mrs. Cankins. We're at the ER. The doctors will check you over. We'll take a few pictures of your injuries."

"Pictures?"

"Yes, ma'am. To document what happened. We'll file the complaint. A warrant will be issued for Mr. Cankins' arrest."

Her bruised and bloody lips trembled. "He won't hurt me no more?"

"No, ma'am." Logan led the domestic violence victim into the ER while Brad parked the car.

He spotted a wheelchair and helped lower her into it. She grimaced, holding her ribs. When they'd arrived, Vernon Cankins was kicking the hell out of his wife on the front lawn.

The police were familiar with Vernon's drinking

and quick fists. Uniforms were dispatched regularly to the Cankins' house. Loretta never would press charges, though. Her injuries usually occurred below the neck—out of sight and easier to hide.

Tonight had been different. Vernon started by using his wife's face as a punching bag. Logan doubted if they'd be able to save her left eye. She also had missing teeth. One arm hung awkwardly, probably broken. Part of him wished the law would allow Loretta to repay Vernon with the same injuries. That would be justice.

As he pushed her to admissions, she said quietly, "I was leaving him. That's why he snapped. Said I wouldn't leave the house alive." She attempted a grin. "I did leave that house alive. I made it to the front yard."

"You'll make it the rest of the way, ma'am," he assured her.

They reached the check-in desk. The clerk had Loretta whisked away. Logan pulled a nurse aside to let her know it was a domestic violence case and what they would need. She assured him the patient would be handled with kid gloves and treated like a princess.

Brad joined him. "Got out the APB on Vernon. I told them to start with his favorite watering hole. I'm sorry he slipped past me. Trying to give chase in Gucci loafers is not a great idea. How long until we can see her?"

"It might be a while. She has numerous injuries."

His partner shuddered. "Did you see her eye? What kind of guy would do that to someone he loves?"

Logan shrugged. He'd never understood violence in general and domestic violence, in particular. Not in Atlanta and especially not here in the Springs. Growing up, Walton Springs seemed to be an idyllic community. Now that he worked for law enforcement, he witnessed the dark underbelly present that could be found in every city.

His thoughts turned to Karlyn Campbell. She'd been in the back of his mind since they'd met. Maybe he'd run up and see how her father was doing.

"I'm going to head over to ICU for a few minutes. Get the photos of Mrs. Cankins. I doubt we'll be able to get a statement now. I have a feeling Loretta's going to need some fast work and plenty of strong meds."

"Mr. Campbell?"

He nodded. "Yeah. As long as we're here, I thought I might check and see how he's doing. I won't be too long."

Logan hit the elevator bank. When the doors opened on the ICU floor, his gut told him he saw too much activity for this time of night. He hurried down the hall and spied Karlyn and Martha Campbell huddled together.

He stood a moment and decided to leave. It looked as if Broderick Campbell was in crisis. He didn't need to invade the family's privacy.

Then his eyes met Karlyn's. Hers shone like large emeralds. Drawn to them, his feet automatically stepped toward her.

Staff in scrubs began filing out of the room. Martha Campbell edged closer to the door but he and Karlyn remained locked eye to eye. Logan sensed a doctor coming out, taking Martha's elbow, and leading her back to Karlyn.

"I'm sorry, Mrs. Campbell. His heart gave out."

The older woman wrapped her arms around her daughter and cried softly. Karlyn remained dry-eyed, staring up at Logan.

The doctor touched Karlyn's shoulder. "I'm sorry

for your loss, Miss Campbell. You'll need to see the desk nurse regarding making arrangements for your father."

The physician left. Martha pulled away from her daughter and entered the room. Logan watched as Mrs. Campbell went to her husband and fell across the bed, dissolving into tears. He looked back at Karlyn.

Without hesitation, she walked to him. Logan folded her into his arms.

9

Atlanta was sprawling. Impersonal. After the seven murders in the city, he decided to challenge himself. Up the ante. Mortonville proved a great hunting ground. Not far from his residence. But he played by his rules.

Number One Rule—Never shit in your own back yard.

He'd always followed the rules.

He looked around and decided this medium-sized suburb would take more skill to keep from being detected. He'd found several specimens that would do nicely.

Like Ted Harrison.

Variety proved key in this series. Good old Randy had been fifty-one. A widower with no kids. Ted here was only twenty-three. A fireman. Engaged to a breathtaking blonde whom the guy had just fucked three times in the last two hours. The blonde had left twenty minutes ago. She lived with her parents, so he guessed they expected their baby back home on a weeknight.

That was fine. Ted lived alone. And it was only nine-thirty.

Plenty of time to have some fun.

He eased the closet door all the way open from the slit he'd watched through as Ted and Blondie did it twice in *front of him. He'd heard the first time when they arrived hours earlier.*

They hadn't made it upstairs. And when they did, he'd enjoyed the show they put on. Especially knowing it was the last time for them to be together.

Maybe he could attend the funeral and comfort the blonde.

Part of him wished he could've killed the fiancée, too. But that would disrupt the pattern. The pattern was the most important thing about this series.

The Rainbow Killings.

His most famous group yet.

He smiled as he heard Fireman Ted singing joyfully in the shower.

Ted would be singing a different song. Very soon.

His own blood sang in his veins as he began to think of all the wonderful things he and Ted would accomplish tonight. As a fireman, orange definitely would be his specimen's color.

He couldn't wait for Ted to walk through the door so they could get started.

10

Karlyn glanced at the navy suit she'd picked up off the rack at a local department store. She hadn't brought much in the way of clothes, despite the fact that she'd been told her father's condition was serious. Maybe she'd been in denial as she packed.

She headed downstairs, which bustled with activity. Caterers had arrived from Atlanta an hour earlier. Broderick Campbell left strict orders as to what foods should be served after the funeral, down to the condiments.

Her mother, looking lovely in a lilac suit, stood with Graydon Snow. The editor had deep circles under his eyes, but he was impeccably dressed, down to the navy silk handkerchief jutting from his pocket.

She went to greet him. "Hello, Mr. Snow. Thank you for coming."

He kissed her cheek. "Hello, Karlyn. I'm sorry about Broderick's passing."

Karlyn wondered at his words. Meetings between the two were legendary—and loud—as Graydon tried to give editing advice to his famous client. Broderick refused most of it, claiming Graydon messed with true genius.

The elderly editor brightened. "Your father does have one last novel slated for fall. It's his most accessible work ever."

"Meaning people will actually understand what it's about?"

"Don't be disrespectful," Martha warned her.

Graydon waved away the words. "It's dense as ever —but the biting sarcasm is more discernible. It will outsell anything he's done."

He smiled at her. "You're having a wonderful career. I hear one of your Matt Collins books is going to be made into a film. Who's writing the screenplay?"

Karlyn shivered involuntarily. "I'm supposed to. I haven't touched it since I've been in Walton Springs. I need to get back to New York and—"

"You can't leave me!"

Her mother's words startled her. Martha Campbell never gave her daughter the time of day, much less longed for her company.

"Move in with me, dear. At least for a few weeks. With your marriage ending, you're at odds and ends. The house has plenty of room. You could use your father's office to work."

Sit in his chair while she crafted her first screenplay? It seemed almost sacrilegious.

That only made her want to do it.

It would be easier to meet with Chris if she remained in Georgia. Plus, she wouldn't have to waste time finding a place to live back in Manhattan. She could finish the screenplay. Wrap up her novel. Figure out what she wanted to do with her life.

"If you want me to."

"You may stay as long as you choose, Karlyn. We'll get to know each other again."

"You've never known me," she whispered under

her breath as Martha offered Graydon a cup of coffee
before they left for the service.

It was worse than Karlyn imagined. She should have
hired security. Who knew a funeral in a small town
would be turned into a zoo? She'd thought a few reporters from New York might attend. Broderick was
well known but it wasn't as if a former president or
Oscar winner had died.

When they turned the corner, she spied photogra-
phers lined outside the church, snapping away at
everyone who entered St. Michael's Episcopalian. Fortunately, their driver bypassed the crowd and drove
them to a rear entrance. A mousy associate pastor led
them in a side door and to their seats inside the
packed sanctuary. At her urging, he promised to notify
Chief Risedale of the situation immediately.

The service began. The head clergyman opened
with remarks describing what a warm, caring man
Broderick Campbell had been. Karlyn tuned out his
words. Her father was cold, aloof, and had perfected
the art of being a bastard.

Instead, her focus turned to Logan Warner.

Ever since her father died and she'd been encom-
passed in the handsome detective's arms for a brief
moment of comfort, she couldn't rid herself of his. It
seemed shallow to have the type of thoughts that
flitted through her mind concerning the lawman, but
she couldn't help it. He oozed sex appeal. Images of
having mind-blowing sex with him wouldn't go away.
She felt herself flushing with guilt.

The funeral service ended. She took her mother's
arm. Graydon Snow captured the other side. Together,

they guided Martha down the aisle and out into the cool, overcast March day. Immediately, flashbulbs went off, blinding Karlyn.

And then the questions came, fast and furious.

"Karlyn, why did Mario leave you?"

"Karlyn, are you having an affair? Is that what's behind the divorce?"

"Did your father ghostwrite your novels?"

"Who will play Matt Collins in the movies?"

"Karlyn, confirm or squelch the rumors. Are you pregnant?"

That last question took her by surprise. She had always wanted a child. Mario felt a baby would be a distraction from their careers. At this point, she was thirty-two and divorced. A child was the last thing she needed.

But she would have given anything to have one.

She ignored all the shouted questions as she inched down the concrete steps, yet reporters kept firing at her.

"Karlyn, did you write your father's last two books?"

"Who is Matt Collins based on?"

"Is it true your father cut you out of his will?"

She remained dry-eyed and determined to get through the pack of wolves. She noticed policemen stationed in the street this time, directing traffic as people left the church. Chief Risedale must have realized he had one hell of a mess on his hands and sent every available patrolman to the unexpected chaos at St. Michael's.

They reached the car. Karlyn panicked as the crush of the press separated her from her mother and Graydon. She saw them retreat inside the car while she floated away as if she'd broken through the ice on a lake and found herself swept quickly downriver by the rapid flow.

A hand latched onto her wrist. Strong fingers reassured her as they tugged her away from the madness.

It was Logan Warner. He flashed her a determined look that told her he would get her out of there.

Somehow, he did. One moment she'd been on that tide being washed out to sea. The next, she was fed into a dark sedan with orders to lock the door. Logan managed to make it to the driver's side and slipped in.

"You'd think you were a rock star or British royalty," he said dryly. "That was crazy."

He maneuvered the car a block and turned off the main street. A series of quick turns that would lose anyone who followed.

"Shall we head to the cemetery?"

"No." Karlyn swallowed, glad she could finally breathe. She took a deep breath, inhaling the clean scent of pine that filled the car. Logan Warner seemed like a tall pine at that moment—large, protective, and steady.

"Father's being cremated. He abhorred the idea of mourners stealing his headstone. Or the yearly ritual of visiting his grave by fans and foes alike."

Logan nodded his approval. "Smart man." He headed in the direction of her mother's house and gave her an amused glance. "So, you didn't think security was needed?"

She laughed. "It never entered my mind. Broderick was famous in a dry textbook kind of way. Back there was like media day at the Super Bowl."

"What about at the house? Expecting guests?"

She nodded. "Caterers are there. I don't know how many Mother invited over."

Logan grimaced. "That will quickly get out of

hand. The *paparazzi* will follow the cars there. If they haven't already scoped it out."

He reached for his cell. "I'll keep it off the radio. You never know who's listening to the police scanner. It's a small-town hobby."

Logan apprised dispatch of the situation and had several patrolmen sent to the Campbell homestead. He suggested finding a few off-duty officers to join them, promising they'd garner their usual rate. Karlyn nodded in agreement, eager to avoid a scene like the one at St. Michael's.

"Hopefully, that'll help." He focused on the road ahead but said, "You realize they were there as much for you as for your dad. You got some pretty brutal questions thrown your way."

She shrugged. "I'm left alone in New York. For the record, Broderick wrote his own stuff and I write mine. I left Mario, not the other way around. He had the affairs. And I'm not and never have been pregnant."

He whistled. "Maybe I should write the tell-all about you. I got all the answers I need to pick up a quick buck. Or maybe I can hit the TV circuit and do *Entertainment Tonight*. This could be a whole new career for me."

Karlyn laughed. "I don't think you could make a living off me. I'm boring. I run. I love long, hot baths. Then I write most of my waking hours when I'm not running."

"Or bathing," he quipped.

She smiled. "Actually, I light candles and bring a bath tray with pen and paper into the tub sometimes. I've scribbled some of my best ideas while my toes shrivel."

"So, you brainstorm first and then write. Do you have an outline going in? Or do you wing it?"

"Actually, a little of both. I try to have a detailed road map in order to know the general direction I'm headed." She chuckled. "But sometimes, my characters surprise me."

"I wondered how it worked."

"Everyone's different. Some people start banging on the keys. Others write a forty-page synopsis and block out every scene in advance. I fall between incredibly anal and flying by the seat of my pants." She paused. "Those kinds of writers are called pantsers, by the way."

They drove on and she added, "I read newspapers voraciously, trying to find story ideas. Ways people were murdered. Unusual events. Connections between people that weren't obvious." She looked at him appraisingly. "I might even try to pick your brain sometime if you'd let me, Detective."

He laughed. "Not much happens in the Springs that would make for a good plot." He hesitated and then said, "I did work in Atlanta. I saw way more action there."

"Why did you leave a big city force for a small town? Seems like your job in Walton Springs would be boring compared to a high-profile city such as Atlanta."

Logan's jaw tightened. "I'd rather not get into that."

Karlyn realized she'd barely avoided stepping on a land mine and changed topics. "Are you from here?"

"Grew up in the Springs. My dad's a local doctor. Mom runs a beauty shop. Forgive me, she now calls herself a stylist and it's a . . ." His nose wrinkled in the most adorable way.

"Salon," she provided.

"That's it. To me, it'll always be the beauty shop.

Memories of smelling stinky perms and hair dye that can fry your nostrils."

Karlyn laughed. "The smells are still there. Disguised better nowadays. And smart stylists provide clients with a glass of wine to help forget about them."

Logan turned onto Magnolia Lane. Two squad cars sat in front. A small crowd gathered outside.

He glanced over at her. "Showtime."

11

"Would you like to come in for a few minutes?"

Logan nodded. Little did Karlyn Campbell know, but he'd planned on it.

"Steel yourself," he said as he parked several houses down from the Campbell homestead.

He hopped out and came around to open her door, offering his hand. Her fingers gripped his tightly. A pleasant pulse of sexual energy coursed through him.

Karlyn looked up, surprised, but Logan squeezed her hand lightly. He kept her hand in his as he guided her along at a brisk rate.

"Don't make eye contact," he instructed. "Or answer any questions. And for God's sake, don't smile."

Karlyn tried to hide an emerging smile. "You sound like a defense attorney leading his guilty client up the courthouse steps. In fact, I had a scene pretty much like that in—"

"—*Bells and Whistles*. Guy was guilty of killing his wife and his mistress—all in the same night."

She gave him an appraising look. "You're a fan, Detective? Maybe I'll autograph a book for you before I leave town."

Logan wondered when that might be. Why should

he care? Karlyn Campbell was a New Yorker, not someone who'd stick around a backwater burg like the Springs.

Why did that bother the hell out of him?

He maneuvered her through the throng gathered on the lawn, nodding to the patrolmen saddled with crowd control. They made it to the front door and inside. Logan reluctantly dropped her hand.

Instantly, he smelled the hot coffee and wanted a cup. Although the rain ceased before sunrise, the March day had remained chilly and damp. A woman with her hair in a tight chignon appeared and offered to take their coats. He helped Karlyn slip out of hers and then handed off his.

She led him from the foyer into the great room. A thin man appeared with a tray, offering wine. Karlyn shook her head at the offer. Logan waved him away.

"Would you prefer coffee?" the server asked. When they both nodded, the man said, "Follow me, please."

He led them into the dining area, where an elaborate coffee service had been set up. They each took a china cup. Logan savored the rich taste of Colombian beans in the brew. Karlyn doctored hers with enough sugar to give a dentist a toothache, as well as a huge dollop of cream.

He couldn't help but tease her. "Are you sure there's any coffee in that cup?"

She blushed. "I do take it light and sweet. And I thrive on caffeine. Writing takes up energy. With a Starbucks on every corner in Manhattan, it's an easy habit to slip into."

"What's your favorite? Pumpkin Spice? Vanilla? Mocha Frappuccino?

Karlyn assessed him. "For a man from a small

town with no Starbucks in sight, you know your gourmet flavors."

Logan's teasing stopped. Felicity had been the Starbucks addict, picking up a cup if she dropped the twins off at school. The memory hit him square in the gut, deflating him like a needle jammed into a balloon. He tried never to think of the past. Unfortunately, it had a tendency to creep up and wallop him on the head when he least expected.

The arrival of a wave of people saved him from answering her. They included Martha Campbell and a distinguished man with a trim Van Dyke beard in silver and a blue pocket square peering from his pocket. Others followed behind them.

Karlyn went to greet her mother. Logan moved near a bay window and sat on a piano bench. He'd always been an observer at parties, studying those around him, making up stories about them, wondering how close he came to the truth.

He watched her move about the room, more intrigued with her than before. Knowing she'd be tied up, he decided to grab another cup of coffee before slipping out.

He met Martha Campbell at the coffee urn.

"Thank you for getting Karlyn here safely. I saw you take charge." She frowned. "Broderick was a very private man. He would've viewed that spectacle with distaste."

Logan sipped the hot liquid. "The Springs tried to leave the two of you to your privacy. It's always been a respectful place."

"With Broderick gone, I plan to immerse myself in town life."

Her words took him aback. "You do?"

"My husband withdrew from the world to create

his own on the page. I loved him so I chose to become a part of that solitude."

She gave him an impish look. "It will surprise people to learn I'm quite outgoing. I love social events. Perhaps you can recommend a few activities?"

She rested a hand on his sleeve and smiled beseechingly at him. The Springs would be on high gossip alert now with the Merry Widow out on the prowl before her husband's ashes were delivered to the house.

Logan eased his coffee cup to his lips, forcing Martha to drop her hand. He smiled at her innocently.

"Tell you what, Mrs. Campbell. I'll give you my mom's phone number. She runs the local hair salon."

"Resa Warner is your mother? Oh, she's a lovely woman. Quite talented with her scissors, as well. I get a much better cut from her than I ever did in San Francisco."

"Mom's involved with many activities in the Springs. Garden club. Bible study. Pilates." He set down his saucer and pulled out his ever-present pad and pen, scribbling his mom's contact info.

Karlyn stepped up at that moment. "I see you're entertaining Detective Warner."

"He's helping me make friends in town. I think I'll be best friends with his mother. In fact, I believe I'll ask your parents to dinner tomorrow to get the ball rolling. You must come, too, Logan. Wouldn't that be nice, Karlyn?"

Karlyn's puzzled look spoke volumes. Logan knew he had been taken aback by the suddenly friendly Mrs. Campbell and wondered how much she'd been under the thumb of her much-older husband. She beamed at the prospect of kicking her heels up and starting a social life in the Springs.

"I'll call Resa as soon as my guests leave and tell her it was at your suggestion," Martha promised. "See you tomorrow night. Seven-thirty."

He watched Martha sashay away. His gaze met Karlyn's. They both burst out laughing.

"What has gotten into her?" she asked. "Mother looks like a kid in a candy store picking out all the forbidden sweets she never had."

Logan ventured, "She told me your dad didn't like to socialize. Out of respect, she became a part of the isolated world he created."

He glanced across the room and watched the new widow as she laughed at a comment. "I'd say she's a butterfly emerging from a long stay in a cocoon—and not one of her own making."

"We've never been close," Karlyn confessed. "Mother told me once they regretted having children. That Broderick would always come first. I was left alone while they lived in their own world. I'll have to admit it's a shock to my system to hear her inviting guests for dinner. She's even asked me to stay in Walton Springs."

Logan smiled at her news. "Do you plan to hang around the Springs?"

She nodded. "I will while I'm working on a screenplay. I wrote the novel, but screenwriting is a different ball game. I may ask a studio collaborator to come for a few days. We've talked on the phone. Chris lives in Atlanta. I think we'd get a lot more work done here than if I went back to New York."

She sighed. "Besides, I signed my divorce papers before I left the city. I don't even have a place to live. I might as well put that off and concentrate on what I do best—work."

A pang of jealousy shot through Logan at the mention of some guy named Chris spending time with Karlyn. He couldn't understand why this feeling flooded him. He hadn't been in a relationship since his own divorce became finalized four years ago. He'd had a few dates, mostly set-ups, but work was his life.

Until now. What was so different about Karlyn Campbell?

"Are you free tonight?"

Her words slammed him from his meanderings.

"Uh, yeah."

Great. He sounded as articulate as a rock. Karlyn was used to witty repartee from suave Manhattan men. He wouldn't score many points being monosyllabic.

"I'd like to pick your brain about a scene I'm having trouble with. Do you like Italian?"

"Uh, yeah."

Brilliant. He was on a roll. The English Lit minor dazzled yet again in a stunning show of dialogue.

"I'm a pretty good cook. We could talk over dinner. That is, if you're not busy. Or if it's okay with your girlfriend." She nodded to his hand. "Since I don't see a wedding ring."

"I don't have a girlfriend. Or dinner plans." He glanced at her mother. "Do you think your mom would mind? So soon after the funeral?"

Karlyn frowned. "I hadn't thought of that. How about I take you out? I'm sure she'll be tied up anyway. It'll be my treat since I have lots of questions."

"It's a deal." Logan deliberately didn't say date. He didn't want to attach significance to the fact he would be eating in public with a person of the opposite sex, which hadn't occurred in longer than he could remember.

"Since you know the area, I'll let you choose the

restaurant. Thanks for agreeing to do this, Logan. It's time I got back to work. It keeps me sane."

Which was the last place his mind was right now. Usually, Logan lived for work. All of a sudden, he'd pushed it far away. All he could think about was spending more time with the very sexy author standing next to him.

"I'll pick you up at seven." He drained his coffee and set down the saucer. Logan retrieved his trench coat and made his way through the spectators outside. He couldn't believe he had plans with a special lady.

Even if she did want to talk murder at dinner.

12

Karlyn slid into the chair and watched Logan sit opposite her. The man looked good—Polo button-down, gray slacks, sports coat—and he smelled even better.

All male.

She forced herself not to sprawl across the table and breathe him in.

She glanced at the oak paneling and hardwood floors. Soft piano music sounded from the next room. "Nice place."

"The food has never let me down. And if you have a thing for chocolate, save room for dessert. In fact, I have a friend whose wife always starts with dessert here."

Karlyn laughed. "I've never been brave enough to try that."

"If you're full after the meal, we'll split something."

"As long as it's chocolate?"

He shrugged. "Or their key lime pie. I could live with either choice."

"Hmmm. Maybe we need to order both. What else is good?"

He opened the menu and scanned it quickly. "The

shrimp and linguini. Their scallops and angel hair pasta."

"Seems like you come here often."

Logan shook his head. "A few times a year. But I've eaten at Lombardi's all my life—thirty-five years and counting."

The server took their drink orders and returned quickly with their wine and a breadbasket.

"I've never met a piece of bread I didn't like," Karlyn admitted as she generously buttered a slice of sourdough.

"You must work out. I don't see any bread handles on you," he joked.

"I'm a runner. Picked it up in college from a boyfriend. The relationship ended but the running kept me going." She bit into the sourdough and sighed. "Whenever I'm working on a story idea, I toss on my Nikes and head to the Park."

"Central Park?"

She nodded. "I used to live a few blocks away. I've pounded its pavement many times, characters and scenes whirling in my head."

"I ran track in high school," Logan shared. "I still run. An instructor at the academy preached you never want a perp to get away because he outclassed you in a footrace. I still take his advice to heart."

"Even though you're a detective now? I didn't think plainclothesmen chased suspects. Except in books and movies."

"The former Boy Scout in me likes to be prepared. Besides, I wouldn't want Matt Collins showing me up."

Karlyn laughed. "My readers expect me to put Matt in perilous situations. He has to be able to run like the wind. It's saved his life more than a few times."

Their salads arrived and as she dug in, she said, "Tell me about your work. Any unusual cases?"

He chewed thoughtfully. "Are you milking me for new book material or interested in what I do?"

"Either way, you'll tell me. I'm good at getting what I want," she said with a smile.

"I'll bet you are."

The teasing words didn't mask the undercurrent of sexual energy sparking between them. Karlyn was afraid she'd forgotten how to flirt but she seemed to be doing fine. The flicker in Logan's eyes let her know she was right on track.

He took another bite. "I could tell you about the brawl I broke up last week at the salad bar between two senior citizens during Sunset Hour."

Karlyn chuckled. "Were they fighting over the cherry tomatoes or mushrooms?"

"Neither. It started over who could make the most trips back to the salad bar and somehow segued into a woman they both found interesting. She came in every Tuesday and hadn't showed up yet. By the time she got there and I'd been called, the old coots had demolished all the salad plates and had moved on to the frozen yogurt machine."

"And they say retirement is boring."

"That's about as exciting as the Springs gets. Although we did have a local woman learn that her son hid his bagged drugs in the peanut butter jar. She told us she started hiding her jewelry in it, too, thinking it was a safe place. Naturally, he found it. And sold it."

"At least your life's not dull," she teased.

Logan shrugged. "Most of the violent stuff happened when I was with Atlanta PD. Gang bangers. Meth houses blowing up. Domestic abuse. Robberies gone wrong. I have a thousand stories about that. The Springs has crime but it's mostly on a lesser scale."

Their entrees arrived and their talk turned to books and music. It surprised her how much they had in common. She hadn't wanted to think of tonight as a date, but Logan Warner made for good company.

They decided on the key lime pie and some decadent chocolate mess for dessert.

As they ate, she decided to press him a little about his personal life. "You said you didn't have a girlfriend. Did you leave one back in Atlanta?"

"No. Just an ex-wife."

So, he was divorced. "Any kids?"

Logan grew quiet. "No. You?"

"No. Mario didn't want any. I finally realized that I did want them. Just not with him." Karlyn sighed. "I knew for a long time that we weren't working. Mario was distant or absent for most of our relationship."

She stirred some sweetener into her decaf. "I wasn't the greatest marriage partner, either. I tend to get wrapped up in my work, creating people and places. Especially if I'm on deadline."

Logan looked thoughtful and then said, "I wasn't the best husband myself. Married to the job, like most cops. At least in your work, you can create a happy ending. Matt gets the killer or solves his case. I don't always find my bad guy. Even if I do, the D.A. might not get a conviction."

Karlyn saw how down he had become and tried to lighten the mood.

"Hey, my life sucks sometimes. My characters misbehave constantly. I plan what they should do, then they deviate off-course like clockwork. Eventually, I get them back on track by the end."

Unlike her marriage. She regretted how long she'd

drifted aimlessly, hoping Mario would change. Hoping things would improve between them.

Hoping she could love and be loved.

They finished their coffee and strolled to the car. The night air was clear and cool. Logan opened her door. Karlyn tried to remember if Mario had ever done that for her.

He stepped into the driver's side and turned to her.

"Do you believe people in real life can have that happy ending?"

Karlyn hesitated. "It's possible. But not everyone finds it. Sometimes, life gets in the way."

"Was this a date?" he asked.

She bit her lip and decided to be honest. "I didn't think so. I found you interesting and wanted to talk about my writing with you. I thought I'd ask you a few questions about your profession."

"But we didn't talk much about it, did we?" His moss green eyes drilled into hers.

"No," she said softly. "We didn't. But I did ask you about your work. So, maybe—"

"I don't date," he announced. "I've been out a few times since my divorce, but it seemed pointless."

"I don't date either," she agreed. "The ink's barely dry on my divorce papers. I'm giving myself some time to heal emotionally."

"Then if this isn't a date, I guess I shouldn't do this."

Logan leaned over, his hand cupping the back of her neck. Before she could react, his lips met hers.

Magic.

Instant and real. Karlyn became soft putty in Logan's capable hands. The kiss deepened. She found herself falling, spinning, whirling in a heat-filled maelstrom. His mouth dominated hers, enslaved her, created a longing she'd never experienced.

And as fast as it started, it ended.

Logan pulled away, breathing hard. His eyes glittered with passion.

"If this is *not* dating," Karlyn told him, "I think I'd like to *try* dating with you sometime."

13

"Have a good time?"

Karlyn jumped. Her mother stood at the end of the foyer, a wineglass in her hand. Martha motioned her to follow. Karlyn entered the den and took a seat in a leather wingback chair.

"Need a nightcap?"

She shook her head. "No, I had two glasses of merlot at dinner. I'll never sleep if I have any more."

Martha shrugged and topped off her glass. "Where did Detective Warner take you for your date?"

"It wasn't a date."

Karlyn hoped she didn't blush as she protested. She ran a hand through her hair and glanced at the flickering images on the TV with feigned interest.

Think about anything but that kiss.

Martha's brows shot up. "Logan Warner is an attractive man. The woman that lands him will be lucky."

She looked back at her mother. "I'm licking my wounds from my divorce. I don't have any interest in dating."

Martha set down her glass. "Let's try again. I want us to be friends, Karlyn."

The thought caused her to frown. "Honestly? I don't know if we can."

Martha sighed. "I was so incredibly young when I married Broderick. Twenty-one to his forty-two. Our love was all consuming, like Roman candles erupting when we looked at one another. He was everything I thought I wanted."

Her mother paused, gazing at her steadily. "Then I found I wanted more. I wanted a child, Karlyn. I wanted *you*."

The words shocked her. "Why?"

"After a few years together, I realized what was missing. I knew Broderick would never agree to a child. He considered them too demanding. He wanted the focus on him."

Martha stood and paced the room. "I waited to tell him I was pregnant. He ordered me to have an abortion immediately, but I was past the legal point." Martha's eyes narrowed. "I threatened to leave him. In the end, he agreed to my having you—if I would get my tubes tied and if he would not be responsible in any way for raising you."

Her mother's mouth quivered. "So, I kept you. And wondered if it was a mistake on my part. I was never there for you. I let his selfish desires dictate both my life and yours."

Martha stopped in front of her. "I don't want to know what happened between you and Mario. It doesn't matter. But I'm here for you. From now on."

Martha pulled Karlyn to her feet and hugged her. "This is a new beginning for us. Get to know me. If not as mother and daughter, then as friends. Let me get to know you."

Karlyn made an instant decision. She might regret it down the line, but she was starved for her

mother's affection. And that surprised the hell out
of her.

"All right. I'll stay. For now. I can't make any
promises about what might happen, Mother. But I'll
try."

KARLYN AWOKE before six and decided to go for a run.
Fortunately, she'd brought her training shoes and one
workout outfit. She would need to do some big-time
shopping or send for more of her clothes. Alicia had
graciously stored Karlyn's things in a guest room of
her apartment since Karlyn hadn't searched for a
place to live during the divorce proceedings.

She found her rhythm early and fell into an easy
pace, enjoying the cool breeze. She ran down the main
street of Walton Springs, passing the library and town
center, complete with fire and police stations and post
office. Farther down the block she spotted a drugstore,
grocer, hardware store, and salon. She slowed as she
passed by, wondering if this was Logan's mother's
shop.

Karlyn ran another forty-five minutes, finding a
lone Starbucks. She grinned. A hot detective and a
Starbucks all in the same place couldn't be all bad.
She passed the high school and a huge park, where
she turned off and enjoyed several minutes of solitude
as she pounded along.

Finally, she retraced her steps and returned home.
After showering and dressing, she gathered her notes
and laptop and headed to her father's office. She entered and noted the faint smell of pipe tobacco that
still lingered.

The battered Remington perched in the center, the

only item on the desktop. Karlyn remembered sneaking into Broderick Campbell's study and sitting in the leather monstrosity of a chair when he went for his daily walk, longing to be a writer. She never stayed long, afraid that a warm seat would alert him to her transgression.

Still, she sat in it now, a talented writer and best-selling novelist in her own right. She wouldn't let the chair—or the ghost of a memory—keep her from the business at hand. The screenplay deserved the most attention, so she spent the next hour re-reading what she'd written and then her notes for the upcoming scene. She'd left off in this spot the day she'd met Mario and his lawyer. She couldn't write a word that morning and she'd blamed it on the upcoming meeting. Now, she realized she'd backed herself into a corner. The roadblock glared viciously at her. She could almost taste what needed to happen. Having it occur in the three pages she'd allotted would be difficult to pull off.

Writer's block wasn't new. She raced through some manuscripts lightning fast, while others bogged down with a saggy middle. Sometimes, she put a work-in-progress aside and completed another project or two before ever coming back to what she considered the problem child.

That option didn't exist for this screenplay. Her contract called for a completed draft in six weeks. If the studio liked it, she would polish it and send it to the director. If not, they would award the project to another, more experienced writer. She would get paid regardless but she wanted to be able to bring it home. Matt was her baby. She knew him better than anyone. She could do this.

Two hours later, she realized she needed help.

She stretched and saw it was almost eleven-thirty. Her stomach rumbled. Karlyn puttered into the kitchen and found her mother talking animatedly on the phone.

"I'm sure they had a wonderful time, Resa. Oh, here's Karlyn now, looking hungry as a bear. Listen, I will see you this afternoon for that trim and then we'll do dinner tonight. Talk to you soon."

Martha looked up with flushed cheeks. Karlyn realized her mother was . . . happy. She didn't remember that emotion registering before. Martha had always been, well, Martha. Calm. Reserved. Detached. This woman was younger and more vibrant.

Her mother pulled leftovers from the refrigerator, chattering the entire time. "I spoke to Resa Warner. She and her husband are coming for dinner tonight. I can't wait to have them over. I should call Logan and remind him about dinner." She paused. "Or maybe you could do that."

Karlyn shook her head. "You can. I'm going to eat a quick bite and get back to work."

Martha frowned and turned away. Karlyn felt the wave of disappointment hit her. Still, she stuck to her guns. She would not throw herself at Logan Warner like some desperate 1950s chick—however, she wouldn't mind seeing him two nights in a row.

She excused herself after a few minutes, taking another bottled water and some cheese and crackers back to the study with her. That would allow her to keep working uninterrupted.

She put in two hours of writing, deleting, thinking, jotting new notes, and consulting her outline. Then more writing and deleting again.

"This is ridiculous."

She scrolled her cell contacts for Chris Stevenson.

Karlyn punched in his number and hoped she would get Chris and not his voicemail.

"Hello. This is Chris's phone, Warren answering."

The new voice with the thick Southern twang threw her. "Uh, this is Karlyn Campbell. Chris is—"

"Oh, my god! Karlyn Campbell. *Karlyn Campbell!* I absolutely adore you. I wish that beautiful creation of Matt Collins could step from the pages and whisk me away to Tahiti. And Chris, too. But you don't even know me, darling. I'm Warren Newlin, a terrific hair-stylist, and the love of Chris's life. At least this week."

"Chris is that fickle?" Karlyn had gotten a different impression from the few conversations she'd had with the screenwriter. In fact, she hadn't even known he was gay. Or bi. Or involved with anyone.

"Oh, hush, of course not. Chris is my dream come true. I'm a drama queen, through and through. Everything is larger than life with me because I'm Southern. Chris accepts it so I'm good. He even takes out the trash, which makes him the best man on the planet. Here he is now, coming in from doing that very task. Hold on a minute, Karlyn, I'll get him."

She took a deep breath and shook her head. Warren Newlin was a pure tornado of energy.

"Karlyn? How are you?" Chris's deep rumble sounded over the phone. "I saw the news about your dad. And I apologize for Warren getting ahold of the phone. He's been dying to talk to you ever since I told him we were doing a little work together. He's read all your stuff—historical romances, romantic suspense, the mainstream stuff. He desperately wants to meet you."

"As long as he doesn't turn into a Category 5 hurricane, I'd love to meet him."

"I assume you'll go back to New York now that the

funeral's over. Where did you leave off? Last time we talked, you'd finished the scene with the Mafia don and dominatrix that Matt stumbled into."

"Actually, that's why I'm calling. I've decided to stay in Walton Springs for a while. And the Big Ugly is standing in my way and won't let me write around it. I wanted to see if you're free. Maybe you could come up for a few days and help me out. You'll get a co-credit when I deliver the screenplay to the studio. And you're welcome to stay here. There's plenty of room."

"Walton Springs is only thirty miles away once you get outside Atlanta. I'd love to work together in person. Are you sure your mom won't mind?"

"The house is huge, and Mother enjoys entertaining. I think it would help her keep her mind off things."

"Hold on. Yes, I'm going up." Chris paused. "I'll ask." He sighed. "About how long are we talking?"

"A few days. Maybe a week at the most."

"Think there's room enough for two?"

"Absolutely. Warren sounds like a breath of fresh air. Whenever you can make it. You're the one doing me the favor."

"I can drive up this afternoon. Warren says he has a few appointments he can't break but he can make it by Saturday afternoon. Can I bring anything? Living with a born and bred Southerner, he's taught me I always need to bring something when I come a-calling."

Karlyn laughed. "All I need is your talent. And inspiration. Bring your own laptop. I'm a little possessive about mine."

"I'll run a few errands and be there by six."

"Sounds terrific." She gave him the address. "I'll let you read what I have when you get here. We've got company coming for dinner, a local detective and his parents. Maybe we can pump him if we need some of the crime details tweaked."

"I love talking to experts but I'm not sure this guy would've seen a lot in Walton Springs. It's a little like Mayberry. Matt's a New York guy, through and through."

"Logan spent several years with Atlanta PD. He knows his way around gangbangers and homicides. He could be a good resource." She laughed. "Besides, he's read my novels and likes them."

"We all need that ego booster around, especially when the creative juices dry up. I'll see you by six."

Karlyn hung up, feeling more confident. She needed to let her mother know that houseguests would arrive soon. Before, she might have hesitated with such news. Now with the new and improved Martha 2.0, she believed her mother would be in the thick of things.

She decided to stop working. Chris would jump-start her professionally. She felt an easy rapport with him.

And hopefully, Logan Warner might jumpstart her personally.

14

Logan shut down his computer and turned off the monitor. Ever since the mayor's efficiency expert studied the work habits of city employees, they'd received almost daily emails on how to save energy. He grimaced. If he won the race for police chief, that kind of bureaucratic crap would be unavoidable.

Brad sauntered into the squad room. "Just landed a hot date tomorrow with that new receptionist. You doing anything this weekend?"

Logan stood. "Having dinner with my parents tonight."

His partner's eyes lit up. "Your mom making roast beef by any chance?"

Brad often wrangled an invitation to dinner at the Warner household. Resa loved to see a man with an appetite appreciate her cooking. Brad Patterson came with an empty stomach and a mouth full of pretty compliments.

"We've been invited by Martha Campbell to have dinner at her house. She wants to get more involved in town now that her husband's passed."

Brad chuckled. "And Resa Warner is the busiest soul in Walton Springs. Frankly, I can't believe she's never run for mayor. Maybe Mrs. Campbell will be-come her new bestie and finance a mayoral campaign."

Logan saw the look in Brad's eyes. "Don't think you can crash this dinner party, partner."

"Will the lovely Karlyn Campbell be there?"

"I suppose," he admitted grudgingly. He hadn't liked the interest Brad showed in Karlyn, he had yet to lay eyes on her. Brad was a solid partner but a total womanizer. Karlyn, rebounding from divorce, needed to give men like Brad a wide berth.

Especially since Logan wanted to stake a claim with her first. He'd spent a restless night thinking about the explosive kiss they'd shared. He remem-bered the countless times he'd read *Sleeping Beauty* to Ashley. She clamored for the story again and again and watched the DVD religiously. Ashley had even gone through a phase where she wanted everyone to call her Aurora, Sleeping Beauty's given name.

His kiss with Karlyn last night had awakened him, as sure as the prince's kiss has stirred Aurora back to life.

Logan wanted more. Much more. With her.

Brad pulled out his phone as he hit a few keys on his computer, pulling up a file. He smiled and punched in a number. Logan seethed, knowing ex-actly how this would play out.

"Mrs. Campbell? This is Brad Patterson from the Walton Springs Police Department. I was calling to check on you, ma'am."

He didn't bother listening to the rest. He'd seen Brad's charm in action before. Logan walked out, knowing Brad would be sitting at the Campbell dinner table later tonight, flirting outrageously with both Karlyn and her mother.

He promised himself to stay pissed on the inside and be cool to the world on the outside.

Most of all, he would make sure Brad didn't make any headway pursuing Karlyn.

KARLYN JOINED her mother and Chris in the living room, glad that Chris fit in effortlessly upon his arrival. Martha was delighted to play hostess for the writer and his partner.

"Would you like a drink?" Chris moved to the bar. "I bartended for years in New York before I moved to Atlanta. It kept me going before I sold a screenplay and could give it up to write fulltime."

"I'll take a pomegranate martini," she told him. "Thanks."

"I think I'll try one, as well," her mother said.

Chris mixed the drinks and handed them over.

She sipped it. "Perfection."

The doorbell sounded. Martha excused herself to answer it.

Karlyn told Chris, "Thanks again. You've entertained Mother since you got here. The best medicine for her is to be around others right now."

"She's an interesting lady. Lots of good stories. She's met everyone—Capote, Clooney, Clinton. She should write a book."

"My father knew everyone, even if he didn't care much for the company of others."

Logan walked into the room, escorting his mother and father. A man she didn't recognize followed them. Karlyn noted looking at Dr. Warner was like seeing Logan twenty-five years down the road.

Mrs. Warner came straight to her and shook her

hand warmly. "Miss Campbell, I'm Resa Warner. You're the only author I read. And your haircut is re-markable. I love all those messy layers of honey blonde."

Karlyn pushed a hand through it. "It's actually starting to get a little long. Logan tells me you have your own salon. Since I'm staying in town for the near future, I'll need to book an appointment with you."

"You do that, hon. And who is this young man? I must say your hair is impeccable. Resa Logan. I'm a hair stylist, in case you hadn't figured it out by now."

Chris extended his hand. "Chris Stevenson, ma'am. And credit Warren Newlin with my hair. I haven't had a bad hair day since Warren took over."

Resa brightened. "*The* Warren Newlin? His last book on blow-outs opened my eyes. The tresses of Walton Springs owe a lot to Mr. Newlin's influence on my work."

Resa turned and introduced her son to Chris. Karlyn added, "Chris is a screenwriter and my collab-orator on my first attempt at a screenplay."

The stranger stepped up. "Nice to meet you, Kar-lyn. Chris. I'm Brad Patterson, Logan's partner in crime. Or I guess in solving crimes. I called to see how your mother was doing and she was kind enough to invite me to dinner tonight."

Karlyn caught Logan's eye roll and stifled a smile. She made a mental note to ask him about Brad.

The group adjourned to a large, walnut-paneled dining room. No shortage of laughter occurred. Chris told a handful of Hollywood stories of stars on the set and their tantrums. Martha added her own twist with anecdotes from the literary world. Mitchell Warner entertained the group with tales of camping trips that went awry, while Resa caught up Martha and Karlyn on local town gossip.

Over coffee and dessert, Logan spoke up.

"I'd like to run something by you." He shifted in his chair. Karlyn could see he was unsure where to start.

"Spill it, Logan," Brad chided him. "They probably already know if they've gassed up at Casey's the last couple of days."

Logan sighed. "I was afraid of that." He sat a little taller. "I'm planning to run for police chief in the upcoming May election."

Resa beamed her approval. "I think you'd make a fine chief, sweetie. More importantly, you have big city experience that Seth Berger doesn't have. I'm sure he's your main competition."

"Berger's no competition," Mitchell Warner noted. "He's a nondescript paper-pusher. Logan here knows how to solve cases. He's got the practical experience to back it up."

"I need to get five hundred signatures in order to run." He extracted a sheaf of papers from inside his jacket and looked at his father.

"I'd be honored, sir, if you were the first registered voter to sign my petition."

Karlyn saw the doctor's eyes mist with tears. He pulled a pen from his pocket and scrawled his signature. He eyed Logan with a bit of mischief.

"I suppose this means I'll also be the first person you hit up for a campaign donation."

His son grinned. "Great idea, Dad!"

Resa smiled as her husband passed her the pen and petition. "You definitely need a haircut, Logan. Citizens in the Springs will want a well-groomed chief."

"Does this mean I have to get a manicure, too?"

Resa laughed. "I'd say yes. If you look good, it's good advertising for me."

Both Brad and Martha signed. Chris and Karlyn apologized that they couldn't.

"That's okay. I'll hit the square tomorrow for the rest. It'll have a lot of pedestrian traffic since it's a Saturday." He blew out a long breath. "I guess I'm officially in the race."

They raised their coffee cups in a toast.

"If I can keep crime down between now and the election, I think I'll have a good chance," Logan declared.

"That's if we can keep the Rainbow Killer out of the Springs," Brad muttered.

Chris shivered. "Those are some pretty violent murders. Everywhere I go, that's all people are talking about."

Karlyn frowned. "The Rainbow Killer? I've been busy writing lately and haven't caught much news. Feed me some details."

Chris explained. "They started about five months ago in downtown Atlanta. A couple a month since then. They've taken place in various parts of the city until the last one. It occurred in Mortonville. First time a Rainbow Murder took place outside the Atlanta city limits, in a suburb north of the city."

"That's only about twenty minutes from here," Karlyn remarked. "I passed through it on my way here. Why are they called the Rainbow Murders?"

"After killing his victims, he paints them from head to toe in a solid color of the rainbow," Logan said. "Cops nicknamed him Roy G. Biv because he's stuck with that order—red, orange, yellow, green, blue, indigo, violet."

"The pattern wasn't obvious until after the third murder," Brad added. "He completed the cycle of seven murders and then started repeating the colors with a new set of victims."

"Who are his victims? And why hasn't this gotten more press?" Karlyn asked. "I'm surprised the media isn't all over this. They love it lurid and violent."

"The mayor of Atlanta has tried to keep it quiet. They don't want people to panic as they did with the Atlanta child murders years ago." Logan sighed. "The biggest problem is that there's no profile victim. Roy has killed an elderly widow. Two gay men. A hooker and a lawyer. Then an accountant and a plumber. You name it. Roy's victims are a hodgepodge of people."

Karlyn thought a moment. "You know, John Grisham did a non-fiction book about murder in Oklahoma. I would love to sink my teeth into something like that. Maybe I should write about this Rainbow Killer."

"Don't do it," Logan warned. "We don't know who this guy is, much less why he does it. If you get involved, it raises the profile of the entire case. Hell, you could even wind up as a victim yourself, Karlyn."

Chris added, "Logan's right, Karlyn. Besides, you've got the screenplay to finish. Dabble with Roy later. If then."

"You're also three-quarters through a new stand-alone, dear," her mother reminded her. "No time to get involved in these grisly murders."

Karlyn disagreed but it was obvious she wasn't finding any support around this table. "Maybe you're right," she said. "Anyone need a refill?"

She rose to get the coffeepot but as she walked to the kitchen, she couldn't help but think how much Roy G. Biv intrigued her.

15

T he minute he saw her, he knew she had to be Yellow. He'd done a Black teacher in Atlanta. Retired. Had kids and grandkids. Feisty for a woman on Social Security.

But Jeanine was forty years younger. White. An elementary art teacher in his new hunting ground—Fountain Valley. A specimen he couldn't resist. He'd watched her for weeks. Knew in his gut that this strawberry blonde was the next one.

Bumping into her at the grocery store had been genius. He gave his sheepish smile and struck up a conversation, pretending not to know the difference between a melon and cantaloupe. She helped him. Teased a little with him. Rewarded him with a genuine smile. Was at a point where he knew she wanted him to ask for her number, so he pretended he got a call and excused himself. Noted her disappointment as he hustled from the market.

Now, she was a bit tipsy from drinks with a few friends. She'd remained behind to hit the restroom. He knew her car. He knew her house. He knew everything about her.

Especially how good she was going to look in all yellow.

She exited the restaurant. Headed for her car. He'd parked next to her. Just before she approached, he stepped from a doorway and stood next to his car. Watched her approach. Saw her do a double take. Let a smile escape as their eyes met. He'd feed her a line about being stood up by a blind date. How embarrassed he was. How he was still hungry. Ask her if she was. Suggest to her that they get a pizza—no melons involved.

She'd laugh. He'd nudge her some. Make her think going back to her place and having pizza delivered was her idea.

They'd eat. Drink a little wine.

Then he'd have the time of his life.

Jeanine? Not so much.

16

"What do you think?" Karlyn asked.

"You nailed it." Chris wrapped her in a bear hug. "Matt pops off the page. The dialogue is crisp. The pacing is terrific. The studio will want more. This has sequel—no, series—written all over it."

She sighed. "And it only took a week. Your suggestions had me pouring words onto the page. I wouldn't have completed this without you, Chris. You saved the entire project."

He squeezed her hand. "You're a dream to work with, Karlyn. Organized. Original ideas." He laughed. "Most of all, you listened to my suggestions. You wouldn't believe the screenplays I've tried to punch up with the writer fighting me tooth and nail."

Karlyn inserted the flash drive into her laptop. "I'll save it and email it to Alicia. She's a fast reader and eager to get this. We'll have her feedback by this time tomorrow."

"Ahead of schedule. The studio won't expect that."

"It's a relief to finish. I feel we did Matt justice. Now, if I could help cast him? Icing on the cake." She ran her fingers through her hair. "When will you head home? I'm not trying to get rid of you. Mother and Resa will simply die when Warren leaves with you."

Chris shook his head. "I can't believe he's stayed so long. He's had a blast hanging with Resa at the salon and going to all the social events with her and your mom. We do need to get back to Atlanta, though. I'll give him the news and start packing."

Her cell phone buzzed in her pocket. She answered it as Chris slipped out.

"Hello?"

"Hello, my beautiful."

Freaking Mario was calling her?

"I'm definitely changing my cell number."

"Karlyn. Always so dramatic."

"No, that was your specialty. Tantrums. Mood swings. Excuses for sleeping around. I'm hanging up. Goodbye."

"Wait!"

Karlyn knew she should cut the connection but the writer in her thought she might get something good from whatever her ex-husband wanted. He was a recipe for disaster. Might as well see what he asked for. Maybe he'd provide fodder for a creepy character down the road.

"My Karlyn, I have missed you."

"Cut to the chase, Mario. You want something. What?"

He began cursing in Spanish, his mother's tongue. Then Italian, which he'd picked up in art school in Florence. She rode out the torrent of words, waiting for him to wind down.

"You are so petty, my darling."

"You treated me like shit, Mario. Stomped on my heart. Spit it out. How else would you expect me to be toward you?"

"Well, I do have a small request. I want to see you. I heard your father passed. I should comfort you and your mother. And possibly borrow a bit of money. Maybe as a commission."

She expelled a loud breath, furious at his nerve. "You have got to be kidding." She almost went on her own cursing rant but decided a cool head would prevail. She'd take a firm tone with him, like a parent with a naughty child. "We are divorced, Mario. I gave you the condo. The furnishings. It's over between us. I'd give a homeless person my last dime before I'd see it in your greedy hands."

Her ex-husband let out a long string of profanity in multiple languages. Karlyn hung up and turned off her phone rather than listen to his tirade. She knew it would infuriate him—which gave her pleasure. He didn't have the unlisted number of the Walton Springs' house landline. He'd always left details like that up to her. She made a note to change her cell phone number tomorrow.

Yet, she was curious. How could he go through that kind of cash so fast, assuming he'd listed and sold the condo? Gambling? A mistress?

She didn't care enough to Google it. Mario was the past. She looked forward to her future.

Karlyn thought about it. Georgia was growing on her. Technology made it easy to stay in touch. She could write anywhere. Look at Chris. He pulled seven figures easily and lived over two thousand miles away from the major studios.

Maybe she could buy a Victorian home in Atlanta. She loved the architecture and pace of the city from book tours she'd done. The outstanding food and terrific museums made the city an attractive place to live.

Still, she had to admit she felt the tug to stay close

to her mother. Maybe the time had come for a fresh start in their relationship. Walton Springs was an idyllic town with big city conveniences a short drive away. It might be the place to put down roots.

And Logan Warner's face kept popping up in the equation. True, she was nowhere near wanting to become involved with a man but if she were? The gorgeous detective would be a good place to start. And end. What was not to like? Intelligent. Sexy as hell. Dedicated to his job.

Maybe she would stay in the Springs.

"THE WITNESS IS DISMISSED. Court is adjourned for the lunch break and will reconvene in two hours."

Logan left the stand and exited the courtroom. He saw Brad sitting on a bench, talking on his cell. Logan headed that way.

Brad caught sight of him and waved. "Okay, babe. Looks like it's my turn to testify. My partner's finished. See you tomorrow at eight." He pocketed his phone. "Everything go okay?"

Logan nodded. "You know me. With my detailed notes, I'm the last person that some public defender would trip up."

"A true-blue Boy Scout to the end. Maybe that could be your campaign slogan. Has a ring to it. Of course, nothing will ever beat *I Like Ike* or *Tippecanoe and Tyler, Too.*"

Logan ignored the comment. "The judge sounded the lunch horn as I was leaving. I guess you'll be stuck here until mid-afternoon. Want to grab a bite during the recess?"

Brad shook his head. "I got a call a few minutes

ago to pick up my car. I dropped it off this morning and had new tires put on. I'll grab a sandwich and the car. Then return here and testify. I'll see you back at the house."

Logan exited the courthouse, stepping into a sweet spring day. Not a cloud in the sky and only a slight breeze. He decided to see if Rick Mabry was available. They'd graduated from the same patrol class in Atlanta. Both gravitated back to their hometowns after time spent on the job in Atlanta. Rick made lieutenant a few months ago and ran a squad room not two blocks from the county courthouse.

He dialed the number. "Hey, Rick, it's Logan. I wrapped up testifying and wanted to see if you were free for lunch."

"Perfect timing. Ensenada okay? Order me the daily. I'm leaving now."

"Will do. See you in five."

Logan cut around the corner and entered the restaurant. He grabbed a booth and ordered two iced teas and two daily specials. By the time the chips and salsa arrived, Rick slid in across from him.

"How's Fountain Valley these days?"

Rick shoveled in a few chips. "Busy morning. Had to deal with an EEOC discrimination charge, which meant I spent a couple hours in HR, digging through personnel records. I think it's all settled. How about you?"

Logan grinned. "Got the number of signatures I needed and paid my filing fee. I'm officially a candidate in the May election. You might be sitting with the next chief of police in the Springs."

Rick let out a low whistle. "That's awesome. You have what it takes to lead a department, Logan. Have you started campaigning yet?"

"No." He laughed. "I know I'll need signs. I moved enough of them around twenty years ago. Might as well give other enterprising teens the same opportunity."

Rick thought about it. "Set up some informational meetings. You know, your ideas on what you'd change. And a website is a must. Maybe some flyers. And tweet. A lot."

"I met an author recently. I know she has a website. Maybe I can pick her brain about how to engage voters through social media."

His friend's eyes gleamed. "A she? Who's this author? And why would she take up with a sorry SOB like you?"

"It's Karlyn Campbell, the—"

"—mystery writer. No way! She's amazing. Her novels keep me guessing until the end." He eyed Logan. "And those back cover photos? Scalding hot, bro. Those brilliant green eyes scream, *'Fuck me, baby.'*" Rick studied him. "So, you know her well enough to pick her brain? You've been holding out on me, Warner."

Logan shrugged. "We've had dinner a couple of times."

Rick leaned across the table and punched him on the shoulder. "Dinners. Yeah."

The server arrived with their platters, preventing Logan from answering. His friend doused the entire meal with salsa, while Logan busied himself buttering a corn tortilla and rolling it up.

The men ate in silence a few moments, savoring the best Mexican food in the area.

"I think it's good you're having dinner with a lady."

Logan raised his eyebrows.

"Seriously. It's been a long time between dates. You

need to get out more. Hell, I can't wait to tell Hildy you've been seeing Karlyn Campbell."

Before Logan could reply, Rick's phone buzzed. Logan busied himself with the last bites of his meal while Rick took the call.

"God, no. Not here. Who did? Okay. Be there in ten. Don't let him talk to anyone but Brady and Malone. I'll check the crime scene first and then come back to see how the interview went." Rick ended the call and sat there, an odd look on his face.

"Bad news?"

His friend grimaced. "Looks like Roy G. Biv has hit Fountain Valley. An art teacher didn't report for work this morning. Didn't call in for a sub. Wasn't answering her phone. Her principal went to her house to check on her. Saw the body through the window, in all its painted glory."

Rick tossed his napkin on the table. He pulled out a twenty and dropped it there. "I got it. You up for heading over there with me?"

"Sure."

It was the first—and last—thing Logan wanted to do.

17

S ilence permeated the car. Logan took slow, even breaths. Murders rarely occurred in these little havens outside Atlanta. Detectives handled burglaries. Drugs. A few sexual assaults. If he'd been a patrolman in the Springs, he might've cleared wrecks or dealt with teenage drinking.

Murder—in this neck of the woods—brought a deep unease. More importantly, this wasn't the drugstore variety of murder. Instead, it was the work of a savvy serial killer who had murdered over and over again.

This would be Roy G. Biv's tenth victim.

Rick pulled into a cul-de-sac, waving at a patrolman moving sawhorses to block vehicles from approaching. Of course, that didn't stop the foot traffic. Logan saw a crowd of stay-at-home moms and retired citizens already gathered.

A paunchy officer with a receding hairline met them on the front sidewalk. Mabry made a quick introduction and motioned for a report.

"Twenty-eight, white, divorced. Taught at Wilson Elementary the last three years. Neighbors said the ex is out of the country working for an oil company—"

"—in Qatar," Logan finished. "It's Jeanine Tyler."

The officer nodded. "Cell phone's ICE had a Walton Springs number. You know her, Detective?"

"A long time ago. I played high school football with her brother, Gregg. Jeanine was probably ten the last time I saw her. Gregg died in a car accident shortly after we graduated. This'll be rough for the Tylers. She was the only child left."

"Canvass turn up anything?" Rick asked.

"Not yet. Lady next door said Tyler was a runner. Up about five-thirty most mornings. Said she pounded the pavement like it was her ex's face. The neighbor said the husband had cheated on the vic. She even took back her maiden name after the divorce. Neighbor's retired, didn't hear a peep, and she seems the nosy type that would know."

"What about Brady and Malone?"

"Took the principal downtown. He barfed in the bushes after catching sight of the body. Can't blame him, Loo."

The patrolman's pained face said it all. Logan mentally prepared himself as they moved toward the front door.

Dread seeped through his veins. In Atlanta, he finally realized that he could never get used to it, only hardened. Answer enough calls and even the grisliest scene becomes old hat. He'd throw a switch and automatically be in homicide mode. Couldn't look at the dead as a person, at least not then. A cold dispassion took over. Study the scene. Think like the killer.

Only later did he allow himself to think of the vic as a person. Someone who loved and was loved. Someone robbed of time.

Still, he was glad he was out of practice. He

wouldn't trade going back to that work life in Atlanta in a million years.

The hum of activity never changed. Rick took the lead as they entered. Logan knew the details about Roy's victims. A macabre interest drove him to read the police reports, along with the FBI profiles, circulated to local law enforcement. He knew Jeanine would be hand-painted a garish yellow as Roy cycled around the rainbow to his latest innocent.

An average living room held the requisite sofa, coffee table, and entertainment center. Everything clean and orderly. No newspapers scattered about or clipped coupons or magazines in sight. He remembered Jeanine being neat, her hair always braided, a matching ribbon to her outfit woven into it. She hadn't been a grubby child with skinned knees or untucked shirts. Obviously, she hadn't changed as an adult.

Logan soldiered on behind Rick, down a hallway. A small bedroom converted into an office came first, followed by the primary bedroom at the end of the passage. As they stepped inside, both men automatically reached into their pockets to slip on gloves.

The amount of blood surprised him. Roy had strangled some of the previous vics with piano wire, a rather neat way to leave a crime scene. Some had been tortured with a knife, but Roy was careful. No arterial spray. This scene, though, had a huge amount of blood spatter. Blood soaked the mussed bedsheets, as well. Jeanine lay atop them, her nude body coated in bright yellow paint. He watched the ME check the corpse and had to look away, saddened at the end the neat little girl came to.

He forced himself to look at the wall next to the bed. High above the headboard glared the killer's trademark signature. A tongue fastened to the wall with what would undoubtedly be a knife from the kitchen. This detail had been withheld from the press, kept in reserve so only law enforcement knew about it. At least until the last murder. The leak hadn't been discovered yet, but a reporter had made it public.

One difference leaped out at Logan. He looked back at the body on the bed. Jeanine's eyes were missing.

Mabry nudged him. "The knife matches a steak set from the kitchen. What do you make about the eyes? He hasn't taken trophies before. You think he's escalating?"

Logan voiced a thought. "What if it's not Roy this time, Rick? What if we have a copycat on our hands?"

Rick's mouth tightened. "Hard to say. They still can't find any link between the vics. Usually, the pattern becomes evident with this many killed. Not with Roy. He's killed male and female, every race. All ages."

The ME snapped off his gloves. "I'd place TOD between midnight and two this morning, based on lividity and her body temp. Throat was slashed, probably with her own knife. Roy hit a major artery, hence our Jackson Pollack display." The examiner's mouth hardened. "He's changing things up, gentlemen. And that's not good."

They stayed a few more minutes before Rick said he wanted to get back and talk to the principal. They drove in silence, each man lost in his thoughts.

Logan knew serial killers hit a point where they began to unravel. It looked as if Roy had reached that place in his lengthy crime spree.

Someone had to stop him. Soon.

~

KARLYN LACED up her running shoes and stretched. She pocketed her cell and keys and started out. The morning smelled fresh, crisp after a shower last evening. She wove her way through residential streets before moving toward town.

A coal black Lab fell into step with her. He startled her the first time he did so, but they'd become regular running buddies since she'd been in Walton Springs. Karlyn checked his tags and took him home the first time it happened. His owner, Jonas Watkins, explained that Hugo loved to run.

"Belongs to my son, actually. He got transferred overseas for a year. I try to walk him, but Hugo moves too fast for me." Jonas patted the Lab's head. "He's a good boy. Roams a bit but he always comes home."

After that, Karlyn didn't mind the friendly dog's company. She always made sure to loop by Jonas' house to return the dog. Hugo would fall out and rush up to the door. More often than not, Jonas sat on the porch, sipping an iced tea, and shouted his thanks.

Rounding a stretch that headed up to Main Street, she spied Logan and wondered why he was out before six in the morning. He looked her way, a deep frown crossing his brow.

"What side of the bed did you crawl out of?" she tossed out jokingly as she approached.

Karlyn would've kept going but Logan stepped out and blocked her way. She came to an abrupt halt, Hugo running ahead and then circling back, his tail wagging impatiently. She jogged in place, not wanting to interrupt her rhythm.

"Don't tell me you're out here at this time every morning," he ground out.

"No. Sometimes, earlier. Sometimes, I write first

and then run mid-afternoon. I don't have a set time. Why?"

"Stop!" Logan put his hands on her shoulders. Karlyn quit moving her feet.

"What's wrong?"

His fingers dug into her shoulders. "That hurts," she told him. She took a step back. Hugo froze at her tone and stared quizzically at Logan, his head cocked at an angle.

"Don't you ever listen to the news? Didn't you hear what happened yesterday?"

Karlyn drew a blank. "No. Chris and I kicked around some ideas last night since he's leaving around noon today. I didn't catch the news."

Logan expelled an exasperated sigh, running a hand through his coal black hair. "A Rainbow Murder happened in the next town. Fountain Valley. A teacher whose little kids aren't going to understand why she's not in her third-grade classroom anymore. I saw her body, Karlyn. It wasn't pretty."

Confusion filled her. "Why are you mad at me? Maybe I'm slow in the mornings, Logan. What's the connection?"

"She was a runner. Ran each morning."

"So?"

"So? Maybe Roy watched her. Saw she always ran alone. You shouldn't do that. The Springs gives people a sense of false security. But if the Rainbow Killer struck a few miles from here, he could hit here, too. Hell, he could even live here, for all we know."

Karlyn snorted, her fisted hands coming to rest on her waist. "First of all, I ran all the time in Central Park. That's big, bad New York City, Detective. I've taken a self-defense course. I'm more than capable of taking care of myself."

She glanced down at the lab. "And if you haven't noticed, I do have a running partner. This is Hugo."

"I know Hugo. The entire town knows Hugo." Logan leaned over and scratched between the dog's ears. "He's the sweetest mutt around. If someone attacked you, Hugo wouldn't be much help."

"No one will come near me, Logan Warner. I'm fast when I turn the speed on. If Roy G. Biv were after me, my adrenaline rush would make me fly."

Karlyn placed a hand on his forearm, finding it rock-hard. "I know you're upset. I don't blame you. But Roy isn't going to tackle me and paint me in public. Can I move on?"

She saw he still struggled, his face pained.

"I worry about you, Karlyn. That's all."

She squeezed his arm. "It's nice to have someone worry about me. No one has in a long time."

"Would you like to go for a motorcycle ride tonight?" he asked out of the blue. "When I'm troubled, I take my bike out and think."

Her insides coiled in anticipation. Her body next to his. Her arms wrapped around his waist. "I'd like that."

He grinned. "Seven? We could grab a burger while we're out."

"Only if it has cheese on it. And tons of grilled onions."

"I can manage to find us a burger joint." Logan patted Hugo's head. "Take care of her, boy. Don't let her do anything too crazy."

Karlyn took off. Hugo fell into step as she ran down Main Street. It was sweet that he worried about her safety. Mario never had. Her parents hadn't, either. Other than Alicia worrying about Karlyn hitting her deadlines, she couldn't think of the last time someone had been concerned about her.

She smiled. Logan Warner might be a little bossy, but in a good way. Now, her biggest problem was thinking how to avoid flat hair when she took off her motorcycle helmet tonight.

18

L ogan glanced in the mirror and ran a comb through his hair.

"I may not be as good-looking as Matt Collins, but I make up for it with my sparkling personality," he said aloud.

He picked up Karlyn's latest book, featuring her famous private investigator. He wanted her to autograph the hardback but had nowhere to put it since they were taking out the Harley.

Logan turned the book over. Karlyn's emerald, green eyes shone with a little bit of mischief and a whole lot of sex appeal. Her picture alone revved up his pulse.

And the lady could kiss. He thought of their brief encounter in his car and hoped they could repeat that —and more—tonight. Her slender, athletic body snuggled next to his on the bike would probably ignite flames that people could see from here to Lexington.

Logan tossed the book aside and grabbed his keys. He locked the apartment and headed down to the diner, moving fast. He didn't want to stop to talk with any customers. He was too eager to see Karlyn.

"Hey, sugar pie. Heard you might need my autograph. And it's chicken and dumplings tonight."

Mandy stood behind the counter, her eyes dancing with a come-hither look as she rested a hand on her hip. Logan hated squashing her hopes. She always had a ready smile for him and practically begged him to ask her out on a regular basis with those sparkling baby blues.

"I'd love for you to sign my petition, Mandy, but I don't have it with me. I'll bring it next time." He raised a hand to wave goodbye.

"Logan Warner, your political consultant would have your head," she scolded.

He shot her a look. "I don't have a political consultant."

"Well, you do now," she said. "First, don't look like you're in such a hurry when you're talking to a potential voter. Stop. Chat. Smile. Even flirt a little."

"Flirt?"

"Yes, flirt. You're a nice-looking man, Logan. That'll win you votes. Plus, politics means power—and power is an attractive thing to a woman. And *always* keep your petition with you. You never know who you'll run into. I won't even charge you for the advice."

"You'll want your name listed on my campaign website?"

"*Head* political consultant." Mandy smiled. "I like the ring of that. Go get the petition, will you?"

Logan saluted her and headed back upstairs. He would get his list and pick up a helmet for Karlyn, which he'd forgotten. Of course, his new head political consultant would wring out of him that he was taking a female friend for a ride. That tidbit would spread like wildfire all over town.

He grinned. If he set up a table on the square tomorrow, he guaranteed a couple dozen would stop by to find out what was brewing between him and Karlyn.

He might as well get their signatures at the same time.

Logan folded the petition and slid it into his inner jacket pocket. He found the extra helmet and returned to the diner.

Presenting Mandy with the petition, she whipped out a pen from her apron and signed it with a flourish.

"Hmm. Extra helmet. Are you offering free rides for signatures?"

"Would that be a good idea?"

She studied him. "You're freshly showered because you're hair's still damp." She breathed in. "A hint of cologne. I'd say our next chief of police has a date with that writer I've heard about."

"You're right. Shouldn't that raise my profile with the voters, Madam Consultant?"

"Only if you'll get out of here and let me spread a little gossip, honey." Mandy's eyes skimmed the café. "Hmm. I spy Casey Attaway." She grinned. "I think I'll go pour him some more coffee."

Logan exited the diner. And bumped into Seth Berger.

"Evening, Warner."

"Berger."

He viewed his colleague with new eyes since they were now opponents in the race.

What he saw didn't wow him. Berger was lanky. A little under six feet, with a walrus mustache and mud-brown eyes. He rarely smiled, probably to hide his crooked front teeth. He was a loner. Divorced for a decade with no children. Kept to himself—at work, at church, and in his leisure hours. Berger liked to hunt and fish. Always alone.

Maybe that's why Logan thought Berger was missing the trust factor. Usually, small town policemen were friendly with fellow officers and townsfolk alike. They had a bond and enjoyed service to others.

Berger rarely spoke to anyone. He went out of his way not to speak at the station. He liked working cases alone, with no input from his colleagues. Seth Berger trusted no one, while no one on the force seemed to trust him.

"Heard you're running for chief," Berger ground out.

"You heard right."

"I'm expecting a fair fight."

"I wouldn't give you any other kind."

Berger's eyes narrowed. "Let the best man win." He brushed past Logan to enter the diner but turned back.

"If I win, I'll expect your resignation. Don't need wannabes in the Springs. I don't care where you go. Maybe run to Fountain Valley with your little pal Rick Mabry. But I don't want you here. Understood?"

"You'll have to win. I don't aim for that to happen." Logan hurried away, anger seething as he cut down the alley to his bike.

Resign?

Like hell. He planned to win. Big. Seth Berger be damned.

~

LOGAN PULLED to the curb in front of the Campbell house and saw Karlyn waiting for him on the porch swing. She came down the steps, her hair pulled back in a low ponytail. Tight jeans molded to her hips and butt left little to his imagination.

She reached for the helmet he offered and swung it onto her head.

"I am starving, Warner, so this hamburger joint better be good."

"Then we'll eat first and cruise after."

Karlyn snapped the strap in place and threw her leg over the bike. She snaked her arms around his waist and locked her fingers together. Her floral perfume wafted around him, revving up his own engine.

"Hang on," he warned. "We're gonna fly."

Logan gunned the motor and enjoyed the rush of wind that came. The open road. A beautiful woman nestled against him. It had the makings of a perfect night.

They arrived at Aunt Ju's fifteen minutes later. He killed the motor and let Karlyn climb off before he did. She lifted the helmet, her smile broad.

"I've never been on a motorcycle before. I might have to buy one."

Logan gave her an appraising look. "A bike virgin, huh?" He stroked the seat of his Harley. "This is the best baby on the road, but it takes a lot to control her. You might want to stick to your convertible."

"It's rented. I don't own a car. Actually, I need to think about that."

Logan escorted her inside, where a jukebox played country tunes and over half the red vinyl booths were filled. "Have you made any plans about where you'll end up?" He waited, on edge, hoping to hear that she was staying put.

Karlyn nodded. "I need a clean break with my past. Plus, I want to know Mother better." She brightened. "Maybe I can establish residency and vote for you in the next election."

"I'll need every vote I can get but let me try to win this one first." He described his encounter with Seth Berger after they were seated.

"What an asshole. Could he force your resignation? Or fire you?" She bit her lip. "I mean, not that I think you'll lose."

Logan laughed. "Thanks for the vote of confidence. He'd need plenty of documentation to fire me. The thing is, Berger could create an uncomfortable work environment that made me want to leave voluntarily."

She shuddered. "He gives me the creeps. Mother pointed him out at the hardware store. We went to get keys cut for me. He was buying paint and fertilizer. I told her who knows—he could be the Rainbow Killer."

"You've got a vivid imagination, Karlyn. I know it serves you well in your writing but Seth Berger as a killer? Come on. I'd like to think Roy G. Biv had a personality."

They ordered and Karlyn asked, "What can you tell me about this latest murder? I could tell it upset you."

He stretched out both arms along the edge of the booth's back. "I knew the latest victim when we were kids. She was a good person. It's hard to believe she's gone. Especially in such a brutal way."

Karlyn leaned closer. "I scoured the internet looking for info on the previous cases. I can't find any kind of link between the victims. They vary in age. Ethnicity. Occupations. The only thing consistent is Roy working his way through the colors of the rainbow. In order."

Logan nodded. "Cops are baffled. They've tried establishing connections between the vics. Three and eight joined the same health club. Two were gay but didn't have any friends in common. Three were Baptists, but in Georgia? That's nothing new. They worked in different areas, belonged to different libraries, had varying incomes. No obvious connections."

The server arrived with their platters and beers. Karlyn bit into her Swiss mushroom burger. "Grilled onions on a burger should be a national law."

"The fries are pretty amazing," Logan added as he doused his in ketchup.

Karlyn returned to Roy. "He must be strong since several victims have been strangled. That's not an easy death to pull off, especially with the size of some of the male victims. I know that from my research."

Logan put down his burger. "Can I count on your professional discretion? This goes no further."

"Of course. He's escalated, hasn't he?"

He admired how perceptive she was. "He slashed Jeanine's throat. His previous scenes have been gruesome. But pristine. This was messy." He paused. "He also took a trophy for the first time."

"That makes sense. Serial killers usually do. I was surprised Roy never had. Or with the previous victims he took some personal item from them, and it hasn't been discovered yet. But was she still painted?"

"Yes. Yellow, just as the sequence required. That part hadn't changed."

"That's two murders outside of Atlanta now. That means new jurisdictions that'll need to coordinate. Mortonville and Fountain Valley. All that bureaucracy will make him harder to catch."

Logan agreed. "We have no description. None of the vics was seen with anyone prior to their murders.

And now, he's started collecting trophies. It doesn't look good for catching him."

"Do you think he's starting to lose control?"

"I have no idea." He sighed. "How did we start such pleasant dinner conversation?"

Karlyn shrugged. "It's fascinating to me. It's my life."

"As long as you don't try to write it as true crime. Roy's been slick enough to avoid the law this long. You don't want to go up against a clever monster like that."

"I've never delved into true crime before. Right now, I don't have time to think about it."

"Have you finished your screenplay?"

Her face lit up. "Yes. Chris gave it a final read and said it passed his litmus test. I've sent it to my agent. I also have a non-Matt standalone manuscript close to completion. I'll finish that novel before I consider my next project."

"Chris seemed like a decent guy."

"He gave me perfect suggestions and let me do most of it on my own. I would kill to work with him again."

He laughed. "Mom would love to have Warren Newlin visit again. Do you know he stopped by her shop and did free cuts? He invited her to his Atlanta salon. She can't wait to go and watch him give Jennifer Lawrence or Jennifer Aniston or Jennifer Lopez a trim and blow-dry. She says he's the It Guy as far as the stars are concerned."

They moved away from the murders and discussed life in Walton Springs. Karlyn expressed interest in visiting Anne Stockdale's antiques store, as well as eating at the diner.

"I've heard it's the best food this side of the Mississippi. Of course, I can think of a few New York critics that might differ with that opinion."

"Nelda would let her food do the talking. Of course, she's never been bashful about her cooking."

"She's your mom's best friend, right?"

"They've been thick as thieves since the sandbox. It's like having two moms."

Karlyn pushed her empty plate back. "I'm stuffed."

"No dessert? Remember, I'm a chocoholic."

"Maybe after we ride around. We could pull into Dairy Queen for a chocolate sundae or cone."

"I have a better idea."

He paid the check and they climbed on the bike again. The evening had turned cool. Logan knew he took a big risk, but this woman had gotten under his skin.

The worst she could do was say no.

The best would be a huge yes.

He tooled down the highway a few minutes and then pulled into a small parking lot. He cut the engine and waited a beat.

"The Cavalier Motel." Her voice was low. Her arms still locked around him. He could sense the tension scrolling through her.

Logan got off the bike. Lifted her off. Pulled her to him. Heard the hitch in her breath.

"I haven't slept with anyone since my wife. I've never pulled into a no-tell motel on a first date." He drew her close. "But my blood races every time I'm around you, Karlyn Campbell. You're all I think about. I want to taste you. Touch every inch of you. But the ball's in your court.

"Dessert—or no dessert? The choice is up to you."

19

Logan's words scared Karlyn to death.

But she'd wanted him from the beginning.

He gave her control now. She could say thanks—but no thanks—and they'd ride back to Walton Springs. He might call again. Or he might not.

She wouldn't take that chance.

Karlyn had never been a risk-taker. She enjoyed being a perfectionist. Making lists. Leading a normal, ordinary life. Her adventures came through Matt or her other characters.

Here was a chance to be the real-life heroine in her own story.

He didn't have to ask twice.

She unstrapped her helmet and tossed it to the ground. He met her challenge and did the same. She pushed up on tiptoes and wrapped her hands around his neck. Pulled his lips down to hers.

And kissed him with everything she had.

Her blood heated as the kiss grew urgent. Their lips warred with one another, seeking, demanding. His hands pushed into her hair, kneading her scalp. She clung to his shoulders, not sure if she had the strength to stand on her own if he released her.

Logan pulled his mouth from hers, his eyes sparkling with mischief. "Wanna get a room?"

"Yes." The effort getting out the single syllable left her spent.

He released her. Reached down for their helmets. Gave her a smile that made her insides tingle with anticipation.

Five minutes later, they entered a clean, nondescript room. Logan pitched their helmets aside as she put the *Do Not Disturb* sign on the knob and locked the door. She turned. He moved into her space. His hands flattened against the door on both sides of her. His body pressed against hers as his lips met hers.

Karlyn wrapped her arms around his waist. The scent of his leather jacket and cologne surrounded her like an invading army. She surrendered to the demands of his hungry mouth. Time stood still. There was only his kiss. His scent.

His lips moved to her neck, to that sweet spot that made her pulse jump as his hands caressed her arms. Then he slipped the buttons through the holes and had her blouse open, his lips trailing to the valley between her breasts.

Logan peeled her shirt away. Then her lace bra.

"Beautiful," he murmured as he gazed at her. His mouth came down on her nipple and began laving and sucking. Her insides flipped as if she'd gone upside down on a roller coaster. She whimpered. A throbbing between her legs began, raging out of control. Karlyn thought she would come then and there.

Logan's mouth deserted her for a moment. He whipped off the leather jacket and drew the polo shirt over his head. Her first jumbled thought was that a Greek statue had come to life. She glimpsed sleek muscles and a fine layer of dark hair on his chest before he pressed against her again.

"Hot," he panted as he returned to her breast.

The heat of his mouth coupled with his body scorching hers lit her on fire. She latched onto him, kneading him, wanting more. Now.

She must have voiced that aloud. He paused. Gave her a crooked grin. Bent to peel her jeans down her legs, his tongue trailing the newly-exposed skin. He got them off and yanked hard on her thong. It snapped apart in his hands. His eyes met hers, a mischievous look dancing in them. He threw the ruined thong over his shoulder.

And then his tongue went to work.

Karlyn leaned against the door, gasping, her heart pounding, as he worked a spell on her like no other man had. She gripped his shoulders as he burrowed closer, his tongue never ceasing, causing her to lose all inhibition. Suddenly, she was jerking, moaning in pleasure, crying.

Then spent.

Logan's mouth worked his way back up her trembling body. It arrived at the starting point, kissing her deeply as his thumbs wiped the tears from her cheeks. She shook with emotion from his unselfish lovemaking.

He stopped and glanced over his shoulder.

"You know, we did pay for the bed. Maybe we should check it out."

She bit her lip. Nodded in approval.

He swept her up effortlessly and placed her on the bed. He shed his own jeans and boxers. Logan Warner could give Michelangelo's *David* a run for the money. As he stood there, she smiled.

"You look like you're ready for Round Two," she

teased, hoping she could accommodate his large erection.

Thankfully, she did. And then some.

～

THEY CHECKED out of The Cavalier three hours later. It hadn't all been sex. Logan appreciated the in-between pillow talk as much as their robust physical activity. Karlyn talked about the publishing world. He shared about growing up in the Springs and playing football in college. Blushed as she joked with him how he knew he'd get lucky multiple times when he pulled out a few condoms from his wallet.

"A Boy Scout learns to be prepared. That's the life lesson Scouting taught me. I like to go into every situation knowing I have options." He laughed. "Even if it meant driving to Fountain Valley to buy a box of condoms to avoid hometown gossip."

They showered together and dressed again. He'd already paid in cash when they registered. They both decided they should return to their own beds tonight.

After he got her to promise that a repeat performance would be scheduled soon.

Logan thought sex with Felicity had been satisfying. His ex had a nice body and lots of stamina—but sex with Karlyn had been off the charts. He didn't know if it was the newness of the relationship or not, but the connection between them sparked emotions he'd never experienced.

It was enough to make a man fall head over heels in love.

Which he couldn't do. She was newly divorced and not looking for anything permanent. She wouldn't leap into a relationship with someone she barely knew.

But enjoying sex on a regular basis? It was a start.

He was a planner by nature. The plan now was to win Karlyn Campbell's heart. However long it took. He could be patient. He would be patient.

She would be worth whatever wait.

They climbed back on his Harley. Logan couldn't believe how much had changed in the space of a few hours. He cut down a few back roads before arriving at the one leading to the Springs. They rode in silence until he slowed the bike and brought it to a stop.

"What's wrong?" she asked.

Logan cut the engine and got off. "Something caught my eye." He pointed to a grove of trees. They heard movement more than saw it, due to the lateness of the hour. They both headed in that direction.

A whine tore at his heart.

"It's a dog!" She ran ahead.

"Wait! Don't touch it," he warned.

He caught up with her. A chain attached the canine to a tree. At the end, it held the most pitiful pup he'd seen. No tags. Bone thin. The dog cowered.

"Someone left him out here to die." She bent and touched the dog's head. He whimpered again.

Logan managed to get the chain off and scooped up the pooch. A wave of emotion rolled through him. Pure love. He didn't know if the animal would survive but he would make every effort to see that it did.

"Will you keep him?" she asked softly as she rubbed the dog's ears.

"Yeah." He stroked the pup, whose heart pounded wildly. "I'll take him in to Jesse Alpine tomorrow. He can check for ticks and clean him up. Give me an idea if this little guy'll make it. But he's coming home with me tonight."

They returned to his motorcycle. He cradled the puppy as Karlyn slipped her arms around him. Logan suddenly experienced longings he'd shut out long ago when he'd given up Boomer to Felicity in the divorce.

He wanted a dog. A home. Not a couple of rooms over the diner. A place where he could mow his yard and grill steaks and watch his kids play.

There, he'd finally thought about it. Kids. He *wanted* kids again. No child would ever replace Alex and Ashley, but he realized he could open his heart and let another in.

And another wife. Logan longed to be married again. He wanted to share his innermost thoughts with a woman. He wanted to love and laugh and live.

He realized this half-dead, Heinz 57 mutt made him decide to join the land of the living again. Logan wanted the dog.

And the woman behind him.

20

Logan awoke to heat along his side. The scraggly pup refused to stay in the box lined with an old flannel shirt. He'd given up and let the dog sleep with him. He scratched the soft belly. The mutt gazed at him with adoring eyes. He'd gotten the dog under a warm shower last night and scrubbed gently. He hoped the vet wouldn't find any little critters on him.

His cell buzzed. He answered it.

"This is Dr. Alpine's office," said a robotic female voice. "We received your message and have a cancellation at eight-thirty this morning. Would you like that appointment, Mr. Warner?"

Logan agreed and rolled out of bed. "Looks like you've got a date with destiny," he told his scruffy new friend. "Let's find you something to eat while I shower. Without you, this time, I might add."

He rummaged through the refrigerator and came up with the tail end of some meatloaf. The dog devoured it and looked up expectantly.

"Hmm. Cheese made Boomer fart so let's don't go there. All I have left is yogurt and pinto beans. We'll get you some dog food today. And me some people food."

Logan dressed in nice black slacks with a sharp crease and a sports shirt he'd ironed last night when he got home. He hoped he looked ready to impress as he launched his campaign into full swing today. He grabbed the petition sheets, scooped up the dog, and went downstairs.

"Where on earth did you get that . . . thing?" Nelda Vanderley exclaimed.

"He—or she—is my new best friend. Clean but scrawny. We're headed to Jesse Alpines's for a check-up."

"I guess I never shared the part about no pets allowed," Nelda said wryly.

"I've decided to buy a house. This little friend has spurred me into action."

"I'm not running you off, Logan," Nelda protested. "You can keep a dog upstairs. I was only kidding."

"It's time, Nelda." He winked at her. "Doesn't mean I won't stop eating here even when I do move out."

He left the diner and lowered the dog to the ground. Immediately, it scurried to a nearby tree.

"Be glad you didn't need a poop bag."

Logan wheeled and saw Seth Berger. "Or you'd ticket me?"

Berger shrugged. He indicated the sheaf of papers in his hand. "Gotta see if anyone in the diner wants to sign for their next police chief."

Logan pushed aside his anger at Berger's needling. He retrieved the pup and drove to Jesse Alpine's office, a converted one-story brick home from the late sixties. Alpine had taken over the retiring vet's practice upon graduating from vet school a couple of years ago.

He climbed the steps, admiring the large porch filled with rockers. He guessed on a busy day, clients waited outside.

He entered and saw the receptionist frown. She pointed to the sign. "All animals on a leash." She squinted a moment. "Why, it doesn't even have a collar."

Logan groaned inwardly. It was the monotone voice from earlier. "I found him last night, ma'am. I'll outfit him today with the works—leash, collar, toys, bowls."

"Your name?"

Logan told her.

"The dog's name?"

He shrugged. "I don't know yet."

The receptionist glared. "I must have a name for my records."

"I'll tell you one as soon as we have it."

She sniffed. "Room two," and indicated a door.

He happily escaped and closed the door behind him. He placed the dog on the steel table and stood next to it, talking softly, trying to reassure the pup. Less than a minute later, a young man in his late twenties sporting a dark goatee entered.

"Good morning. Jesse Alpine. And you're Logan Warner and the nameless beast, according to my receptionist."

Logan shook the offered hand. "She's not pleased with me."

Alpine snorted. "She's never pleased with me, and I sign her checks. I inherited her along with the practice. Every Sunday in church I pray she'll tell me she's retiring, come Monday. Hasn't happened yet but it's made me a regular at First Baptist."

The vet turned his attention to his new patient. "Well, hello, little one," and ran his hands over the dog, feeling the ribs, checking inside the ears. "So,

your message says you found"—he paused and looked
under the tail—"her on the highway."

"Yes. Someone chained her and abandoned her. I
tried my best to clean her up and get some food in
her."

Alpine continued his exam. "She's about four
months old. A little on the small side, but with good
food and a lot of love, she'll be fine. She's a mix, for
sure. Some cocker. Maybe even golden retriever. I
think she'll be good-natured, though."

He looked at Logan. "Let me keep her until this afternoon. Give her some shots, a medicated bath, trim and
fluff her up a bit. We carry the food she'll need to be on."

"Can I wait on her name until I pick her up?"

"Only if I let you sneak out the back door. Ramona
is all policy and procedure. I've never met a more by-
the-book person." He laughed. "Come around three
and you can have this little sweetheart back."

The vet picked up the dog and led Logan down a
hallway. "Here's your exit."

Logan chuckled at their subterfuge and thanked
him. He headed to his car and met Jonas Watkins
coming up the sidewalk.

"Hello, Jonas. Hugo. Here for a check-up?"

"Hugo needs his yearly shots. Everything okay at
Jesse's?"

Logan grinned. "Found a stray last night.
Scrawniest mutt ever and a real heartbreaker. I
couldn't pass her by."

He patted Hugo's head. "If you're out walking later,
stop by the square. I'm running for police chief in the
May election. I'd appreciate your John Hancock on my
petition."

Jonas' eyes lit with pleasure. "Will do."

Logan drove to the center of town. He popped the trunk and removed a card table and two folding chairs he'd loaded last night and set up under a shady elm.

Show time.

~

KARLYN PULLED ON HER VISOR, ready to run. Her cell rang. It was Alicia.

"About time you called. What do you think of the screenplay?"

"That you have a knack for it," her agent said. "No one would guess this was your first attempt."

Karlyn laughed. "I credit Chris Stevenson for pushing me. He's amazingly talented."

"He thinks highly of you. His agent told me Chris has an offer to write an original screenplay for Scorsese, based upon a story idea by the great man himself. Chris wants *you* as his collaborator. If you're free."

"You're kidding!"

"I never kid about business. Chris is polishing another project first and thinks he'll be ready to start the new material in early September. That's when Scorsese wants to meet and discuss the characters and direction of the story."

"That gives me from now through summer to finish my novel and outline my next Matt book. Tell him yes, Alicia." Karlyn did a quick happy dance, holding in her squeal of joy.

"I'll do that. I wanted to ask with summer coming, are you vising me in the Hamptons?"

"Probably not. I'm planning to relocate to Walton Springs. I've got to buy a car and find a place to live. I don't think at thirty-two I should be living with my mother."

"I can understand wanting to get away from New York and Mario. By the way, that SOB contacted me twice, wanting your mother's number. I told the cheating scumbag to go to hell."

"That's because I changed my cell number. He called. Wanting money. How could he already be broke?"

"You must not get the tabloids in magnolia land. Mario's seeing some high-strung model. I think she'll bleed him dry and move on. Either that or she'll drop dead. Rumor has it she's big into drugs."

"He won't squeeze another cent out of me. Switching subjects, what do you think about true crime?"

"Why? If you're thinking about venturing into the area, I'll be frank. It doesn't sell well, Karlyn. By the time an author researches, writes, and gets into print, the crime and trial are old news, thanks to the internet, podcasts, and Court TV. Why?"

"I'm interested in a serial killer in Atlanta. The Rainbow Murders. Roy G. Biv. I thought they might be challenging to write about."

"Stick to your familiar guns, darling," Alicia advised. "Original crimes and original characters. That's what'll keep you on the bestseller lists. Besides, you've got your budding screenwriting career to consider. Listen, I've got to run. I'll contact Chris' agent now and tell him you're in on the Scorsese project. *Ciao*."

No one wanted her to get involved in the Rainbow Murders.

She decided to finish her current work-in-progress and then give Roy G. Biv a long, hard look to see if he would be worth her time.

21

Logan smiled. Ninety minutes into getting signatures and the petition was almost complete. Mayor Vick beamed at him like a proud troop master at an Eagle Scout ceremony as he signed his name. Chief Risedale told passersby what a great cop Logan was and what an excellent chief he'd make.

Antique store owner Anne Stockdale emerged and crossed the street. "I'd be happy to sign your petition, Logan. I know your parents are so proud."

He handed her a pen. "Thanks, Anne. Would that mahogany dining table and chairs still be available?"

"Yes. Are you interested?"

"Mark 'em sold if you can house them for me for a while."

Anne smiled. "For our next chief of police? Happy to do so. I want to remain on your good side."

"I'll stop by Monday with my checkbook. Thanks for your signature. Be sure to vote—for me—in May," he reminded her.

"Bring a campaign sign for my front window. The square gets lots of activity so it would be seen a lot. See you later, Logan."

"I'd like a sign for my front yard."

Logan grinned hearing the familiar voice. "Why, Miss Galaway. Good to see you. How are integers these days?"

"Since you have plenty of practice putting signs in my yard, Logan Warner, you may place one of yours there. Just keep the *For Sale* signs out of the mix this time."

His face reddened at the memory of his middle school prank.

"And integers are lovely these days, as are co-efficients. Now, let me sign your petition."

He teased, "Sorry I don't have a red pen. I seem to remember it's your favorite color. I saw plenty of it bleeding on my papers."

Miss Galaway sniffed and scrawled her name. "I don't grade in red anymore. I mark papers in green felt tip now. I'd say I'm good for another ten years. Maybe more."

Logan laughed. "I'll bring a sign by as soon as I have some made up," he promised.

"I'll take a sign for my yard," Bridget Marley said, stealing the pen. "How are you, Logan?"

"Good. How's—"

"—your little one, Bridget? Heard Doc Warner went over to treat the child for chicken pox." Casey Attaway nosed in and waited for an answer.

"Casey, you know every happening in the Springs," Logan marveled.

The gas station attendant shrugged and took the pen from Bridget Marley, who waved goodbye. "People need gas, Logan. And everybody has something going on. The two go together, I'd say."

Casey signed his name to the petition. "Looks like you're about done. Tell your mama and daddy hi for me. Gotta get to my shift at the station."

"Will do." Logan caught sight of Marge Strombold exiting her car. He signaled the realtor.

When she reached him, Logan said, "You don't have to sign anything, Marge. I'm looking to buy a house."

She brightened at the prospect of a sale. "Three or four bedrooms? Single-story or two? Garage or carport?"

"I'll know it when I see it. Remember, though, I'm on a public servant's salary."

She pulled out her iPad. "You'll make considerably more if you win this election. You have any time open today? Say around three-thirty?"

"Only if I can bring my dog. She's at the vet. I'm supposed to pick her up at three."

"That's no problem. We'll go over a few properties at my office and set appointments to see the ones you like." Marge picked up a pen from the table. "And if you're buying a house from me, you've got my vote. Especially since Seth Berger's your opponent."

Logan laughed. "Then I'll be sure we've closed before the election. See you later."

He glanced down and saw only one more signature left before he would officially be able to enter the race. He looked back up and saw Karlyn jogging toward him. She stopped at his table.

"Almost done," he indicated. "Not even noon yet. Want to go grab a bite once I get the last signature?"

"No one would seat me looking and smelling like this," she teased as she jogged in place. "Why don't I—"

"Hey, Logan."

He did not want to turn in the direction of that girlish voice. Beth Marie Sizemore had done everything short of flashing him since her divorce came through from her no-good, used car dealer husband. Logan had no interest in dating her and Beth Marie couldn't understand. Or wouldn't.

Reluctantly, he turned from Karlyn. "Hello, Beth Marie. Have you met Karlyn Campbell? She's new to the Springs."

Beth Marie's smoky eyes looked Karlyn up and down as she bobbed in place. "Nice to meet you," she said dismissively and turned back to Logan. "I hear my ex-beau is running for Chief of Police. An even better idea than when you ran for Student Council president senior year. I remember—"

"Did you know Karlyn's a famous writer?" Logan interrupted, not desiring a trip down memory lane. That was all Beth Marie seemed interested in whenever he saw her.

"Oh." She looked blankly at him. "I don't read." She looked back at Karlyn. "What do you write, Carolyn?"

"It's Karlyn. I write novels. And screenplays."

"Huh. Well, that's real nice," she said as she wrote her name across the final blank of Logan's petition. "Say, Logan, maybe after you're through here—"

"I've got a million things to take care of, Beth Marie. The vet. Grocery store. Saturday errands."

His former flame looked back at Karlyn, assessing her again. "I see. Well, call me sometime, Logan. I'd love to get together for a drink. Or . . . whatever." She gave him a seductive smile.

He watched her leave, hips in full swing.

Karlyn stopped moving and pursed her lips, trying to imitate Beth Marie's sexy pout. "Since you've got so many errands to run, we should have lunch together some other time. Besides, Ms. Sizemore was doing more than sizing me up."

He took her arm. "Give me a break, Karlyn. She was my girlfriend for about two weeks during our senior year in high school. And that's only because it took her that long to work her way around to me. Beth Marie nailed anything male back then. She's been on the prowl the same way since her second divorce last year."

He took a step closer. "I wasn't that interested back then. I'm definitely not interested now. I have better things to occupy my mind."

"Like winning an election? Training a stray dog?"

"Getting to know you." His gaze held hers. "Why don't you run home and jump in the shower? I'll pick up some barbecue sandwiches for lunch and then we can go shop for my nameless dog. She needs everything a dog could want, and I plan to give it to her."

"Lucky girl. She's found herself a sugar daddy."

Logan exclaimed, "That's it! Lucky!" He planted a hard, fast kiss on Karlyn. "You named my dog. Should've known a writer could come up with a great name."

He liked the look in those shining green eyes of hers as Karlyn waved and took off running again.

"Lucky, it is."

LOGAN BROUGHT the promised lunch by the Campbell house. When he learned Martha was out for the afternoon, he said, "To hell with the sandwiches."

He snagged Karlyn around the waist. His lips nibbled along her ear and ventured to her neck.

"Why do I suddenly feel like I'm lunch?" she teased.

Logan's reply was to sweep her off her feet and exit the kitchen. He headed for the stairs.

"You can tell me which bedroom is yours. Or we can do it in every bed in the house." He gave her a knowing look. "I've heard this is one of the larger homes in the Springs."

"I'm the last on the right, Detective. Let's start there."

He took his time, removing each piece of clothing from her slowly. Her lightly-tanned skin gleamed in the sunlight that shone through the window. Logan marveled at her tight, firm, athletic body. He captured her runner's calves in each hand and squeezed them, admiring their curves.

Karlyn's emerald eyes burned with intensity as she looked at him. "Lose the clothes, Warner. Fast."

He did the opposite, slowly stripping his shirt over his head. Taking his time to fold it neatly and place it in a chair. He continued to remove each item as if in slow motion, enjoying her burning gaze.

When nothing remained, he joined her on the bed. "I plan to kiss you everywhere, Miss Campbell. If I happen to miss a spot, let me know."

He didn't.

While their first night together had been fast and furious each time they made love, this afternoon involved leisurely exploring her body. When he finally entered her, he forced himself to continue slow and steady. She whimpered. Begged him to speed up. He stayed the course, moving like molasses, until she panted and moaned.

"Oh, Logan. Please. Please. I can't take it anymore."

"Really?"

"Really."

He increased his thrusts, moving faster and harder

until he felt as if he flew through the air. Karlyn called his name as she came, her nails buried in his shoulders as they both rode through the pleasure storm.

Logan collapsed, nuzzling her neck, licking her sweet, slightly salty skin. He rolled and brought her with him so that she rested on top.

Her disheveled hair added a sexiness that he liked. He reached and pushed it back from her contented face.

"You. Are." She took a deep breath and let it out. "A. Mazing." Her head fell to rest on his chest. "I don't think I can move."

"Good."

Karlyn lifted her head. "That sounded like a very satisfied *good*."

He grinned. "It was. Because you. Are. A. Mazing. Too."

She slapped at him playfully. "What did the vet say about Lucky?"

"What time is it?" He reached for the wristwatch that he'd left on the nightstand. "Okay, pretty lady. We've got to go." He rolled out of bed and pulled her to her feet. "We've got to shop for Lucky and go pick her up."

"I say we grab those sandwiches and eat in the car. You certainly know how to work up a girl's appetite."

They dressed and picked up what Lucky would need before they stopped by the vet's office to claim her. Logan couldn't wait to show the dog all the new toys she'd scored.

Karlyn remarked how pretty her fur shone after her bath and trim. Jesse Alpine assured Logan that Lucky was in decent shape despite being rail thin. He told Logan to schedule follow-up shots with Ramona, and he would take a look at Lucky's weight then.

"Beef her up some but no table scraps," he warned. "Don't start bad habits now that are impossible to break down the road."

Ramona seemed mollified now that Lucky had a name to go on her file. The receptionist loaded Logan up with dry and canned food while Karlyn attached the new collar and leash to the pup.

Logan drove them straight to Marge Strombold's office, explaining to Karlyn how he'd decided to buy a house.

"It's smart to put down roots," she observed. "You have a history here, but it'll be important to some voters to see you're a homeowner and a taxpayer. Besides, Lucky needs a big yard to play in, don't you, girl?" She ruffled the dog's coat and was rewarded with a sloppy kiss.

Inside the realtor's office, Logan introduced the women. Marge immediately recognized Karlyn's name.

"You're not on my good list, Karlyn," Marge told her. "I read after your next Matt Collins book, you're taking a break. I need my Matt fix."

"I've finished a screenplay of the first novel. Maybe seeing Matt on the big screen might make you happy."

Marge sighed. "I don't think God's made the man that could stand up to the Matt I've created in my mind," she confided.

The realtor sat them at a round table and called up several listings. "Look through these. My associate's drawing up papers for a closing and I want to check on that. I'll be back soon."

They clicked through several listings before he stopped.

"Huh. This is the old Kinyon place." He studied the page. "It's about six blocks from you. The Kinyons lived into their nineties. They died within a day of each other at the end of last year."

"You hear about that happening all the time," Karlyn commented. "I guess the survivor is sad thinking of a life without his spouse."

She scrolled to the specifics. "Nice size primary bedroom. Three other bedrooms. You could make one into an office." She clicked through more photos. "The eat-in kitchen is huge. But outdated."

"I love a big kitchen," he said. "Every good party winds up in the kitchen. Despite eating most of my meals at the diner, I like to cook." He frowned. "It needs new floors throughout. Definitely a paint job. I'd also want to re-landscape the front."

She smiled. "It sounds as if your heart's set on this Kinyon house."

He shrugged. "Let's keep looking."

By the time Marge returned, Logan picked out two other possibilities. All three were in his price range, even including what he might want to do to update the Kinyon property.

"You've made some good choices, Logan. The last two houses both have open houses tomorrow. We can hit both if you'd like."

"When can I see the Kinyon place?"

Marge glanced at her watch. "Tell you what. I have plans with my supper group tonight. I need to get home and throw the rest of my dish together. Since it's unoccupied, I'll give you the code to retrieve the key and let you check it out on your own. We can meet back here around one o'clock tomorrow and see the other properties together."

She wrote a few numbers on a piece of paper and handed it to him. "Remember, it needs updating. That's why their son set such a reasonable price. He's in his seventies and doesn't want to tackle it. He wants the property off his hands so that the next owner can do the remodeling."

"Thanks, Marge. Enjoy dinner. We'll see you tomorrow at one."

He escorted Karlyn and a well-behaved Lucky back to his car.

"We?" Karlyn asked.

Logan nodded. "Definitely we. You can advise me on what I'll need to do. I have a feeling you have pretty good taste."

Her eyebrows shot up. "You think so?"

"Hey, you're hanging out with me. I'd say you're showing remarkable taste."

22

A voice inside his head screamed he was breaking a cardinal rule.

He ignored it. Why should he follow rules? He was Roy G. Biv

No one could touch him.

He looked at her again. Full-breasted. Tiny waist. A short skirt that showed plenty of thigh. Lips painted a glossy, fuck me red. She hadn't let herself go after her divorce. If anything, she looked hotter than ever.

He'd never killed someone he knew. Not in the Rainbow Murders. Nor any of the ones before. Ever.

Could he do it? Could he get away with it?

Running into her in Atlanta was in his favor. No one would know they'd hooked up. She lived in a secluded place just south of the Walton Springs town limits. She'd spilled that her nearest neighbors had left on vacation.

An electric thrill ran through him. He could follow her home. It was late. No one would see him pull into her place. Or leave. He could play to his heart's content and then head home, no one the wiser. Still meet up with his friends tomorrow. He'd pulled all-nighters before. They'd become routine since he'd started his hunts all those years ago.

Beth Marie gave him an alluring smile. He returned it.

Brushed his fingers lightly against her knee. Ran his hand up her silky thigh. He couldn't wait to be inside her. Feel her shudders. Have her watch him through heavy-lidded eyes.

Then watch those eyes pop when he pulled out his piano wire and knife.

23

L ogan surveyed the madness around him coming to an end. In the course of three weeks he'd bought the Kinyon place, discussed ideas to fix it up with Karlyn, and then sweated like a working-class dog to make them a reality. Yesterday and today a brigade of friends helped complete the last-minute details.

Karlyn and his dad had finished the trim work and carted all the paint cans, rollers, and brushes to the garage. They returned and Mitchell Warner surveyed things.

"When I retire, I'm becoming a painter. That is, if Karlyn partners with me." He gave her shoulder a squeeze.

"Considering what this place looked like a week ago? It looks lovely," his mother said.

Martha Campbell chimed in, "The curtains Resa sewed make the place. I think we were right to use—"

Logan drifted away from their conversation. He'd had enough domestic talk to last a lifetime. How big were the closets? How much pantry space did he have? Should he get the sixty-gallon water heater or go larger? Should they strip the wallpaper in the dining room? It made his head hurt.

He escaped to the kitchen, where Brad washed his hands. His partner had spent hours after work helping him put in the new flooring. They'd always been friendly but rarely saw one other outside of work. He appreciated Brad's efforts.

Logan slapped him on the back. "You did an amazing job, buddy. Karlyn claims the floors are the centerpiece of the house. I appreciate the time you spent on them."

"Hey, everybody."

Logan saw Mandy coming through the doorway with two huge bags. He and Brad strolled out to meet her.

"Nelda sent fried chicken, mashed potatoes and gravy, green beans with bacon, and some pies. I had to leave those in the car."

"I'll fetch them," Brad volunteered. "You are lookin' good, Mandy."

She handed the sacks to him. "Don't flirt with me, Brad Patterson. I heard you have a hot date tonight with some ad exec you chatted up at Home Depot."

"How'd you hear about that? I only told Resa."

"I may have mentioned it to Nelda," Resa said, looking guilty.

"Nelda told me," Mandy added. "And Casey Attaway was standing there, so by now half of the Springs knows."

They dined on paper plates provided by Nelda since Logan wouldn't move in until next week. He owned all of two dinner plates—both chipped. He would need Karlyn's advice on kitchenware since that had been Felicity's domain.

Thoughts of his former wife stirred up bitter feelings. Once he'd led a magical life, with a loving wife and two happy kids. But the twins were frozen at six years, thanks to Carson Miller. Logan's marriage collapsed under the strain of their murders. Felicity blamed him for being a cop, making her babies the target of a killer. She remarried a year after their divorce, telling Logan she couldn't stand being alone. He'd left her that way plenty after the twins died, burying his grief in case after case.

At least Felicity had moved on. Started a new life. Logan figured it was time he did the same. He needed to leave yesterday behind and forge toward a new tomorrow. That now meant this house. Possibly a new job with new responsibilities.

Logan wondered if it would mean Karlyn, as well.

As they ate, he watched her, remembering the slightly prickly author who'd arrived in the Springs. Karlyn was now flushed, happy, joking with everyone. She'd come out of her shell since she'd arrived in town. He hoped he'd played a small part in that transformation. He'd backed off, trying to give her some space. But pretty much every waking moment his thoughts came back to her.

He decided in that moment he had nothing to lose. He had planned to take things slowly but didn't want to waste any more time. He would pursue her like a mad dog. If she said no, he wouldn't sit around and wonder about what ifs. He believed they both deserved some happiness. With each other.

It was time to make his daydreams a reality.

"Any other plans for the house, Logan?" his dad asked, dragging him back to those gathered. "Besides giving this sweet girl a place to run herself ragged." He patted Lucky's head and slipped her a bite of chicken.

"Some landscaping while the weather's good so

things'll take root. I'd also like to replace the fence soon since it's in bad shape."

Karlyn laughed. "Oh, he's got more plans, Dr. Warner. He wants to build a deck. He's also got his eye on a monster gas grill at Costco."

Brad whooped. "Beer and BBQ. That's what makes the South what it is. Add football in the mix and you've pretty much got perfection."

"What about the main bathroom, Logan?" his mother asked. "Karlyn mentioned you had plans to rip out the tub."

He nodded. "That'll come later. I want to replace it with a large Jacuzzi bath."

"Did you know they put a new bathtub in the White House for William Howard Taft?" Brad asked. "He was over three hundred pounds and didn't fit into the one Teddy Roosevelt used."

"Let's hear it for a new tub." Logan raised his Coke can. "Taft won't have anything on me when I'm through with what I've got planned."

"And to our new chief of police," Mandy threw in as the group raised their sodas. She continued, "Talk at the diner's running three to one in your favor, Logan. You have this election in the bag."

Karlyn laughed. "If I were writing this story, Logan would either be killed—or his opponent would be murdered, with Logan becoming the prime suspect."

"I hate to interrupt your get-together, Logan. The door was open, so I came on in."

All eyes turned to the current police chief, Bobby Risedale.

"Pull up some floor, Chief. We've demolished the chicken but there's pie left."

Risedale shook his head. "Roy's struck again." His face was grim. "In the Springs."

Silence blanketed the room. Both Logan and Brad stood, leaving their food and drink on the ground.

Resa voiced what everyone must be thinking. "Was it anyone we know?"

"It's the Springs, Resa. Everyone knows everybody here." Risedale sighed. "We've notified her family. It was Beth Marie Sizemore."

Logan and Karlyn locked eyes.

"I CAN'T BELIEVE IT," Brad said as they drove to the crime scene. "I saw Beth Marie at the diner two days ago. She asked about you. Still carrying a torch for her Mr. Quarterback."

Logan remained silent. He remembered Beth Marie signing his petition to run, flirting openly with him in front of Karlyn, still hoping they could make a run of it since her second marriage soured.

Now, she was gone. Thanks to the Rainbow Killer.

"It might not be Roy," Brad said. "What if it's the ex she had trouble squeezing alimony payments from? Dick Sizemore could keep all his money if Beth Marie were out of the picture. What if he's played copycat and made it look like Roy left Atlanta and moved north for the last few murders?"

"Stop second guessing until we see the crime scene," he growled.

His partner mumbled something. Logan quickly apologized. "Sorry. I know you've seen some of the murder scene pictures, Brad, but when Rick took me to Jeanine's, and I saw it in person—someone I knew —it changed everything. And now Beth Marie. We need to get this bastard."

They pulled up at the small cottage Beth Marie

rented, which stood behind a much larger house. Risedale had told them the owners were on vacation in Spain. Logan remembered Beth Marie bragging at how private it was, inviting him to dinner several times.

Somehow she'd hooked up with a killer. Beth Marie hadn't stood a chance against Roy.

The coroner's van was parked in the circular drive. Risedale had two patrolmen stationed to keep prying eyes away.

As they walked through the front room, Logan became convinced Roy was at work. Everything was in place. Roy was an orderly guy. Each previous scene echoed the same pristine neatness. Beth Marie had been a slob. Logan wondered how long it took Roy to bring order to the place—and why it was important to him to do so each time he killed.

The chief called out, "In here."

They followed his voice to where Risedale stood outside the bathroom.

"She didn't show for a lunch date. Her friend said she was flaky that way, so she didn't think much of it. Texted her several times to give her a hard time but Beth Marie never replied. The friend said her phone was always near her so unanswered texts concerned her. Decided to check on Beth Marie. Got the key from the flowerpot when no one answered the door.

"And found this."

Risedale stepped aside so they had a view of the body. Beth Marie was somehow propped up, so she stood in the shower, painted a garish green. The color of money. From the looks of it, Roy was back to using piano wire to strangle his victims as Logan searched her from head to toe. Both her eyes were intact, and

Logan hoped her tongue remained attached in her mouth.

"Definitely Roy's work." He looked at the crime scene tech dusting the tile for prints. "How's she held up?"

"Super glue," the tech said. "Must've used a ton to get her attached to the tile like this."

24

Karlyn closed her laptop, unable to focus. Thoughts of Beth Marie's death clouded her brain. She'd spent last night and this morning scouring everything she could find about Roy's victims and methods, still toying with the idea of a non-fiction book on the elusive Rainbow Killer.

She thought of meeting Beth Marie, who'd flirted outrageously with Logan, hoping to renew their relationship. Karlyn hoped she and Logan were in the process of starting up their own relationship, but this interruption from Roy arriving in Walton Springs would put that to simmer on a back burner. Logan would be a man obsessed until Roy was in custody.

Her cell rang. She grabbed it, ready for some human contact.

"Hello?"

"Hey," said Logan. "Sorry we had to bail last night."

"That's okay. I locked up for you. By now, the paint's dry. You're ready to move in, Detective."

"Yeah, right. I have no glasses. I need plates and silverware. Pots and pans. Not to mention furniture to fill the place."

"I know you're busy. Want me to go online and pull samples of things you need? I'll even hit a few furniture stores and take pictures if you trust my taste."

"You're a lifesaver. Brad and I are leaving to meet with the Atlanta task force. My friend Rick Mabry from Fountain Valley is also attending. Right now my priority is catching Roy. The house, the election—all that's on hold."

"I understand. I'll pull stuff together for when you're ready. Remember, you don't need a totally furnished house. A man starts with a recliner, his TV, and a bed. Anything else is secondary."

"I appreciate you doing this, Karlyn."

"I enjoy stuff like this. Besides, it will give your family and friends ideas on what to buy for the surprise housewarming they're giving you next Saturday. Which I thought you'd better know about."

"Like I'm in a party mood? I have a serial killer on the loose!"

"You might have Roy in custody by then."

"I wish."

"And Lucky went home with your parents last night."

Karlyn heard his sharp intake of breath. "Damn. I forgot I had a dog. With this investigation, I can't spend a lot of time with her. Maybe they can keep her for me."

"I enjoy Lucky's company. Mother's always gone these days. She could go on runs with me."

"You wouldn't mind?"

"No. Besides, Jonas Watkins will be relieved. I think he believes I want to steal Hugo from him. He's accused Hugo of favoring me over him."

"Poor Jonas. He'll miss that dog once his son returns from overseas. Listen, Karlyn, I've got to go. I'll call when we get back from Atlanta."

"Good luck there. I'll collect Lucky. Talk to you soon."

Karlyn couldn't imagine the pressure Logan would be under with Roy having committed a murder here in Walton Springs. She noticed that he didn't mention Seth Berger attending the task force meeting. Which meant Berger would use the time to campaign. With the election in two weeks, Logan needed to be hitting the pavement and knocking on doors.

But catching a killer would come first in his book.

She dialed the Warner residence. Dr. Warner answered.

"Hi, it's Karlyn. Logan called and said he's swamped with this investigation. I volunteered to keep Lucky and lavish attention on her. Is that all right with you?"

"Sure is. I just put her in the back yard since we're headed to church. Come get her whenever it's convenient. If she stayed with us, she'd be ten pounds heavier from table scraps, which I hear is a big no-no in the dog world these days."

"Lucky could stand to gain a few pounds. I'll stop by while I'm out running."

"I'll put her leash on the front porch in the mailbox. You'll need to get her food at Logan's place."

"Thanks, Dr. Warner."

Karlyn changed, stretched, and then set out. As usual, Jonas sat on his porch. Hugo bounded down to join her. She trotted up to Jonas.

"I'm off to pick up Logan's dog, so Hugo better stay here today. I'll bring Lucky around soon so they can sniff each other out."

"Sounds good," Jonas told her. "I'll distract this big

lug so you can take off." He looked at Hugo. "Want a Milk-Bone, boy?" Jonas opened the door. Hugo raced by. "Safe to go," he called.

She ran to the Warners' house and collected Lucky's leash before going around the back. The dog ran over to greet her.

"Let's go have some fun," she told her.

She put in another two miles and returned home, sliding her key in the lock.

When she turned it, though, she noticed the door was unlocked. She knew she'd locked it when she left. Maybe her mother had returned home and forgotten to lock it as she often did.

Karlyn entered the kitchen cautiously. Lucky's ears perked up, as if the dog listened to the sounds of the house. With the Rainbow Killer having been in Walton Springs the day before, an unlocked door was an invitation to trouble. She patrolled downstairs. No murderers lurked in the shadows. She returned to the kitchen and gave Lucky a bowl of water while she downed a Gatorade.

Karlyn headed upstairs, leaving Lucky to explore the house. When she reached her bedroom, she peeled her T-shirt off and was about to do the same with her sports bra when she screamed.

Mario Taylor sat perched in the middle of her bed as if he hadn't a care in the world.

25

Karlyn exploded as she came out of the bathroom, dressed only in her underwear. "Why the hell are you here? How did you get in? Get off my bed! Get out of here!"

Mario laughed. "You've always been an Ice Queen, my love. Little to no emotion. Suddenly, you are now a Drama Queen? Why the change?"

He hopped off the bed and moved toward her, eyeing her appreciatively. Karlyn grabbed a T-shirt off the floor and pulled it on. Sex had never been their problem. Just the fact that he liked to have it with women other than her.

And the only man she wanted to be intimate with was Logan.

Lucky appeared at the door, a low growl sounding in her throat as she stared at the stranger.

Mario chuckled. "What a scrawny mutt. Not your style at all. You deserve a regal Great Dane or German Shepherd by your side." He turned his nose up. "Not . . . this mongrel."

He grasped her elbow. Lucky growled again, her eyes bouncing from Karlyn to the man as she assessed the threat.

Karlyn remained calm. She didn't want to set off the dog. She should have predicted Mario would show up when he found it impossible to reach her.

"Leave now," she said in a non-threatening tone, "or I will press charges against you for breaking and entering."

Mario produced the house key from his pocket. "From the proverbial flowerpot. I don't think you could make a case."

"A lucky guess."

"Or the beautiful Martha told me where to find it."

Her heart skipped a beat. "She wouldn't," she ground out. At least Karlyn hoped her mother wouldn't.

Lucky bared her teeth. Karlyn was afraid Mario would hurt the dog if she tried to protect her. Lucky was still an underfed baby. He could issue a swift kick to the pup's head that might kill her. She wouldn't put it past her ex.

"Let go of me. I'll get Lucky. You'll leave."

Karlyn moved the minute Mario released her elbow. She stepped back and swept Lucky into her arms. She glared at her ex, anger permeating her body.

He smiled, his white, even teeth perfect against the dark Spanish looks inherited from his mother. His height and lean build came from his father, an American art professor who met his wife while on sabbatical in Spain. Unfortunately, the couple died in a car accident. Mario's aunt spoiled him from the age of four, giving him a sense of entitlement he never lost.

She missed that when they met. All Karlyn saw was charm, intellect, and a sweetness she now knew to be false. Mario missed his calling when he chose to paint. He should have become an actor instead. It surprised her he hadn't thought of it himself. He would relish walking the red carpet. Gaining attention from the *paparazzi*.

"You came for money. You're out of luck," she said bluntly.

"I came for you, *mi querido*. Life without you?" He shrugged. "I had the love of my life and foolishly let her go."

"Did you mention me to the hot model you're banging?"

He shrugged. "She's gone from my life. I love no one but you, Karlyn. I worship your beauty."

Karlyn snorted. "I'm above average if I apply mascara and fix my hair. Don't act like I'm some Greek goddess you can't live without. You sniffed out other women on our honeymoon."

"You've never been average, *querido*."

"I'm not your darling, Mario. I'm not your anything. What I am is serious. Get out. Leave town. It's over." She sighed. "*So* over. And give me that key."

Mario eyed her with interest as he placed the key in her upturned palm.

"You've found someone new. I can tell because you're blushing. You can't lie to me, Karlyn. I know you too well."

He continued to study her. "You're cautious by nature. Somehow, you look different. Could you already have slept with him so fast? Hmm . . . who is he? A small-town banker, perhaps. Or a news editor. A literary type would appeal to you."

Karlyn decided to tell him about Logan. Maybe if Mario could get through his thick skull that she'd already moved on, he would do the same.

"I'm seeing a detective who will arrest your sorry

ass for trespassing in a nano-second," she said evenly, still trying not to alert Lucky. "I'm able to keep Lucky back but with Logan? There's no holding back." She grinned. The thought of Logan making mincemeat out of Mario appealed to her immensely.

He gave her an indulgent smile. "If you change your mind, I'm staying at a charming bed and breakfast on Maple. Mrs. Camille Attaway's. *Ciao.*"

Karlyn counted to fifty as she listened to him go down the stairs and open and close the front door. Tension coiled through her shaking body.

Lucky stared sadly at her, as if she could feel Karlyn's emotional pain. She buried her face in the dog's fur. "I'm not mad at you, girl. I'm mad at him. He's a loser who knows how to push my buttons. That makes me mad at myself."

Either she would be the death of Mario Taylor—or he would be the death of her.

~

"CALL HER, buddy. You know you want to."

Logan stopped at the light and looked at Brad. He wore a knowing grin.

"I can tell. You guys are getting tight. Besides, today's been a long day." Brad ran a hand through his hair. "If I even hear the name Roy in the next forty-eight hours, I will run screaming from the station. Much less think about serial killers and murders and decent people losing their lives to this drifter."

"What do you mean? Drifter?"

His partner shrugged. "I don't mean it in a literal sense, like he's blowing through and will be in another state next week. I'm thinking how he's drifting north after so many murders in the city. Moving up the map. You gotta wonder why."

The light changed. Logan moved with the traffic. "In all the years I've seen this kind of stuff, I've never understood why."

"Why?"

"You know. Why a person would harm another person. I don't see how they can look at someone and perform such savagery."

Brad sighed. "Research proves most serial killers were abused as kids. Maybe they aren't treated as human from a young age. In turn, they don't see others as human. But why they mutilate, stab, burn? Enough of the gory talk." He pulled out his cell. "What's Karlyn's number?"

Logan told him. He concentrated on the road as Brad dialed, trying to push away thoughts of what Carson Miller had done to Ashley and Alex. In his book, Miller wasn't human. He was an animal.

"Hey, Karlyn. It's Brad. Yeah. Doing good. We sat all day looking at gruesome pictures and hearing all kinds of nasty things. I think Logan could use a break. They didn't feed us. You can probably hear our stomachs growling over the line."

Brad paused and laughed. "Well, I could. Anything. I would eat garbage if it had garlic sprinkled on it. Hmmm. That sounds nice. Thanks." He looked at his watch. "Probably twenty, twenty-five minutes. Okay. See you then."

Brad pocketed his phone. "Karlyn's taken pity on both of us. She's ordering two extra-large pizzas. They should be there by the time we get to her mom's place. Hope you don't mind me horning in. I'll eat and run. Promise."

"That's fine." Logan was glad Brad had pushed to call Karlyn. He'd missed her all day, especially since it was a Sunday and he'd hoped they could go for a motorcycle ride that afternoon. At least now he could salvage some time with her during dinner.

Maybe more. Once Brad left.

Logan pulled into the drive. A Honda with pizza advertising on its roof arrived at the curb.

"I'll get it," his partner said. He handed cash to the delivery guy and brought the pizzas to the porch.

Karlyn opened the door before Logan rang the bell. He drank in her face, glad to see someone who hadn't had their throat cut and wide, staring eyes. He mentally shook off the image and gave her a quick kiss. As he pulled away, she pulled him close again by grabbing his tie and kissed him once more.

She broke the kiss. "Mmm. Smells heavenly." She motioned to Brad. "Bring those into the kitchen. Beer? Iced tea?"

They devoured the pizzas as Karlyn explained how her mother had left on an impromptu trip that afternoon.

"A new antiquing friend got a wild hare to go shopping in New York. Mother jumped at the chance. She was excited about buying new purses and seeing *Hamilton*."

"How long will she be gone?" Brad asked.

"Maybe a week. Maybe longer." Karlyn laughed. "This flying by the seat of your pants thing is new for her."

Logan said, "Lucky will be good company then. I'm glad you agreed to keep her a few days while we're running down leads on Roy G. Biv."

She frowned. "I had an unexpected visitor today.

Having some protection around the house will be nice."

He caught the bitter tone in her words. "Who was it?"

Her mouth tightened. "My ex-husband. He found the spare key while I was gone. Let himself in and made himself at home. I threw him out."

Logan's shoulders tensed. "Why is he here?"

"Bottom line? He wanted money. What he said was he wanted me back but that's a joke."

He looked into her troubled green eyes. "Do you want to file a temporary restraining order against him?"

Karlyn hesitated. "Let me think about it. He's staying at a B&B here in town. If he continues to pester me, I'll do it."

"I disagree," Brad said. "File the order now, Karlyn. Don't wait for trouble to come knocking. Be proactive." He glanced at Logan. "I can start the paperwork tonight."

"No," she said firmly. "You've both had a long day. I can come to the station tomorrow morning if I decide to go that route."

"If for any reason Brad and I aren't there, don't let Seth Berger handle it," Logan advised. "He files away every tidbit of info. It wouldn't surprise me if he sold what you said to the tabloids."

"Good advice. That guy creeps me out. He won't get a handful of votes against you, Logan."

"Do you know he saw Beth Marie Sizemore a few times?"

Logan looked at Brad in surprise. "What? How do you know?"

"I heard him brag about it in the locker room. That they'd gone through a six-pack together." He paused and added, "Capping the night off in a fun way. And the way he said it? His meaning was clear."

Karlyn shivered. "That creeps me out even more."

"We need to question him now that she's dead." Logan met Brad's eyes. "Makes me think about Berger in a whole new light."

26

L ogan stared into the mirror. Dark circles screamed his lack of sleep, thanks to Mario Taylor hanging around town. He'd spent the night with Karlyn, in case her ex decided to pay another visit. He doubted an undernourished puppy would be enough protection. He insisted she set the little-used alarm system before he kissed her goodbye this morning and returned to his apartment.

His shower sparked some life into him. He nuked the pizza she sent home with him for breakfast. He was eager to arrive at the station this morning.

And get Seth Berger into interrogation.

Logan would play it strictly by the book. He had a reputation for making sure every *T* was crossed and each *I* dotted. He didn't want Berger to accuse him of any impropriety, especially with the election looming.

He decided to grab a coffee in the diner to help jump-start him. He zipped down the stairs and sidled up to the counter.

"Coffee'll do it today, Mandy. I need to get to work."

Her brow wrinkled. "I heard. Beth Marie." She filled a to go cup for him.

Logan sensed eyes on him. He turned to survey the diner's patrons. A stranger with dark, good looks and burning eyes met his with contempt.

"Here you go, Logan." Mandy leaned in as he took a long drink. "The guy looking at you?" she asked. "He's been asking about you since he got here."

Logan didn't bother with mixing anything into the coffee and took a large swallow. He felt the rush of caffeine hit his system and fan out.

"I know who he is. Thanks for the coffee." Logan tipped her and went to introduce himself to Mario Taylor.

He pulled out a chair and sat opposite Karlyn's former husband.

"I'm Detective Logan Warner, Mr. Taylor. I don't cotton much to assholes. Which means you should head back to New York."

Taylor smiled, his white teeth dark against olive skin. "Two powerful men. In love with the same fierce blonde. Whom will she choose?"

Love?

Logan hadn't said the words to Karlyn because he didn't want to frighten her off. But he knew it was true. He'd fallen in love with an amazing woman. He'd do anything to protect her. He stared at her ex-husband. A strong wave of possessiveness washed over him.

He loved her. Period. And he wanted to mop the floor with this jerk.

"Karlyn will toy with us while she makes up her mind," Taylor informed him. "She may have you fooled into thinking she is kind and demure. Actually, she is quite fickle. Whatever the outcome, rest assured it'll appear in her next book. With Karlyn—like Taylor Swift—there's always a price tag attached."

Mario pushed his eggs around with a fork. "I hear

you are not only fighting for love but fighting for political office, Detective Warner. And struggling to put a killer behind bars."

The artist paused and took a bite. "Of course, you have yet to find the killer that murdered your two beautiful children."

Rage raced through Logan. He jumped to his feet and threw back an arm to punch out this bastard's lights. Then dropped it. That's what this bozo wanted. Mario Taylor would be sue-happy. He could ruin Logan's present. And future.

"I Googled you, Detective, and found out—"

"Leave. I don't want trash like you in my place."

Logan found Nelda Vanderley standing next to their table. The diner's owner glared at Mario. "I heard what you said. You're no friend of Logan's—or Karlyn's—and you won't find any in the Springs."

Mario stood. He yanked out his wallet.

"No," Nelda warned. "I don't want your money. Or your kind. Now, git!"

He stormed out without a backward glance. Logan tried to relax his clenched jaw.

"Thanks, Nelda."

She patted his arm. "Go to work, honey. I know you've got a lot on your mind. That scumbag won't come back here."

Logan picked up his coffee and left. He saw Taylor scurrying down the sidewalk east of the square.

He arrived at the station and grabbed Risedale's arm, pulling him aside into the empty break room.

"We need to talk before roll call."

As they walked to the chief's office, Brad entered the station. Logan motioned to him. The three men closeted in private. Brad repeated to the chief what he'd told Logan the night before. Risedale's eyes widened.

"Kid gloves, fellows. No accusations in the interview. This could be an explosive situation. I'll watch outside Interrogation One." He gripped Logan's shoulder. "Go fetch Berger. I saw him come in a few minutes ago."

Brad said, "I'm grabbing coffee. I'll meet you there."

Logan entered the squad room and found Berger at his desk, reading the sports section and eating a fried egg sandwich. He took the last bite as Logan walked over and mopped the grease from his chin.

"Interrogation One. Now."

Berger sized him up. "Yeah, Mr. Golden Boy. I heard you're working the Sizemore homicide. I know Risedale handpicked you and Patterson for the area task force." He sneered. "You think that'll make you more qualified to run this town? Election's in less than two weeks. Better catch Mr. Roy G. Biv, Warner, because if you don't? You won't get a dozen votes in this town. I've got a blitz prepared that'll—"

"I said move your ass."

Berger leaned back in his chair, hands behind his head. "I'm not working the case. Go fuck yourself, Warner. I won't do your work and let you take the glory. Find another sucker to milk dry."

"You're part of the case now. You slept with Beth Marie. We have a few questions to ask. We better get answers we like."

Color flooded Berger's face. "I'm a cop. You couldn't think *I* killed her?"

"I'll be asking the questions. Not you."

Logan stepped back and allowed Berger to lead the way. No one had witnessed their confrontation in the squad room because of the early hour. Roll call for patrolmen would be in a few minutes so they were either in the locker room or headed to their briefing.

Berger walked stiffly. Logan wondered if this man, whom he'd worked next, could be a cold-blooded killer.

One who had the gall to run for police chief.

Berger reached the interrogation room and entered, slamming the door back against the wall. Brad waited at the table, stacks of filled manila folders and yellow legal pads in front of him.

He brightened at their arrival. "Glad you could make it, Berger."

Logan frowned at the sarcasm. Risedale wanted it clean and mean. Logan intended to keep it that way.

Berger sat across from Brad. Logan closed the door and remained standing. Brad looked to him to take the lead. He leaned over and turned on the video camera.

"Let the record reflect that it is Monday, May tenth, at 6:49 A.M. Present are Detectives Brad Patterson and Logan Warner interviewing Detective Seth Berger regarding his relationship with homicide victim Beth Marie Sizemore, killed two days ago."

"You haven't read me my rights." Berger glared at Logan, his thin face drawn and suddenly much older than his years.

"We don't suspect you of a crime," Brad informed Berger. "Yet."

"This is strictly for standard background information," Logan added. "You don't need your rights read to you."

Berger looked both of them over. "Maybe I should ask for an attorney anyway."

Logan shrugged. "It's up to you, but this is merely routine questioning, Seth."

To be on the safe side, he proceeded to read Berger his rights and asked if Berger understood them. He paused, then aimed for a friendly tone. "We're looking into Beth Marie's background. Charting her moves. Seeing if we can find any patterns. How she might have come across Roy G. Biv."

"Well, I'm not a murderer. Especially the Roy G. Biv variety. The only thing I've ever killed is deer. *In* season."

"Could you tell us how you met Beth Marie Sizemore?" Logan sat next to Brad.

Berger shrugged. "It's a small town. I can't remember a time when I didn't know her. Did we meet in the sandbox or at Vacation Bible School or the Fourth of July parade? I don't know. We've had a passing acquaintance for years."

Logan's hands balled into fists under the table. "When did your relationship move beyond acquaintance? Especially since you have to be a good dozen years older than Ms. Sizemore. I doubt you were playground buddies."

"We ran into each other at the drugstore a few weeks ago. Talked a bit in the toothpaste aisle. I asked her out. She said okay. We went."

"Where did you go?"

"Took a picnic over to the lake one Saturday afternoon. She fried chicken and made potato salad. I picked up the beer and some cookies at the bakery. We ate, talked. Left when the mosquitoes started eating us up."

"Did you see her after that?"

"Once. She mentioned she liked a movie called *Love, Actually*. I found the DVD in a bin at Walmart the next day. Called her up and said I'd bring it over. Picked up a six-pack on the way."

"And?" Logan prompted when Berger didn't continue.

"We watched it. Pretty lame. Drank the six-pack during. Then moved into the bedroom after." Berger snorted. "For all her talk, Beth Marie wasn't all that hot in the sack. I didn't call her after that. Was a week later that she turned up dead."

"And you had no contact with her after that Sunday?"

"No. No desire to."

"How many relationships have you been involved in, Mr. Berger?"

Berger glared at him. "None of your damn business."

Logan pressed on. "Wouldn't you characterize yourself as a bit of a loner? I haven't heard of you dating anyone since your divorce ten years ago."

"I go out some. Truth is, I like my own company best. I'm quiet by nature. Like to fish and hunt on my own. Work pretty much fulfills my socialization needs. I enjoy being by myself."

"Can you verify where you were this past Friday night?"

"No. Didn't know I'd need an alibi."

Logan stared at Berger. The silence hung. Finally, Berger started up again.

"I left work about six-thirty. Grabbed a cheeseburger and shake at the diner. No, wait. It was meatloaf because that was the special. Had the cheeseburger Thursday night. Made it home around eight. Didn't see anyone or leave again until the next morning around four when I went fishing. By myself."

Logan watched Brad scribble a few notes. He knew from reading the crime scene reports that no physical evidence tied Berger to Beth Marie's homicide.

Nothing circumstantial linked him to her or any other victim in Roy's crime spree. Seth Berger was a cop. If he were Roy, though Logan doubted he was, he would know how to beat the system.

"Have you two interviewed Dick Sizemore? He was giving Beth Marie fits. Holding out on alimony. She was ready to drag him into court. You need to give him a hard look. The ex is always a solid suspect in my book. Of course, I do have more experience than you do."

Logan let the sour remark slide. "Thanks for your time. You're free to go." Berger didn't hesitate and exited the interview room quickly. Logan turned off the camera.

Brad pitched his empty cup into the trash can. "Does he think we're idiots? Naturally, we talked to Sizemore right after we saw the crime scene. Besides, that idiot isn't smart enough to plan and execute what we saw. The fact that he was banging the dealership's receptionist most of Friday night and all day Saturday sure cleared him."

Brad slammed a hand on the table. "Back to square one."

Risedale walked in. "That was a big fat nothing. And let's face it—Berger's too slippery to be nailed in a simple interrogation."

"I don't think it's him," Logan said. "Gut feeling."

"If it wasn't Berger, who was it?" Brad asked.

27

K arlyn hummed along to Coldplay as she drove north on the interstate. She'd spent the day in Atlanta looking at furniture for Logan. She found it strange shopping for big-ticket items for a man she hadn't known a month ago.

She wondered if she'd done the right thing, leaping into bed with him. It was so out of character for her—no matter how attractive or intelligent he was.

As she headed back to Walton Springs, she hoped Logan would have time to have dinner with her tonight and scroll through the various shots of furniture she'd taken. She already had a handle on his taste. If he could make some decisions, the "surprise" housewarming on Saturday would allow the guests to find his den furnished. Every store she visited assured her that delivery could be made during this week.

Thankfully, the trip kept her mind off Mario. Karlyn couldn't have stayed home to write today knowing her ex might show up again, uninvited.

She entered the city limits and thought about pulling into the diner for a slice of pie when she saw Seth Berger entering. That made the pint of Ben and

Jerry's Cherry Garcia in her mother's freezer sound more appetizing.

Suddenly, her eye caught Mario exiting the bookstore, a sack in his hand. When had her ex ever read a book, much less one of hers? More than likely he'd stopped in for a *Playboy*, his favorite reading material.

He saw her as she passed and waved jauntily. He called out, "Remember, Mrs. Attaway's bed and breakfast on Maple. See you soon, my darling."

Karlyn gave the convertible the gas, burning rubber like there was no tomorrow. As she drove away, she grinned. So, this was the rush Matt got when he blew by people in her books. Imagine the fun she would feel seeing him do that on screen.

She slowed and decided to circle back, avoiding Mario. She would stop at the police station and look into the restraining order that Logan and Brad suggested last night. It wouldn't hurt to see what the process involved. Besides, she could always work the information into a book down the line. That was the great thing about being a writer. She could mine information anywhere.

She approached the square from the opposite direction and found a nearby parking spot. She stopped at the front desk.

"I'd like to see Detective Warner."

The rotund sergeant manning the desk broke into a huge grin. "My stars alive! Karlyn Campbell in the flesh. My wife told me she saw you the other day. We love Matt Collins. Is it true they're making a movie about him?"

She appreciated running into grateful fans. "I finished the screenplay not too long ago." She confided, "I can't wait to see Matt on the screen myself."

"It's nice to have you in the Springs, ma'am. Let me call back for Detective Warner."

He dialed the extension. "Got Ms. Karlyn Campbell here, Detective. Uh-huh. Okay, will do."

Looking at Karlyn he said, "That was Detective Patterson, Detective Warner's partner. He's coming to get you." He scribbled her name on a peel-off tag with a Sharpie and handed the visitor's badge to her.

"We're a little more careful these days." He chuckled. "Not that I expect the Springs to become a hotbed for terrorist activities in the near future."

She saw Brad approach.

"Thanks, Sarge. Come on back, Karlyn. Logan's tied up on a conference call with an FBI profiler that spoke to the task force yesterday."

Brad led her through a series of halls and settled her in a chair next to his desk.

"Can I get you something? Bad coffee? A Coke?"

"No, thanks. I guess you know why I'm here."

"Your ex breaking into your mom's house was pretty ballsy." He frowned. "Are you ready to file and go to court?"

Karlyn hesitated at the mention of court. "Could you explain the process first?"

He leaned back in his chair. "Sure. In Georgia, we use the term Temporary Protective Order. The judge issues it after you make an appearance in court to ask for one. Mario wouldn't be present for this. It states that a person is to refrain from particular acts and stay away from particular places."

"Such as?"

"Your residence. Your place of employment. It would go into effect when it's served on him. Puts him on notice."

"That's it?"

"No, it's more complicated than that. The next step is an Order to Show Cause hearing. This time both of you would appear to explain why a permanent order should or shouldn't be issued by the court. The law states this should be done within thirty days of issuing the original TPO, but we usually can get you in with the judge in half that time. In the meantime, the temp is in effect."

"How does the judge decide how to rule?"

Brad sipped on his coffee. "You present evidence at the hearing. Try to show sufficient cause. And if you get it, it's in effect immediately. You also can renew it for an additional period of time. In some cases, it can become permanent."

"What if Mario violates it?"

He grinned. "He would be in contempt of court. We'd slap his ass in jail. Charge him with a misdemeanor or felony, based upon the violation. He'd be sentenced to serve time and possibly pay a fine."

Brad leaned over and typed a few things into his computer. He clicked and then turned the screen toward her.

"This is the eight-page order you use to petition the court. You note that you're past spouses and what acts of family violence he's previously committed.

"You share that, as the petitioner, you have a reasonable fear of your own safety and that you feel it likely that Mario would commit violent acts against you in the future."

Brad finished his coffee and pushed the mug aside. "If you decide to file the papers, I'll need his info— date of birth, Social, physical description, where he's employed. That kind of thing."

She blew out a long breath. "That's part of the problem. He's an artist who blows through cash like water for chocolate. He's here to squeeze me from money. This TPO wouldn't apply. He has a temper, but he's never been violent toward me."

He thought a moment. "We could file under Georgia law for a Stalking Protection Order. That lasts twelve months and can also be extended. Georgia defines stalking as following you or contacting you with the purpose of harassing and intimidating you. Contact includes in person, over the computer, by phone, mail, email.

"If you got this—and Mario broke it—the state could put him away. They also give you notice of when he's released if you give them a landline number."

Brad studied her. "Is this something you'd like to move forward on? I can get the paperwork started. We could grab a court date in the next day or two to file. Just say the word."

Karlyn fidgeted in the chair. "Can I think about it? I believe when Mario sees I won't fork over any more money, he'll leave town. He's not the kind to rock that boat."

"I respect that, but I've seen this before. It's smart to be safe. Not sorry. My advice is do it. The sooner, the better."

He glanced over his shoulder. "Door's still closed. I'm not sure how much longer Logan'll be on that call." Brad laughed. "Knowing the Feebies, he's been on hold the entire time."

She stood. "Have him call me, okay? And thanks for explaining everything to me so thoroughly." She smiled. "Who knows? I may have to use you as a law enforcement reference for a future novel."

Karlyn returned to her car, restless. She thought she'd go over to the antique store and see the dining room set Logan had on hold. He'd mentioned needing to set up delivery of it. Maybe she could arrange that for him.

She drove to the square. When she entered the shop, Anne Stockdale called out a greeting.

"Hello, Karlyn. I'm on hold with a customer. Feel free to look around."

"Can you point me in the direction of Logan's table and chairs?"

Anne held a finger up. "Yes, I can get that for you in about a week's time, Sandra." She pointed to the far right of the store, so Karlyn made her way there as Anne continued her conversation.

The table was a beautiful mahogany with eight matching chairs. Karlyn could easily picture it in the large dining room of the old Kinyon house. She ran a hand across the smooth wood, imagining it with a lace runner and fresh floral centerpiece.

The bell rang, announcing the arrival of a new customer. A large man waddled in, wiping his flushed face with a handkerchief. He noticed Anne on the phone and began wandering around the store until he spotted Karlyn and headed her way.

"You must be the little lady everyone's talking about." He thrust out a meaty hand. "Mayor Joe Vick. Don't read books, but if I did, I'm sure I'd read one of yours."

She shook the offered hand. "Karlyn Campbell."

"Might I ask if you're staying in town, seeing as to how you and Logan Warner are stepping out?"

She blushed at the quaint description, still surprised how everyone seemed to know each other's business in a small town. "I'm considering it."

Vick beamed at her. "I can't say enough good things about the Springs. And if a strapping fellow like Logan isn't enough of a temptation, think about the quiet and solitude of a small town. Perfect for a writer. I'm sure that's why your father moved here."

Karlyn decided to change the topic. "Are you browsing or shopping?"

Vick mopped his brow. "Got an anniversary coming up." He gestured widely. "From the large to the small, there ain't nothing here that wouldn't please Mrs. Vick."

"Then let me suggest jewelry, Joe," Anne smoothly interjected as she came their way. "I have a few new pieces. Come look in the case."

The mayor ambled over as Anne joined Karlyn by the dining set.

"Isn't this a beautiful table? The chairs have been reupholstered. I love these rich colors."

"I do, too," Karlyn agreed. "Logan was excited that this set was still available. Do you think I could set up delivery for him?"

"Let's check my calendar. We can also help Joe make a decision. If we don't, he'll be in here until his next anniversary."

Anne went to her office while Karlyn pointed out some items to the mayor. The store owner joined them and confirmed Wednesday.

"I have a father and son who deliver for me. They can be there around one. I'm glad Logan bought the Kinyon place. That dining room is the perfect place to showcase this set."

Vick asked to see a bracelet. Karlyn looked in the display case. A locket caught her eye.

"Anne, would you mind getting that locket on the end? I'd like to see it."

The owner retrieved both pieces. Vick agreed he couldn't do better, so Anne began ringing up the sale.

Karlyn studied the locket, turning it over and then opening the catch.

"Twenty-four karat gold," Anne told her as she gave Vick his credit card back and slip to sign. "Belonged to a relative of Margaret Mitchell. Supposedly, the great author gave it to the girl on her sixteenth birthday. No provenance, but it's a nice story all the same."

Karlyn nodded, thinking how she loved *Gone with the Wind* as a teenager and had read it several times.

"I'll take it." She retrieved her credit card.

Anne laughed. "You two are easy to please. I hope you come in more often."

The bell sounded. "What a pleasant surprise."

Karlyn cringed at the voice. She refused to turn and acknowledge her ex. He'd probably seen her car out front and guessed she was inside.

Mario came closer and greeted the others. "This must be the lovely Mrs. Stockdale." He looked around the store. "You have a treasure trove of items here. You could compete with the best stores in New York."

He offered a hand to Vick. "And you must be the mayor of this humble abode. Mario Taylor, sir."

The two men shook hands. Anne finished with the transaction and handed both Vick and Karlyn their packages.

"Buying yourself a treat, my sweet? Or do you gift your lover with something new?"

She saw Anne's brows raise in interest. The mayor's jaw simply hung open. Karlyn hated the gossip that would result from this encounter. She tamped down the anger that threatened to flare out of control and took a deep breath.

Calmly, she faced her ex. "I will say this for the last time. We are divorced, Mario. Financially, I gave you much more than you deserved. You won't get another dime from me. I never wish to see you again. Go back to New York. Find some sugar mama to take care of you."

Mario stepped toward her. His fingers latched onto her elbow. "I have seen your detective. I am ten times the man he is. You are blinded by infatuation now." He smiled benignly at her. "I will wait. You will come to your senses. Then all will be well with us again."

The bell tinkled as Nelda Vanderley bustled in. "Hey, Anne. Are you bringing your bacon spinach dip to bunco tonight?"

Nelda froze as soon as the words left her mouth, and she took in the scene unfolding.

Karlyn angrily jerked away. "When will you get it?" she said, her voice trembling with rage. She didn't care if witnesses were present. She needed to get this off her chest.

"You are a user. You took my money and self-esteem, and God knows what else, but no more. Do you hear me? No more! I wish you'd drop dead, so you'd stop pestering me."

Her fingers tightened around the sack she held. She pushed past her ex and hurried from the store.

She unlocked the car door and sank into the seat, her whole body shaking.

Then Karlyn laughed aloud. She'd certainly given the bunco group plenty to chew on tonight.

28

Logan emerged from his conference call with the FBI profiler with a pad of scribbled notes and no idea where to pick up in the investigation. He tossed the legal pad on his desk and went to the break room to refill his coffee cup. The pot was empty. He leaned his hands against the counter, head down, and wondered what the hell he should do now.

Brad entered with his empty mug. "Rutherford have anything enlightening to say?"

"Rutherford refined the profile. After making me wait forever."

His partner grinned. "What did you expect? Bill Rutherford is like every federal agent. He hates locals. Locals hate the bureau. The Feebies milk us dry. Steal all the info from the legwork we've put into an investigation. Then a break in the case occurs. They catch the bad guy. They get all the credit. End of story."

Logan cracked his knuckles. "I don't care who gets the credit. To get Roy off the streets and behind bars is what's important. He's in our town, Brad. *Our* town. He killed someone I've known since she was in diapers. And I haven't been able to do a damn thing about it."

Brad added fresh coffee and programmed the coffeemaker. The drip began. The aroma filled the small break room.

"What's the updated profile?"

He ran a hand through his hair. "Still thirties, though more likely late thirties. With the possibility that Roy could be in his forties. Maybe."

"Hmm. Real certain there. I'll bet he was at the head of his class at the academy. Rutherford. Not Roy."

"Still a white male who appears stable to outsiders. Educated, though not necessarily formally."

"As in college?"

Logan nodded. "Rutherford's on a new kick now. Thinks Roy might have military training. Said there's a precision to his work that could indicate a military background."

"Great. I can see the headlines now." Brad lifted his hands in the air to frame his imaginary copy. "Former Navy SEAL claims he's Rainbow Killer. Grew up hating his mother."

Brad dropped his hands. "Or his sister. Or kinder-garten teacher. Whatever. If he's killing women, the Feebies always go Freudian and think he hated some woman at some time in his past. I don't always buy that." He stopped and poured a cup of coffee. "Besides, Roy has proven to be an equal opportunity killer. He kills indiscriminately. So, it's just not his mama he hated as a child. It was every man, woman, short, tall, fat, thin, left-handed, right-handed person he ran into."

Logan asked, "Who do you think Roy is? Or what causes him to do what he does?"

Brad grew thoughtful. "I think he gets off on it. Pe-riod. He's killed from every age and ethnicity. Every socioeconomic group. I think the freak enjoys torture.

Or maybe he likes feeling superior to the police. When he's finally caught—and I'm hoping it's when and not if—he won't have a thing to say. I believe Roy's totally, one hundred percent apeshit nuts."

His partner paused. "That's what scares the devil out of me, Logan. I'm afraid he'll get off because he's loco, plain and simple. And they'll lock him away like they did Reagan's attempted killer. You remember that guy from Dallas? John Hinckley. He was released from institutionalized psychiatric care. Some fat-assed judge said Hinkley was no longer a threat to himself or others. At first, he was ordered to live with his mom. Then he got a full, unconditional release regarding where he lived.

"To top it off, the freak can now use his own name on his art, writing, and music instead of publishing anonymously as in the past. A guy who tried to kill the fuckin' President of the United States—free on the streets!"

Brad looked Logan in the eye. "Promise me something."

Logan sensed the atmosphere in the room change. "What?"

"That if we find Roy—you and me—that we'll shoot him. No going to trial. No finding him insane. No putting him in some psychiatric facility. We remember all of the families of Roy's victims. We take him out. No questions asked. You in?"

He thought about the pain he still faced daily at losing the twins. At the empty hole Carson Miller left in Logan's life. At how it tore his marriage apart. And thought of all those families shattered beyond repair, thanks to Roy.

"I'm in."

Logan stood there a moment, not quite believing

he'd agreed to execute a man instead of arrest him and bring him to trial. He was supposed to be one of the good guys. For law and order. For Pete's sake, he was even running for chief of police.

Yet if he confronted the Rainbow Killer face to face, Logan knew he would remember his promise to Brad.

And keep it.

If caught on his watch, this serial murderer would not get away.

He returned to his desk and thumbed through his messages. Brad followed with coffee for them both.

"Karlyn came by while you were tied up with Bill Rutherford."

Logan glanced up, his thoughts turning to Mario Taylor. "She okay?"

"Yeah. She had a few questions about restraining orders against her ex. I walked her through things. It would be easier to get him on stalking laws."

He thought a moment. "I think you're right. Did you convince her to file?"

"She wanted to talk with you first. But she seemed pretty upset with the creep."

Logan's desk phone rang. He picked it up. "Detective Warner." He paused a moment. "Nelda, slow down. Okay. Just now? Got it."

He hung up. "Karlyn had it out with Mario Taylor in Anne Stockdale's store a few minutes ago. Nelda witnessed the tail end of it."

"And?"

"Karlyn wished him dead and stormed out."

Brad stood and lifted his jacket from the back of his chair. "Let's go assess the situation."

They signed out. Logan instructed Brad to stop at the antique store first.

"I want to hear Anne's version of things before we confront anyone," he explained. "Nelda said Anne heard the entire encounter."

They drove to the square and saw Mayor Vick outside the store, jabbering on his cell phone. He caught sight of them and quickly pocketed it.

"Heard the whole thing, boys," Vick assured them. "That man is slimier than—" Vick paused. "Don't want to insult a snake. I think it'd have more integrity than this old boy. Miss Campbell just stuck up for herself."

"You were there?" Logan asked. Nelda hadn't mentioned Vick's presence.

"Miss Campbell was helping me pick out a present for my upcoming anniversary. If I want another forty with the missus, I know to come through on the big occasions."

Vick's cell rang, and he grabbed for it. "Yes, I was there, Casey. She wants that man dead. D-E-A-D, dead."

Logan signaled for Vick to hang up. No way for damage control now. The mayor had probably been on the phone with his wife when they pulled up. She was bound to call every woman in her bridge club. Casey Attaway would spread things from his end like a brushfire out of control.

"Gotta go. I'll stop at the pumps and tell you everything about it later."

"Have you talked to anyone else about this, Mayor?" Brad asked.

Vick didn't bother to look sheepish. "Well, Anne and Nelda. They're still inside. And I called my wife. And Bobby Joe. I figured the chief might want to hear about it. Even if he is out sick today."

Logan knew all about Risedale's "sick" days. They had become more frequent as his time in office drew to a close. Most of them involved getting therapeutic time on the golf course now that the weather had turned nice.

He glanced at Brad. Risedale had probably gone straight into the Nineteenth Hole for a beer and to pass along the news. By sundown, most of the Springs would have heard that Karlyn had tried to kill her ex in the antique store with a butcher knife. Gossip had a life of its own in the Springs.

Brad nodded. "Mayor Vick, if you'll come over to the car with me. That'll afford us a little privacy. I'll take your statement so you can be on your way."

Logan entered Anne's store. She and Nelda spoke animatedly. As he approached, their conversation died.

"Nothing to get excited about, Logan," Nelda assured him. "I just thought you needed to know what happened. No laws were broken. She just told that sumbitch a thing or two."

He looked from her to Anne. "Start at the top. Don't leave anything out."

Anne composed herself. "Karlyn came in and we agreed upon a time for your dining room set to be delivered this week. Then she and Mayor Vick looked at some jewelry for his wife. Joe found a lovely bracelet, and I rang that up. Karlyn spotted a locket and purchased that.

"As I finished the sale, that horrible man came in. He asked Karlyn if she were buying something for her . . . *lover*."

Anne turned a rosy shade. "Karlyn told him in no uncertain terms that they were divorced, and it was none of his business. That she had given him a lot of money, and he needed to go find a sugar mama to take care of him."

"Go on."

"Well, he told her that he'd seen you and that you were no big deal, Logan. That Karlyn would come to her senses and come back to him."

Anne looked at Nelda. "As if Karlyn would ever think of going back to such a man. And dump our Logan?"

"Never," Nelda agreed. "And then I came in when Karlyn told him that he was a user and she wished he *were* dead."

"She stormed out," Anne concluded. "Poor thing. She was shaking like a leaf on a blustery March day, but that girl didn't cry. She held her head high and marched out proudly."

"Then her ex began ranting. It was some foreign language," Nelda said. "Maybe Spanish? Or Italian?"

"I think it was a little of both," Anne chimed in. "He grew all red in the face and stormed out without a by your leave to us."

"You're absolutely certain Karlyn didn't threaten to kill him?" Logan asked.

"Not at all. She said she wished he were dead so he couldn't bother her anymore. And my stars, he was so darn rude. I'm sorry Karlyn was married to the likes of him," Anne said. "Smart woman to get out of that situation."

"We want you to talk to him, Logan," Nelda added. "Let him know there's no reason to stay in the Springs any longer. And then you'll need to comfort that dear girl." Nelda paused and assessed him. "A chief of police would be well thought of settling down with someone of Karlyn's caliber."

Logan finished his notes and slid his notebook into his pocket, ignoring Nelda's last words.

"Thank you, ladies." He turned to go. "If this incident comes up, be clear that Karlyn didn't threaten Mario in any way. I don't want people to get the wrong impression."

Both women nodded guiltily. Logan wondered whom they'd already spoken to. He could hear the town taking sides now, even if most of them didn't know either Karlyn or Mario.

He exited the store and saw Mayor Vick already a block away, waddling as fast as his legs could carry him. Logan returned to the car and slid into the passenger's seat.

"Anything?"

Brad consulted his notes. "No threats on either one's part. Mario dissed you and seemed to want money from Karlyn. She gave him shit and told him she wished he were dead and slammed out of there like a cyclone."

"That's pretty much what I got. Except the ladies felt we need to visit Mario and gently nudge him out of town before I race over and comfort Karlyn."

"No harm, no foul. No threats. I don't see a reason we can talk to him. Officially, that is." Brad shrugged. "But if we happened to run into him off the clock?"

Logan glanced at his watch. "Let's call it a day. Drop me at the station. I want to head over to Karlyn's."

Brad grinned. "Yeah, you probably need to work on some of that . . . comforting. Unfortunately, I'm between ladies. Guess it's a beer and the DVR for me tonight."

He didn't respond. Brad always chased skirts. His partner liked the no-strings approach. It left him free to scratch his itch when he felt like it and then move on.

Logan drove straight to Martha Campbell's house once Brad dropped him at his car. He went around to the back and knocked at the kitchen door, knowing how Karlyn liked to hang out there.

She opened the door, a spoon in hand, and motioned him in. An open container of ice cream sat on the kitchen table. She grabbed a second spoon from the drawer and handed it to him.

"I've never found a problem that Ben and/or Jerry couldn't solve."

Logan dug in. "Mmm. Cherry Garcia."

"I'm sure you've heard about my altercation with Mario."

He spooned another bite into his mouth. "Nelda called and filled me in."

"I was minding my own business—actually, yours —when Mario walked in and began ragging on me. He said I could do better than you." Karlyn waved her spoon in the air as she spoke. "Can you imagine that? You're smart. Funny. Drop-dead gorgeous. How could I do better than you? And—"

Logan cut her off with a kiss.

Karlyn tasted like the ice cream. And much more.

She tasted like home.

29

He watched Camille Attaway putter in the kitchen, clearing the table and loading the dishwasher. It was her bridge night, thus the early dinner provided to her lone guest. She would ready herself. Put on that vivid orange lipstick she always wore in public. And head out for what the town knew was more sampling of wines than hands of bridge. She'd come home fuzzy-headed and go straight to bed.

Never knowing what had taken place in her absence.

He waited fifteen minutes. Moved from behind the chinaberry tree, grateful for the tall hedges that surrounded the back yard. Two windows in the breakfast nook were open. He slit the screen and pushed it aside. Reached around and used his thinly-gloved hand to unlock the back door.

Still daylight. Which added to the thrill of the hunt. He usually worked under cover of darkness. The light ramped up the challenge. Fed his anticipation.

He entered. Stood rock-still. Listened to her clunky heels echoing on the hardwood floors above him. Heard her descend the stairs. The front door opened. Closed. The deadbolt turned and then snapped into place.

She would be gone several hours.

The house remained quiet. He knew Camille Attaway was an excellent cook. He'd eaten her fried chicken and mincemeat pie at church potlucks. She would have whipped up her specialties to impress her New York guest. He'd probably gone to lie down, the meal heavy in his belly.

No squeaks on the carpeted stairs. No stirring from the second floor. He crept down the hall. Spied a closed door. Turned the handle noiselessly. Opened the door.

The specimen lay stretched out on top of a floral comforter. Snoring softly. He'd thoughtfully drawn the curtains. One less thing to do.

He'd already unzipped his special bag. It held everything he would need. He set it noiselessly on the floor. Removed the first item. Quietly pulled on the edge of the duct tape. Trimmed the perfect-sized piece. Hovered a moment above the sleeping specimen, his adrenaline exploding with excitement.

Then he nudged the mattress with his knee. Twice. Enough for the specimen to open his eyes.

Confusion. Then fear.

He slapped the duct tape across the specimen's mouth. Then snapped a handcuff around his wrist. He yanked the arm to the wrought iron headboard and locked the other cuff around a bar. The out-of-towner's free hand attacked the handcuff, pawing at it uselessly.

With a speed that defied logic—but showed his hard-earned skills—he captured the other hand and fastened it in the same position.

And stood back to survey his handiwork.

He could see the fear pillowing in the pit of the specimen's stomach. With a burst of adrenaline, the artist began kicking his legs, trying to knock his attacker aside. He inched away. Teased him with lips that curled into a smile.

The infuriated specimen kicked all the more. Strained against the cuffs as his body bucked on the bed.

Then he slowed as he began having trouble breathing. The duct tape across his mouth was wide. It rose high above his upper lip. The kicking frenzy ceased. He didn't want to suffocate.

As if suffocation were the least of his worries.

"I know what you're thinking," he said softly. "This isn't big, bad New York. Walton Springs is a sleepy little town. Things like this don't happen here.

"But they do. Sometime, to good people. Sometimes, to bad.

"Which are you?"

He held the specimen's gaze. Delighted in the gamut of emotions that flickered across his face. Then reached across and flicked on the light situated on the nightstand.

"I like light. I like to see what I'm doing."

He reached into his bag of tricks and pulled out the long carving knife he'd borrowed from Mrs. Attaway's butcher block. Turned it slowly, admiring it as it gleamed. Chuckled when the specimen's bowels released and he pushed with his heels into the mattress, scrambling as far away as possible.

"You made a mess, Mr. Taylor. Or may I call you Mario? We will be on fairly intimate terms. For tonight, at least."

A flood of hot tears dripped down the specimen's cheeks. He turned his head away.

Using his handy roll, he quickly wrapped layers of duct tape around the ankles and then the knees. The specimen lay helplessly on the soiled bed.

"I am a killer, Mario. I have killed again and again. A fat plumber. Two schoolteachers. An architect. None of them deserved it. But you?" He grinned. "I think you do."

Mario whimpered behind the tape. His eyes darted about the room. The clock on the wall read seven-twenty.

"Mrs. Attaway won't be home for a few hours. And

she'll be sloshed when she gets here. No other guests at the old B&B tonight. Convenient for me. Not . . . so convenient for you."

Mario thrashed about wildly. He let the fit run its course. It eventually died out. It always did.

Once the specimen stilled on the bed, he raised his knife again. *"I am thorough, Mario Taylor. I take my time. I do hope you have a high threshold of pain. It angers me when people pass out. It spoils my fun."*

Mario groaned as the knife entered for the first of many times.

HE APPRAISED HIS WORK. *He wasn't happy he had to complete his task so rapidly. A few hours of play didn't give him much satisfaction. But with the nosy landlady destined to return around ten, he needed to finish up sooner than usual. He couldn't have her arrive and spoil things. If she did, he would have to silence her.*

And that would spoil his beautiful pattern.

This series had been a joy. He'd learned so much with each candidate. A few he'd come to know personally for the sheer fun and challenge it brought, but many remained complete strangers to him. Chosen for one reason alone.

This time, though? It had been a little personal.

He hoped Karlyn would approve of his efforts on her behalf.

He chose to leave the ceiling fan on. He cut all the lights and opened the window. The smell of spray paint hung in the air. Normally, he liked to paint his specimens as an artist did a canvas, brushing the strokes across their chest, up and down their legs, tickling under their chin. But tonight focused more on speed than artistry. At least this specimen kept a neat room. He wouldn't have to waste time straightening things.

He located Camille Attaway's bedroom. At the opposite end of the hallway. If he closed this door, he hoped the harsh smell wouldn't float her way. And if the bitch came home soused as usual, she'd probably fall into bed and not notice anything until morning.

Besides, she wouldn't find a body. Just her comforter and sheets soiled with royal blue spray paint. And quite a bit of excrement.

And blood. Lots of beautiful, beautiful blood.

30

K arlyn sensed eyes on her. She opened her own. Logan gave her a lazy smile.

"Thought you'd never wake up," he said, his early morning voice a sexy Southern growl.

She snuggled closer, her cheek grazing against his stubble. "You could've nudged me awake. Especially if you had any good ideas in mind."

His arms enveloped her. "I've been known to have an idea or two. Sometimes good. Sometimes very good." He gave her a lopsided grin. "Sometimes amazingly great."

He showed her one. Then another.

An hour later, an exhausted Karlyn gave him a long, slow kiss.

"You've worn me out *and* worked up my appetite." She kissed him. "I do love a multitasker."

Logan stroked her back. "I thought I satisfied your appetite. Several times. Last night. And this morning."

Karlyn sat up and smacked him with a pillow. "There's sexual appetite, and then there's my growling stomach. I've found the stomach refuses to be ignored." She slipped from the bed and scooted into the bathroom, emerging in her robe. "Do you feel like waffles? Or eggs and bacon?"

"Hmm." He reached up, playing with her sash. "I guess I'll have whatever you're making."

"Then it's waffles. Hope you like the toaster kind."

Logan leaned down and pulled on his slacks. "And here I was thinking you'd whip up the batter from scratch." He reached for his shirt and began buttoning it.

"When Eggo has already cooked it, frozen it, and let me buy it? No way, Detective."

Karlyn puttered to the kitchen and started the coffee. She retrieved the waffles from the freezer and popped four into the toaster. By the time she got the butter and syrup to the table, Logan was seated, slipping on his holster.

His cell buzzed. "This better be good to interrupt a frozen waffle breakfast." Logan lifted it from his belt. "Warner."

In seconds, Karlyn saw the color drain from his face.

"I'll be right there. For God's sake, keep it roped off. I don't want any kids to see it. Hell, I don't want anyone to see it."

He stood as if in a dream, pulling his jacket from the back of the chair and slipping into it without speaking.

"It's Roy, isn't it?" Karlyn asked quietly. "He's killed again. In the Springs."

Logan nodded, his eyes meeting hers. "It's Roy." He put his hands on her shoulders and braced her.

"He's killed Mario, Karlyn."

He caught her as her knees buckled and returned her to her chair. Logan knelt beside her.

"I don't know many details. I can't stay with you. I have to get to the crime scene."

She nodded, mute.

"I'll call as soon as I can. Would you like me to have Mom come over and stay with you?"

Karlyn shivered. "No. I need to be by myself." She looked up at him. "I'll wait for your call. Be safe."

He brushed a tender kiss against her brow and left.

LOGAN MET up with Brad at the main entrance to the city park. It was still early, not quite six-thirty when he arrived.

Brad fell into step with him. "Jogger found him about half an hour ago as he passed the gazebo. Said he usually cuts through the park on his morning run. Name's Billy Frank Montana. You know him?"

He nodded. "Billy Frank was a couple of years behind me in school. Weird as all get out. To be honest, I didn't even know he was back in the Springs."

"Pretty much what the patrolman taking the call said. Creepy, slow talking, lots of tats."

"Have they got people stationed around the perimeter? A ton of kids cut through here on their way to school."

"As best they can, but it's not like the park has set entrances. The chief's having them bring in some kind of opaque tenting. Anyone walking by will be blocked from seeing the crime scene."

"Good." Logan fell silent as the gazebo came into sight. He saw the material being erected. Risedale barked orders left and right. The chief motioned them over.

"Look it over first, then talk to Tattoo You over

there." He pointed in Billy Frank's direction. Logan saw him sitting atop a picnic table, slack-jawed, his head moving back and forth, still in disbelief.

"Let's go."

Logan led Brad through those gathered and entered the gazebo. They automatically slipped on gloves. Someone handed him a flashlight. He turned it on and stepped forward. The barrier kept out most of the early morning's natural light.

It also kept the public from a gruesome sight.

Logan had seen his share of grizzly in Atlanta.

But Mario Taylor was in a class by himself.

"Definitely Roy," Brad noted. "The knife wounds. The strangling. Has to be piano wire with a line that thin. And the tongue."

He nodded. The tongue had been nailed to Mario's chest. He was also painted a bright blue all over, the next shade in Roy's color canvas.

Logan moved closer, examining the naked body as he went. "Restraints used on the wrists. Probably handcuffs."

Brad's nose almost touched the body. "Look around the ankles." He pointed in an arc. "I think he used duct tape here. Look beneath the paint. No hairs. Looks irritated. Like a bad wax job." He stood. "Probably removed it once death occurred and then did his paint job."

Logan circled around, studying the corpse from every angle. He couldn't count the number of knife wounds or cigarette burns. Mario Taylor definitely suffered. More than Roy's usual victim did.

"I think he has something in his mouth." He noticed that the cheeks seemed to be puffed out.

"I'll check it out for you," Dr. Paul Hughes said as he marched toward them, his gray mane of hair perfectly coifed, as usual. The medical examiner paused as he looked over the body. "I thought poor Beth Marie had it bad. Looks like Roy really had it in for this one."

Hughes opened Mario's mouth. "Tongue's gone but what the—" Hughes leaped back. "What a savage!"

The ME moved in again and lifted an object from the victim's mouth. He held it up before slipping it in an evidence bag.

"Guess in all the paint and muss you boys hadn't noticed his manhood was missing."

Logan shuddered. "Roy's never gotten that personal before. It surprises me. He's escalating, both in time between murders and adding to his MO."

Brad cocked his head. "Could he have known who his victim was? Carried a grudge against Taylor?" He shook his head. "Jeez, second time in the Springs. Since Atlanta, he's only killed one victim per small town and moved on."

"Rutherford needs to be updated. He'll want to see the scene while it's fresh."

"Remember what I said earlier about Feebies taking the credit when they break the case?" Brad asked. "Well, it's fine by me. Let them find this asshole and lock him up in a place the sun don't shine."

"I just notified Rutherford. He's bringing the crime techs with him from Atlanta," Chief Risedale said. "I called 'em the minute I heard it was Roy. Task force wants them on this one since they're familiar with Roy's ways." He motioned the detectives outside.

"Go talk with Billy Fuckin' Montana," Risedale ordered. "Find out something. I'm *not* ending my time in office this way."

They made their way over to Montana. He smoked

a cigarette. His hand shook each time he brought it to his mouth for a drag.

Montana brightened as they approached. "Hey, there, Logan Warner. You 'member me? High school?"

"I remember you, Billy Frank. I thought you left the Springs a long time ago."

He nodded. "Joined the Army. Got trained and all. Didn't last. Wound up in more fights. People always orderin' me around. Wasn't much of a life. Got discharged." He lowered his voice. "Mama said not to tell what kind, but it's not the good one."

"What have you been doing since the army?" Logan asked.

Billy Frank shrugged. "Been here. Been there. Lived up in DC a while. Slept across the street from the White House. Saw the President take his dog for a dump one time. Some Secret Service guy scooped it right up while it wuz still warm." He laughed.

Logan watched him take a last pull on the cigarette and then drop it. He reached his toe over and stamped it out.

"Thanks, Logan. You wuz always nice. Hey, I show you my beauties?" Montana swung his bare arm to the front. Tattoos covered the skin so heavily that it looked as if Billy Frank wore a dark shirt.

"Started getting these babies in the army. Then I got some more when I got out. I pretty much have 'em all over me now. Mama says they make me look like white trash, but I think I'm pretty cool with 'em."

He proceeded to show his other arm, rolled up his pants legs, and was about to take off his shirt when Logan stopped him.

"Tell me about finding the body, Billy Frank." He eyed the man's thin frame. "You out for a jog? I didn't know you were into exercise."

Montana looked a little sheepish. "That's what I tell Mama. That woman pretty durn near drives me crazy. Anytime I can't take no more of her shit, I say, *'Hey, Mama, I'm going out for a jog.'*" He sighed. "I guess you could say I go joggin' a lot."

Logan prodded again. "What about this morning?"

Montana scratched his head. "Well, I got up cuz I couldn't sleep. Probably too many Coca-Colas. I was outta smokes, so I walked over to Casey's gas station. He's always open by five-thirty. Got my Marlboros and thought I'd go sit and soak up some peace and quiet."

"When did you get to the park?"

"Don't know. Sat on a bench and smoked a cig. Thought I'd walk over to the Dairy Queen and maybe get some biscuits and gravy. I wuz cuttin' through when I saw ... *something*." He shivered.

Logan nodded, "Go on."

"I thought it was some kinda bum sleeping there, but he was dark and all. I got closer and saw he was all damn blue. And then I saw his eyes staring and that tongue and the nail and–"

Billy Frank broke down and started crying. Logan put a hand on his thin shoulder and gave it a squeeze.

"He was all dead and blue and gross, Logan. I wanted to get outta there. But then I thought about *CSI*. Mama watches all the repeats. She says Grissom is the smartest man on the planet. I thought I should call the cops. They could call CSI and find out who kilt that poor man."

The tears came again. Brad offered his handkerchief and told Billy Frank to keep it. Logan said they might have more questions later, but he wanted Billy Frank to go back to his mother's.

"Don't talk about this to anyone, Billy Frank. We don't know who this killer is. We don't want him to think you saw much of anything. Keep your lips zipped. Okay?"

Montana nodded. "I will, Logan." He climbed off the picnic table, ready to leave. "I'll talk to you later."

Logan watched him walk off. Montana stopped and turned.

"And Logan? Tell your pretty girlfriend I said hey."

The look in Montana's eyes gave Logan a chill.

31

Logan arrived at Camille Attaway's. She rented out the occasional room since her husband passed a few years before. He doubted any other boarders stayed there at the moment.

Her array of begonias was in full bloom. He wondered what he should plant at the Kinyon place. No, his place. It was hard for him to imagine being a homeowner after years living above the diner.

He'd missed the sweet smell of mowing his grass. Hosting barbeques with burgers and ice-cold beers. Even retrieving the morning paper was a part of the routine he'd missed.

And his kids. God, he missed the twins. Every day, something reminded him of his precious babies—and what Carson Miller did to them.

He wondered again if he had a future with Karlyn. Logan could imagine her pregnant, all sweet and round, with that special glow. But he couldn't rush her. He needed to exercise patience. She was coming off a bad relationship. She wasn't the type to dive into deep waters so soon after being burned.

But for now? He had to get Roy. Nowhere was safe until he brought this serial killer down.

He mounted the porch steps and rang the door-bell. Camille answered in her yellow satin robe, looking a bit pale.

"Why, Logan Warner. What are you doing here? Come on in. I'm having my coffee. You're welcome to a cup."

She ushered him to the kitchen and reached for the coffeepot.

"Mrs. Attaway, I need to ask about one of your guests. Mario Taylor."

The landlady put a hand over her heart. "Oh, Mario. Sweetest soul in the world. He doesn't care much for breakfast. I take him his coffee and juice around ten. He's an artist, you know."

"Did you see or hear anything unusual last night?"

Her brows knit together in thought. "No. I played bridge at Lou Ellen's. Came home a little after ten and went straight to bed."

"Would you give me permission to search Mr. Taylor's room? Without a warrant?"

She frowned. "This about that ex-wife of his? I heard about the trouble yesterday over at the antique store. That boy was so upset. He's a sensitive artist. Born in Spain. Not like that brash New York gal who —whoops."

Her hand flew to her mouth. "Sorry, Logan. I hear you been seeing her."

"This isn't about Karlyn, Camille." He paused. "Mr. Taylor's been killed. His body was found an hour ago in the park."

She floated downward, her mouth gaping open. Logan grabbed her by the elbows before she completed the collapse and steered her to a kitchen chair.

"Would you like to go next door to Maudie's?" he asked.

"No, I'll wait on the porch." Her hands fluttered nervously. "Go on up, Logan. You don't need no warrant."

He escorted her outside to the porch swing. She told him which room Mario occupied, and he reentered the house.

He slipped on a pair of gloves and steeled himself before opening the door.

A brief glance told him the room had been the original crime scene. He made a quick call before he conducted a search to let Risedale know to send a team here ASAP. He wished Roy would leave behind some kind of clue. The piano wire he used. A hair. His paintbrush. This time he'd actually used spray paint. He figured Roy must've been in a hurry since Camille Attaway would only be gone a few hours.

Logan went through the drawers. Scrolled through the cell phone sitting atop the dresser. Nothing. He thought about the profile Rutherford had constructed.

Military. Tremendous precision with his actions and the scene. Could Roy have been an MP?

Or in law enforcement?

Roy knew what mistakes to avoid to keep a crime scene pristine. His thoughts returned to Seth Berger, knowing he was experienced enough about forensic evidence to avoid leaving clues behind. Berger was a loner. Older in age than Rutherford's profile. Logan remembered Berger did a stint in the marines straight out of high school before he returned to the Springs and joined the police force.

The CS techs arrived downstairs. Logan hollered for them to come up. He'd seen all he needed to in the bloody bedroom. He returned to Camille Attaway, who was being comforted by her neighbor, Maudie Howe.

Camille turned a tear-stained face up to Logan. "How could this happen in the Springs?" She shuddered. "I can't go back in there. I can't."

He gave her shoulder a squeeze. "No one's asking you to. Can I call Casey for you?"

"He's on his way," Maudie said quickly. "I been telling this gal forever to sell and move in with me. Widow women should stick together." She patted Camille's knee. "You're moving in with me, hon. Today."

Logan escorted the women to Maudie's house before he returned to the park and touched base with Brad.

"I've canvassed all around the square," his partner shared. "I'm heading over to do the same on the Attaway street. You get anything there? Oh, the ME said time of death was between eight and midnight."

"Do you know where Seth Berger was last night?"

"No. What are you thinking?"

He explained his theory. Brad whistled. "I don't know, but I'll look into it. I guess you want to keep this on the down-low. Especially after his previous interview."

Logan nodded. "I'll talk to Rutherford about it."

"He's inside the tent," Brad informed him as he left.

Logan decided to take a moment to call Karlyn. He explained what they'd found without going into detail.

"Are you all right?" he asked.

"A little shaky, but I'm okay. I talked to Mother. She calmed me down. Wanted to know if I needed her to come home from New York."

"I hope you told her no."

"As a matter of fact, I did. Why?"

"Because you're staying with me tonight. And every night until we find Roy."

Roy had come after Mario. Karlyn was connected to her ex. Logan didn't know why Roy had chosen the artist as a victim. He certainly didn't want Roy to target Karlyn.

He told her he had to go. He returned to the office and went over different files from the various victims that the task force had compiled. He needed to find a way to eliminate so many puzzle pieces. He had to find the link between the victims.

Rutherford arrived with a pizza in hand. "I knew you probably hadn't eaten. I'm waiting for the reports from the crime scene team now."

"Thanks." Logan took a slice and briefed the FBI profiler on Roy's latest strike from his point of view. He also ran his Roy was a cop theory by him.

"Could be." Rutherford chewed thoughtfully. "Roy's been anal. And clever. It wouldn't surprise me if he were a rogue cop. We need a complete picture of Detective Berger."

The agent contacted the Washington office and asked for a full background investigation into Seth Berger. "Uproot every rock. Bring out any skeleton from his closet. I want this in less than twenty-four hours."

32

K arlyn heard the garage door opening and put down her glass of merlot. Another late night for Logan. He'd worked twenty hours a day since Mario's murder, laser-focused on finding—and stopping—the Rainbow Killer.

She walked into the kitchen, Lucky following on her heels. Logan entered, his posture defeated, the dark circles prominent under his eyes. He set a stack of file folders on the countertop. Karlyn hugged him.

"It's nice to come home to you," he said softly. He pulled away. "Sorry I haven't been around much the last few days." He bent to pat Lucky, who moved to her bowl once the attention ended.

She took his hand and led him around the house on a brief tour. "Den furniture all here and in place. Dining room looks lovely, especially with that floral arrangement your mom brought by. Kitchen is stocked with basic pots, pans, and microwaveable dishes. The fridge is full in case you're ever home to eat."

Logan combed his fingers through his hair. "It's been candy bars and bad coffee on the go. Nelda did send over dinner tonight for the guys working the case. Meatloaf, mashed potatoes, English peas. Even apple pie for dessert. I think Rutherford is ready to marry her after tonight's feast."

"I'm glad she's taking care of you."

He slipped an arm around her waist. "Hey, you're no slouch in that department. You've really pulled this place together."

"I've had the time. With everything that's been going on, I haven't been inspired to write." She paused. "Do you remember about Saturday night?"

"My un-surprise surprise party?"

"Yes, the surprise housewarming. It's on for seven, so you need to be here. And that's after you spend the day campaigning."

Logan shook his head. "No, that's done with. Either people will vote for me next Saturday, or they won't. I've got too much to do. I can't run around like some asshole politician."

"Seth will be out in full force."

"Let him." Logan plopped onto the new sofa. "He's taking vacation days this week. I haven't even seen him. And Rutherford's people turned up nothing on Berger that we could use."

Karlyn perched on the armrest. "Then maybe he's not Roy."

He hung his head in his hands. "I don't know anymore. It could be him. I wanted it to be him. But it could be a thousand other guys." He slammed his fist onto the armrest. "It's so frustrating."

Karlyn stroked his hair. "I know. Why don't you go grab some sleep? Maybe something will stand out when you get some rest."

He walked upstairs as if he were a zombie, Lucky following. Karlyn watched them go and then returned to the kitchen. The stack of manila folders proved tempting. She knew they dealt with the Rainbow Murders. Logan had talked aspects of the case with her, but she hadn't viewed any of the evidence.

She brought the folders into the dining room and spread them out. She grabbed a pad to make notes. She wrote about criminals for a living. She constantly forced Matt to get into his enemy's head. Think as a criminal. Catch a criminal.

And Karlyn wanted to help get Roy.

First, she studied the crime scene photos and then the autopsy reports. Roy had cut out the tongue of each victim, mounting it somewhere nearby. He'd also painted each one of them a color of the rainbow, going in the order of the hues. That consistency was across the board for his dozen victims.

Karlyn finally turned to her ex-husband's autopsy report. She tried to view it objectively but found herself wiping away tears at the brutality of Mario's murder.

She decided to line up the snapshots of each victim, looking for some connection. Five were women. Seven were men. Two men were gay. The white architect had a life partner, while the Black bookstore owner had recently lost his lover in a car accident.

Nineteen-year-old Cyndee Washington was the only Asian and youngest victim, a hooker who trolled some of Atlanta's roughest streets. The lone Hispanic was a plumber with five children and another on the way. Mario had been born in Spain, the only victim born outside the US.

Karlyn noted two widowers, the retired teacher and the truck driver. Two, including Logan's friend Jeanine, had taught elementary-aged children. The others ranged from Jared Quincy, a white accountant with three children to Ted Harrison, an engaged fireman who'd recently become a certified paramedic.

The ages were spread out. Three victims were under thirty. Four were in their thirties. Two had been in their early forties. Only the trucker was in his fifties, with the retired teacher being in her sixties.

Karlyn crossed out that line of thinking and moved to marital status. One engaged, two widowed, one married, and four divorced, including the last three. Another dead end.

She played with the stats, grouping them by occupations, residences, and education. Nothing came up. Karlyn placed each victim's picture in the order they were killed, checking for any physical similarities. Cyndee had a bad dye job, her carrot-red hair spiked tall. Jerry was bald. Both Rita and Jeanine had worn glasses. Randolph Van Buren had seen a few fights in his day, his nose obviously broken on more than one occasion. For the most part, they were all average-looking. The exception was the engaged paramedic. He could've been a Ralph Lauren model.

Karlyn found no discernible patterns that tied the victims together. Roy proved to be an equal opportunity killer. He crossed all lines—ethnic, gender, income levels, sexual preferences. None of those gave any clue as to why Roy killed these particular men and women. No single element connecting the victims stood out.

She stacked the folders again in chronological order, as Logan kept them. She had to be overlooking something. It nagged at her, as if it simmered on a far back burner of her mind. She returned the folders to the kitchen and put away her notes.

It would come to her. She was sure of it.

～

KARLYN JUMPED in the shower after a long Saturday campaigning in the heat. She and Lucky went door to door, singing Logan's praises. Most people knew Logan because he grew up in town, but they also seemed interested in meeting her. She decided her small touch of celebrity hadn't hurt his chances at the polls.

The Kinyon place was fast becoming home to her and Logan. Martha Campbell had returned from her travels the day before and asked Karlyn if she had moved in with Logan after she'd found a bare refrigerator and most of her daughter's clothes gone from the guest bedroom closet. Karlyn told her mother she wasn't sure what the status of their relationship was.

She chose a lemon-yellow sleeveless shirt and khaki skirt, pairing it with gold sandals. After all today's walking, she'd save sexy heels for another time.

She hoped the guest of honor would show up for his own housewarming.

Karlyn gave downstairs a quick run-through, freshening the water in the vase that held the flowers Mrs. Warner brought by. She was ready to take food from the refrigerator when the doorbell rang. Lucky trotted behind her to welcome the first early guest.

Jesse Alpine greeted them. "Evening, Karlyn." He squatted next to Lucky. "Hey, girl. You look sleek and well-loved." He ruffled her fur and stood, handing Karlyn a tall gift sack.

"Come in. You're the first."

"It's wine. As a single guy, I'm not too creative in the social department. And a six-pack didn't seem to have quite the same panache."

Karlyn laughed. "Logan would've liked it."

Jesse followed her into the kitchen, and she set the wine on the table.

"I guess this Rainbow business has him pretty tied up. It's all anyone wants to talk about when they come into the clinic."

"With two of the murders in a town this size, what can you expect?"

"It is pretty Mayberry here. I grew up in Atlanta. Went to vet school in Athens. I'm used to big cities. But one of my profs went to school with the vet who was retiring in the Springs. He convinced me to settle here."

"You haven't regretted small town life?"

He shrugged. "My practice keeps me pretty busy. I don't have time to miss big city life although I do miss some of the conveniences. And being single in the Springs doesn't mean a lot of dates. I mostly work, veg out in front of the TV when I get home, and then do it all over again."

"Have you met Brad Patterson? He's Logan's partner. He's single. I know he goes to Atlanta fairly often to hit the bars and clubs. Maybe you can tag along with him sometime. He'll be here tonight. I'll introduce you."

Jesse frowned. "That's not me. Ear-shattering music and girls waiting to be picked up after you've bought them five drinks? The conveniences I miss are Braves games and fast food. I love Nelda's diner, but there are days I long for a Krispy Kreme or Sonic burger and cheese tots."

"That means we need to find you a baseball fan who can grill a greasy burger?"

He grinned. "You're speaking my language."

The doorbell rang. Karlyn excused herself. She liked Jesse. She determined to find him the perfect girl.

Opening the door, she smiled at Mandy. The wait-

ress was single and attractive. She thought the two
might click. Karlyn had never played matchmaker before, but she'd give it a whirl.

"Come on in, Mandy. I've got someone I'd like you
to meet."

Karlyn led the server to the kitchen and made the
introductions. Mandy worked the breakfast and lunch
shifts, and Jesse had only eaten dinner at the diner, so
they'd never met before. They helped her pull platters
from the fridge that contained appetizers, cheese, and
fruit. She told them to go relax in the den while she
opened bags of chips and set out bowls of dips and
pretzels, hoping a little alone time before others arrived would help fan the spark she'd seen in both
their eyes.

By the time Karlyn had the food ready, a constant
stream of people floated in over the next half-hour.
Resa brought Logan's favorite oatmeal raisin cookies
and a set of sheets for the bed. Nelda contributed a
Mississippi Mud pie and a triple layer chocolate cake,
along with new dish towels for the kitchen.

Logan arrived in and pulled her into his arms.
"Good party. Nice going, Campbell."

She gave him a lingering kiss that promised more
to come once they had the house to themselves. "It's
better now that you're here."

Karlyn handed him a can of beer. "I'll fix you a
plate. I'm betting you didn't stop and eat today."

"You'd win that bet. Maybe you should head to
Vegas soon."

"There's my baby," Resa Warner crooned. "Have
you thanked Karlyn and Lucky for campaigning today? They hit the pavement all day drumming up
votes for you."

Nelda added, "Seth had a booth set up in the

square, but he didn't have much of a crowd. Are you any closer to catching this madman, Logan? That's all my customers talk about these days."

Logan waved her away. "I can't comment on an on-going investigation."

"Did you hear that, Resa? Your boy already sounds like a slippery politician."

Karlyn handed Logan his plate and abandoned him to the two women. She drifted through the rooms, making sure everyone had something to drink and then changed the music from Springsteen to *The Big Chill* soundtrack and *Ain't Too Proud to Beg*. She convinced Brad to dance with her. They were soon joined by Jesse and Mandy and Rick Mabry and his wife Hildy.

As they danced, Brad informed her, "William Howard Taft loved to dance. When he was governor of the Philippines, he would dance the native dances with what he called his little brown brothers. All three hundred and fifty pounds of him."

She laughed. "Was he from the South? I believe I've gained ten pounds since I've arrived. Every event revolves around food. The more fattening and fried, the better."

After a few songs, Karlyn needed a drink. She grabbed a beer and tossed down half of it.

"You throw a nice party." Logan slipped an arm around her waist. "Everyone's having a great time. And Mandy and Jesse Alpine seemed to have hit it off."

"Careful planning on my part." She smiled. "It looks like it's taking." She watched Jesse swing Mandy into a low dip. Mandy laughed as he pulled her up.

"Would you like to dance?"

Karlyn took another sip of her beer and set it down. "I thought you'd never ask."

Logan led her to the large entryway and pulled her close as *Tracks of My Tears* started. He hummed along with Smokey Robinson as the song played.

"You're a lot smoother dancer than Brad," Karlyn told him.

"I bet you say that to all the guys."

"No. Only the ones I'm interested in."

He rocked with her slowly and searched her face. Karlyn grew warm under his stare.

"My kids are still the best thing that ever happened to me," he said softly. "But Karlyn Campbell, you are special. I'm glad you've come into my life."

She tried not to show her surprise at hearing Logan had children. He'd never mentioned them before. In fact, she remembered their first dinner date. He'd told her he didn't have kids when she'd asked. She wondered where they lived and when he saw them with the kind of schedule he kept.

And why he'd lied to her.

The song ended. Logan took her hand and led her out onto the wide porch. The May evening had started to cool. Music drifted softly from inside the house. Logan had them sit on the top stair. He kept her hand in his and focused on it as he spoke.

"I was married before. To my college sweetheart. We lived in Atlanta and had twins. Alex and Ashley. Those two little troublemakers were the light of my life. I had everything then. We'd bought a fixer-upper. It was starting to take shape. I'd made detective. Felicity was working part-time from home while the kids were in school.

"And then it all came crashing down."

Logan grew silent. Karlyn squeezed his hand reassuringly.

"They didn't get off the school bus one afternoon. Felicity went nuts. An animal named Carson Miller took them. He killed them. We found their remains in a storm tunnel after three weeks."

Logan dropped her hand and stood suddenly, staring up at the sky. "We never found him. We still don't know why he chose them." He looked down at Karlyn, pain written across his features. "It tore my marriage apart."

He walked down the steps, his hands thrust deep into his pockets. "I finally left the force in Atlanta and came home to the Springs. Buried myself in work." He turned and looked at her. "I hadn't started to live again —till I met you. I rented the room above the diner and worked. That's been my life for four lonely years."

Logan sighed. "Then you arrived in the Springs. Suddenly, it was like waking up from a black and white dream to living color again. You made me want to feel alive, Karlyn. I've got a dog and bought a house and may win this election. I'm part of this community. I have a purpose again."

He took her hands and pulled her to her feet. "And I want you. I want to build a life with you. I want to marry you, Karlyn Campbell."

Karlyn looked into his eyes, brimming with tears. "I want that, Logan. With you."

He kissed her. A long, slow, melt your bones kiss that held a touch of the bittersweetness he'd suffered. Yet she still could taste that it was full of promise.

"I miss my kids, Karlyn. I miss them more than I can ever say. But I'm ready to move on with my life. With you. What I'm trying to say and doing a lousy job of it is that I love you." He smiled at her. "It seems like I've always loved you."

Her tears now mirrored his. "I love you, too, Logan Warner."

She didn't know about the marriage part. For now, it was just enough to love this man.

They embraced one another, the sound of crickets softly chirping in the night, muffled laughter far in the background.

He...

will...

33

Logan awoke drenched in sweat. He couldn't
remember the nightmare, but a kaleidoscope of
images rushed at him.

Roy's victims.

A week had passed since Mario's body had been
discovered. No new deaths. No progress. Rutherford
and his group had returned to Atlanta. The task force
sent out no new memos. Their silence rang loudly.

Logan wondered if the Rainbow Killer would ever
be caught.

He sensed Karlyn's eyes on him and rolled over. He
kissed her, hard and fast, until they were both breath-
less. His hands stroked the curve of her hip. He marveled at her beauty, both inside and out. He didn't
know what would've happened if she hadn't come into
his life.

She pushed the tangled covers aside. "Election
Day, Warner. And you know what that means." She
gave him a teasing smile. "Shower sex."

Before he could reply, she scurried from the bed
and ran into the bathroom. He heard the shower start
and hustled to follow her.

The stall barely held the two of them. But it didn't

stop either of them. By the time the water cooled, he'd come once to her twice—and he still enjoyed washing every inch of her perfection.

They toweled off each other. As he bent and ran the towel down her leg he said, "First renovation will be this bathroom. We need a shower with more room."

"We?" Karlyn ran her fingers through his damp hair, her brow creased.

Logan stood and tossed the towel aside. He enveloped her in his arms. "Yes. *We*. I know you're thinking you've barely been divorced. That maybe we shouldn't rush into anything. But I know what I want, Karlyn."

He brushed his lips against hers. "I want you. The sooner, the better, with my ring on your hand and you in my bed. Forever." He released her and opened the medicine cabinet. He moved a few items around and extracted the ring he'd bought and thought to wait to give her until she was ready.

But why wait when they were so good together?

Logan dropped to a knee and took her hand in his. He slid the diamond solitaire onto her ring finger and grazed his lips against her knuckles.

"You have the ring now, Miss Campbell, and I see it's a great fit. I don't see the point in wasting any more time. I want you in my life. Always. Will you do me the honor of becoming my wife?"

Her smile rivaled a beam of sunshine. "You better kiss me long and hard to seal the deal."

Logan figured he would make a good husband. He followed her directions perfectly.

⁓

ELECTION DAY PROVED SUNNY, which led to a good voter turnout. Karlyn and Logan manned a booth across from city hall's polling booths.

Everyone noticed her engagement ring. Chief Risedale's wife, Louise, tried to pry wedding details from her.

"We're engaged and want to enjoy that for a while," Karlyn said. "When we set a date, you'll know."

"With Bobby retiring after today and Logan taking his place, you'll be awfully busy. Better to set a date now—and be sure it's not during hunting season."

"Let's just hope he gets elected." Karlyn believed Logan would win, but she didn't want to jinx anything by making assumptions.

Anne Stockdale and Marge Strombold got her attention.

"I thought the housewarming was lovely," Anne told her. "The table and chairs were meant for that dining room."

"You've already done such nice things with the house, Karlyn," Marge chimed in. "I knew the Kinyon place would come alive again when it sold to the right people."

"Will you turn one of the bedrooms into an office, dear?" Anne asked. "You need somewhere to write about that darling Matt Collins. I think I would leave Mr. Stockdale for that man. So smooth and sexy."

"And smart," added Marge. "Who's going to play him in the movie?"

"They haven't finished with casting yet. It should be announced soon."

In fact, Karlyn had received a call from Zev Bruner. The producer was flying her and Chris Stevenson to Los Angeles in the morning to view the finalists. Over fifteen hundred actors answered the original casting call. The producer and casting director narrowed their choices and notified the finalists of callbacks. The director wanted Karlyn and Chris present for those. She appreciated having input in the final decision. Though she was reluctant to leave Logan, he'd told her that she knew Matt as no one else did—and she needed to protect her creation so that Hollywood didn't miscast him.

"Hey, Karlyn."

She looked up to spot Mandy, her long, tanned legs in a short skirt and a happy glow on her face.

"I heard the news." She took Karlyn's left hand and studied the engagement ring glittering in the sun. Mandy gave Karlyn's hand a squeeze.

"I had an awful crush on Logan when he was the star quarterback in high school," she confided. "I was ten years younger than he was, but I thought he hung the moon.

"When he moved back to the Springs, I did my share of flirting with him. He was always nice as pie, but he never bit. Then I saw him with you, and I knew what he'd been waiting for."

Mandy hugged her. "And now I've found what I've been waiting for. Jesse," she whispered. "I've laughed more this past week than I have in my entire life."

Karlyn smiled. "I'm glad the two of you have hit it off."

"You nudged us together. I couldn't be happier. It's like in that Drew Barrymore movie *Never Been Kissed*. She tells another girl that penguins wait their whole lives and when they see *the* one, they just know." She smiled. "Jesse's *my* penguin."

"I'm glad you're happy, Mandy. Let's all go out to dinner soon."

"I'd love that. Or down to Atlanta for a Braves game. Jesse and I are both huge baseball fans. That would be a lot of fun. Now, I need to go vote and help your fiancé get elected."

Logan came over. "I don't think I've ever seen Mandy so happy. Could a certain single veterinarian have anything to do with her good mood?"

"We're double dating with them to a Braves game," Karlyn informed him.

"Ah. Then we'll hit up my favorite Chinese restaurant when we go down to Atlanta. It's not far from the stadium, and they have these dumplings that rock my world."

They were interrupted by Jonas Watkins and Hugo.

Jonas shook hands with Logan. "I'd say from all the people here, you might have the start of a victory party. If I could only find the beer, I'd kick off the celebration."

Hugo barked as if in agreement. Logan scratched the dog's head. "Between us, I could use a cold beer with or without a victory."

Logan finally talked Karlyn into heading home. "There's nothing more that can be done."

She grinned up at him. "I can think of a few things to keep us busy while we're waiting for the election results."

34

Logan glanced around his new office, wondering where everything was. Chief Risedale walked out with next to nothing. What he left behind took up most of the space. An administrative assistant had packed up Logan's files and desk for him. All his stuff lay in opened boxes along the wall.

He pushed through another pile of papers, trashing some, setting a few files aside. It would take until Christmas to sort through this unholy chaos.

His phone vibrated. Logan smiled as he answered. "How's the weather in sunny California?"

Karlyn laughed. "Wonderful. And I have even better news. Two words. Dakota Smith."

He pushed a stack aside and propped his feet on the desk. "That's a person?"

"Dakota is a hot hunk. Thirty-two, laid back, but has sharp eyes. Six feet even, rugged, got a Montana Tan with crinkles around his eyes."

"Maybe he should go by Montana Smith then."

"Oh, Logan, it was such a mess. I don't think the casting agent ever read a line I'd written about Matt. The actors she'd lined up for us to see were pretty boys or beefy hulks or just way wrong in so many ways. At least Kit Pelham, the director, and Chris agreed with me."

"So, where did Dakota Smith come from?"

"Don't laugh. I found him at a biker shop off PCH. And don't ask how or why I was there. It was meant to be."

"Has he acted any?"

"Yes. And no. A few school plays in high school. Plus, he admitted he's delivered some smooth lines with the ladies over the years. Believe me, Logan, women will fall for anything this guy says. But he's cool and tough and has his act together. I think guys would like him in the part, too."

"You believe he's the one?"

"Absolutely. We saw some other prospects read, but Dakota blew them out of the water. He's a natural. The camera eats him up. He's a quick study with lines and relaxed when he delivers them. Kit even had him do a few stunts on tape to see how that came out. He's exactly what I imagined. Dakota Smith *is* Matt Collins."

Logan heard the enthusiasm and pride in her voice. "I'm glad you've found the right guy. As long as you remember to come home to the other right guy."

"Are you a little jealous?" she teased.

"Maybe. But I am sitting in my new, messy to the hilt office. I will get a fabulous bump in salary of about five thousand dollars. I also look amazing in and out of clothes, so I think I could give this Dakota Smith a run for the money."

He loved the rich laughter that came across the line. "I love you, Logan Warner. In and out of your clothes." She paused. "How are things on your end?"

"Quiet, actually. Roy is lying low. Since you've been gone, the Springs has been as silent as the grave."

Brad walked in and handed him a file. He mouthed, "Karlyn?" and Logan nodded.

"Let me talk to her."

Logan handed his partner the phone. "Hey, Karlyn, when are you going to come back and straighten up Logan's new office? It needs a woman's touch."

"Hi, Brad. I'm waiting at LAX for my flight home now that we've cast our lead actor."

"You have your Matt. Good for you. Anyone I know?"

"Nope. He's totally unknown. Name's Dakota Smith, and he's from Montana."

"Hey, did you know that Sheriff Bullock of Deadwood, Montana, was a close friend of Teddy Roosevelt's? Bullock was a Rough Rider and even rode in Roosevelt's inaugural parade. And Teddy named him U.S. marshal of South Dakota. There's your Dakota/Montana presidential trivia for the day that you can share with your new star. Here's Logan again."

He took his cell back and waved as Brad left. "I swear, Brad knows more useless trivia. I've told him he should go on *Jeopardy*."

"I wish I would've had Brad as a history teacher. Instead, all I did was memorize stuff. States and their capitals. The Preamble. The presidents in order. What each amendment was. At least Brad has interesting facts to share."

"Yeah, like John Quincy Adams used to swim naked in the Potomac. Did he tell you that one? Or that Andrew Jackson had a chronic cough from a musket ball in his lung that was never removed? I get a different piece of presidential info daily."

"Maybe I can talk him into collaborating on a book for kids that details fun facts about the presidents. I'd love for our kids to read a book like that."

Logan went still. "You really want children?" he asked quietly. They hadn't addressed that elephant in the room.

He heard the long pause on her end before she asked, "Do you think you can go there again? After what happened to Ashley and Alex?"

"The hurt will never go away. But I loved being a father. I want kids again, Karlyn. With you."

Fatherhood came naturally to him. He loved reading bedtime stories and teaching how to tie shoelaces and sharing his love of the outdoors. He couldn't think of anything more wonderful than seeing Karlyn with a baby in her arms. His baby.

"Logan, I would never have asked you for children. But now I know you're open to it . . . it's wonderful. Maybe we'll have a boy that'll follow in your footsteps and be a star quarterback."

He lightened the mood. "Or maybe our girl will be the star quarterback and our boy will be a bestselling novelist."

Karlyn giggled. "And Brad can teach them all about U.S. history."

Logan groaned. "Footloose bachelor Brad with toddlers hanging from each pants leg, spouting trivial trivia. That's a picture I don't think I can handle." He paused. "Hurry home, baby. I miss you."

~

KARLYN SHUFFLED through her notes again, adding to the different stacks on the dining room table. Alicia had graciously boxed up Karlyn's files and shipped them to Walton Springs. She had different types of research piles. New story ideas. Outlines she'd started and abandoned. In other words, a spread-out jumble.

Her cell rang. Seeing Logan's name on the Caller ID brought a smile to her face. She was glad he'd proposed. She didn't care if others thought it too soon. The two of them knew they weren't rushing into this marriage lightly.

Once you found the right person, nothing else mattered.

"How's my favorite man doing?" she purred, hoping she sounded sexy because she was ready for him to come home.

Last night had been an incredible homecoming. Karlyn was hungry for more.

"Busy. That's why I'm calling. I'm sending Brad over to collect some file folders I forgot."

"The blue ones on the kitchen island?"

"That's them. I've got a budget meeting at two. I need to review a few things in them." He chuckled. "Since I didn't have time last night."

"I hope you'll have time to flip through them and sound prepared and chief-like. Is this the city council meeting?"

"It is. Expect Brad in a few minutes."

"He can join the crowd. Both of our mothers will be here any minute. They're coming over to map out a wedding strategy."

Logan snorted. "Remember what we agreed to. Beach wedding. Family only. Reception in the Springs when we return. Hell, the more I think about it, eloping sounds better and better."

"I'll do my best, but your mom is a force of nature."

Logan chuckled. "You're the boss. Not them. Hang tough. I'll see you about six. Sooner if I can break away from the paperwork."

A loud knock interrupted her goodbye. "I think the moms have arrived. Talk to you later."

Karlyn ushered in both mothers. "Let's meet in the kitchen. I've got too much sorting out going on at the dining room table." She motioned at the stacks as they passed through the dining room.

Her mother stopped. "You're worse than your father when he was writing. I didn't think anyone could make more clutter than Broderick."

"Chris and I discussed several ideas while we were in California. I have printouts of all of our notes plus stacks of what I was working on before I left. And my agent sent me my working files from New York. They arrived this morning."

"I hope buried somewhere in there is the start of a new Matt Collins book," Resa said, a hopeful look on her face.

Karlyn nodded. "That's also here." She fingered a few pages. "This group is notes I was working on before I left. I'm still thinking about writing a book on Roy."

"Logan's Roy? The Rainbow Killer?" Resa frowned. "Oh, Karlyn, I know you like to write about crime, but this man has done such unthinkable things. How could you live with that day after day?"

She shrugged. "I floated the idea to Logan. He's not in favor of it. But I've never attempted a true crime story before. I think it would offer me a huge challenge. I would hope for access to interview him. Get into his mind and see why he did it. Include the trial and its outcome."

"That's if he's ever caught," Martha pointed out.

Resa looked offended. "I have complete faith in Logan and his investigating abilities. This murderer will be off the streets soon."

Karlyn smoothed her ponytail, hiding her smile as Logan's mother came to his defense. "I'm sure Logan and the FBI task force will find Roy. At least according to all this research."

Her mother frowned. "What do you mean, honey?"

"Oh, we don't have to get into it, Mother. Let's head to the kitchen and—"

"No way, missy," Martha declared. "We've got plenty of time to talk wedding. I want to hear about this."

She saw curiosity written on both their faces. "Okay, Roy is classified as a serial killer. It takes killing three or more people over more than a thirty-day period to be branded as a serial killer. Usually, the victims have something in common—race, gender, looks, maybe occupation."

Karlyn pointed to another side of the table. "Here's the work I've amassed on Roy's victims. I've tried to narrow down what they have in common. He's selected different races, ages, genders, professions, sexual preferences, education levels. But he chose each victim for a reason. I plan to figure it out."

She moved to a different stack and pointed at it. "Here's my research on the various types of serial killers—organized, disorganized, and mixed."

Karlyn held up a folder. "Disorganized have below a normal IQ. They're impulsive. Opportunity driven. Whatever victim is convenient. They kill, leave the body, and go without getting caught for a while because it's so random. A disorganized is introverted and often has mental problems."

"But that's not Roy?" Resa asked.

"No. Roy is an organized. He's above average in intelligence. He possesses a strong knowledge of forensic science, so he can better cover his tracks. He's more extroverted—has friends, a sexual partner, maybe even a family. He's also methodical. Think Ted Bundy. He usually abducts his victims, kills them one place, then dumps the body somewhere else. His compulsion drives him, and he's more than likely following the media coverage about his exploits."

"That sounds like Roy. At least what's been in the papers," her mother said. "He's probably got a scrapbook of clippings about the case or records the news reports. Broderick and I watched a movie where the killer did that."

"Why do you think he'll be caught, Karlyn?" asked Resa.

"The third kind of serial killer is mixed. He usually starts as an organized, but then he becomes careless. He gets caught up in what he's doing. His success makes him overconfident. He starts making mistakes."

"Thus giving law enforcement a chance to catch him." Brad entered the room. "I think your doorbell's acting up again. I rang and then knocked, but no one answered. Being a skilled detective, I saw whose cars were parked in front and figured the gossip was flying so fast and furiously that you couldn't hear me." He raked a hand through his hair. "I hope you're right, Karlyn. Roy needs to be caught. Soon."

Brad glanced around. "All of this is about Roy? Maybe you need to join the task force." He paused a moment. "So, you three ladies are going to solve who the Rainbow Killer is today?"

Karlyn said, "We were supposed to discuss the wedding and reception. And no, only a small portion of those files are dedicated to Roy. The rest is a hodgepodge of story ideas and previous research on other topics."

His eyebrows shot up. "How did wedding talk turn

to serial killers? Surely, you aren't thinking of asking Roy to be the best man?" he joked.

Karlyn reached for a manila folder. "I was explaining a little bit about serial killers since they were interested in my mess. My third Matt book featured one, so I dug out my research on that. I've toyed with the idea of trying to write a true crime book on Roy—his victims, his capture, and his trial. I haven't decided whether or not to pursue that idea."

She opened the folder in her hand. "This is all about motives. Some serial killers think they're on a mission from God. Or the devil. They might want to clear their area of prostitutes because God tells them it's wrong for a woman to sell her body. Some are on a power trip. Those are usually adults who were abused as children, and they want to hold the power over someone."

Resa peeked over Karlyn's shoulder. "What does this mean? That some are hedonistic."

Karlyn closed the folder before Resa saw the graphic photographs within. "They thrive on the kill. They take pleasure in the torture that leads up to the kill. They get off on the thrill of doing something beyond society's codes of conduct. I think that's Roy."

Brad pointed to the DVDs sitting on the table. "What about the stack of movies?"

She blushed. "Don't discount movies. Those are a few I bought. I mostly Netflix the movies or documentaries I need. Some that really proved helpful included *Copycat*, *Mr. Brooks*, and *The Silence of the Lambs*." She motioned to a stack of books. "I read all the Dexter books. *Darkly Dreaming Dexter* was the best as far as getting into the mind of a serial killer."

Her mother shivered. "I don't like this at all. Honey, is this really how you want to spend your time?" Martha's eyes widened. "Oh! What if Roy found out you were researching him? What if he came after you like he did Mario?"

Karlyn put an arm around her mother's shoulder. "Don't borrow trouble, Mother. Besides, I haven't decided if this is a project I even have time for."

"Sounds like you're seriously committed to the idea of Roy," Brad noted. "You've gone well beyond curiosity."

She shrugged. "I'm exploring the idea. If I don't write Roy's story, I can use the research in a novel. I've been playing with the idea of creating a series with a female detective. Maybe she could have a run-in with a serial killer. Or she could even work for the FBI and specialize in profiling serial killers. Whatever I decide, the research is never in vain."

She paused. "I'm sorry. I rarely talk over my story ideas with anyone. I get a little wound up. Let me get what you came for."

Karlyn disappeared into the kitchen and scooped up the budget folders Logan needed. She returned and handed them to Brad.

"I know you need to head back. With your job, you don't need a lesson from me on serial killers."

He laughed. "Actually, I'd rather hang with you ladies. After I drop these budget files with Logan, I'm heading to the high school. Some teachers have been getting pretty nasty messages on their voicemails." He wrinkled his nose in disgust. "You know me and kids. Not my favorite combination."

Martha reached for a folder near her. "This is much better than killers. It's marriage info."

Karlyn laughed. "That's my marriage stack. To get our license in Georgia, we need proof of identity—driver's license, passport, birth certificates. I also have to provide a copy of my divorce decree."

Brad leaned over and flipped open Karlyn's passport. "Hey, you look pretty good in this picture, Miss Karlyn Pierce Campbell. Not anything like a washed-out criminal, which most passports favor."

"Pierce was my maiden name," Martha explained. "It's a family tradition to make the maiden name the middle name on my side of the family."

He grinned. "You realize you're in excellent company. George Herbert Walker Bush married Barbara Pierce, and she became known as Barbara Pierce Bush. Then they had George W. Bush. He proceeded to have fraternal girl twins, and he and Laura named one of them Barbara Pierce Bush, after her grandmother. The elder Barbara's family came from Rye, New York. Who knows? You might even be distant relatives."

"Leave it to Brad to spin the presidential trivia," Resa declared. "I could use a glass of iced tea, Karlyn. All this talk of killers has me parched."

"Ladies, nice seeing you. I'll be on my way."

"I'll walk you out," Karlyn offered.

When they reached the door, Brad said, "I enjoyed hearing about your possible book. And seriously, if you come up with anything—anything you think the task force could use to catch Roy—holler."

"I will. I've got much better things to do now. I'm off to discuss the merits of buttercream versus cream cheese icing and whether or not we'll do a buffet or plated dinner."

"Either way, I better be invited. Later." Brad waved and left.

Karlyn steeled herself to go up against two strong women and their equally strong opinions.

35

Karlyn leaned back against the pillows and watched Logan zip his suitcase closed.

"I wish it were next weekend," he said. "I wish we were on St. Simons Island right now, repeating our vows in front of the lighthouse. Looking out at that panoramic view of the Golden Islands as the sun sets. Squishing sand between our toes."

He hoisted his suitcase off the bed. "Instead of going to this conference." Logan looked at her hopefully. "Sure you don't want to tag along?"

"Not a chance, Warner. You'll be busy the next couple of days with seminars. And you're rooming with Rick. I don't think there'd be room for me. Besides, it's not as if I've never seen Atlanta before."

She moved off the bed. "I still have some wedding details to finalize for next weekend. I don't want you to have to worry about anything. You had the brilliant idea to get married at the lighthouse."

He pulled her close. "You've been a beacon of light in my life, babe." He gave her a lingering, thorough kiss that caused her toes to curl. "And as soon as Roy's in custody, we'll take the time to go on a real honeymoon."

"Mother and Resa are planning the finishing touches for the reception back here. They want most of it to be a surprise."

He shook his head. "Funny, they've become thick as thieves. And Nelda rounds out the trio." He kissed her again. "I've got to go. I'm meeting with Bill Rutherford and some of the task force today before the conference starts tomorrow. What will you be up to while I'm gone?"

Karlyn fluttered her eyelashes coquettishly. "Why, Mr. Warner, I do declare. I think I might have some writin' to do. Plus, Chris and Warren are coming in tomorrow for the weekend."

"I hope you get a lot done. I should be home no later than seven Saturday night. Tell Chris and Warren hello."

"Will do." Karlyn hugged him one last time. "Stay out of trouble. You'll be running in a tough crowd with all those Feebies." She grinned. "But you'll be dressed better than any of them. Especially if you wear the new paisley tie."

After seeing Logan off, Karlyn spent the morning going over the files she'd compiled on Roy's victims. It amazed her how much information she could access through the internet and social media profiles.

She shuffled her index cards and grouped them by information on the table. Four of the victims held library cards. Rita and Jeanine belonged to the ACLU. Five regularly attended church, with four sharing a Baptist background, but this was the South. *Roy* was probably a Baptist! Six showed up as registered voters —two Republicans, three Democrats, and one Independent. Claudia also held membership in the AARP.

She kept drawing blanks. Two of the Atlanta vics actually used the same vet, but one owned a schnauzer and the other a parakeet. All but motor-cycle driver Ted Harrison owned a car. Their hobbies varied from gardening to community theatre. The only connection common to all? Every victim had a cell phone.

All this info amounted to was BFN. Big Fat Nothing.

Although Roy struck fairly regularly, Karlyn couldn't find a set pattern. Why couldn't he be like se-rial killers in books and movies and strike once every full moon or the third Tuesday of each month?

"Because he's too smart," she said aloud. Since Roy had avoided getting caught, Karlyn surmised he'd learned from earlier mistakes. She believed by the time he started the Rainbow Killings, he had per-fected his style.

And that's what it was. Style. Roy had created a persona in the news, a ghost who left no evidence be-hind, a killer who killed without links between vic-tims, a man with no conscience and a huge stack of press clippings.

The morning had been a waste of time. Karlyn de-cided to go for a run to clear her head. Lucky snoozed in Logan's recliner, so she decided to go alone.

The noon sun burned down as she jogged. She cut through the park and decided to stop at the diner for an iced tea. She stepped inside and immediately got a hug from Mandy.

"You meeting Logan?"

"He's out of town until Saturday night at a regional conference in Atlanta. I'm parched and could use an iced tea to go."

Mandy brought her the drink. "The Braves play on Sunday afternoon. Maybe the four of us can go."

"I'd love that. How are you and Jesse doing?"

The server beamed. "We're not pussyfooting around. I like him. He likes me. We enjoy a bunch of the same stuff. And we're both trying new things. I've got him hooked on HGTV. He's gotten me into hiking."

Karlyn grinned. "It sounds serious."

Mandy nodded. "We feel right together. We're soulmates, even if neither of us has used that word. I figure by this time next year, we'll be married."

"I couldn't be happier for you."

"Thanks. And the tea's on the house. Enjoy the rest of your run. Or in this heat, you may want to walk home."

Karlyn took a long sip and strolled over to the park as the clock tower chimed a quarter after noon. She decided she'd sit in the shade and enjoy her tea before she started back.

As she sat on a bench, a man stepped out from a grove of trees and came to stand in front of her. His unkempt hair, scraggly beard, and faded clothing made him appear homeless. He brought a cigarette up to inhale. She saw tattoos lined his arms.

"Hey, there, Karlyn."

He knew her?

Karlyn swallowed and steadied her voice. "Hello. I don't believe we've met."

The stranger took a step toward her. She gripped the arm of the bench. He frightened her. A fine sheen of sweat covered his forehead. His dark blue eyes didn't seem in focus as he stared at her.

"I'm Billy Frank. I found your dead husband. But you're getting a new one now. Logan. I knowed him forever before he left the Springs to play football. But he came back. He's the police now."

She slipped the lid off her Styrofoam cup. If she needed to, she'd throw the drink in this stranger's face and run like hell. His unsteady speech made her wonder if he were on drugs.

Then a torrent of words came out of Billy Frank. "I was an army guy. Did you know that? I didn't go to college like Logan. But now I'm back. I found your dead husband. He was painted all blue. It was scary. But Logan came and talked to me and said he'd take care of it."

"Mario was my ex-husband. We were divorced."

"I'll be durned." He took a deep drag on the cigarette. "Logan'll be good to you. He's a nice guy."

"He is, but he's a hungry guy. I need to head home and fix him some lunch." She stood and managed a smile. "Nice meeting you, Billy Frank."

He gave her a half-smile and turned away, disappearing back into the thick grove of trees. She took deep breaths, trying to lower her racing pulse. For a fleeting moment she wondered if Billy Frank could be Roy. Could the slow talk and slack face disguise a killer? She needed to talk to Logan to find out if that were possible.

Karlyn downed the rest of her tea. The cool drink had refreshed her. She decided to continue her run. She left the park, keeping an eye out for Billy Frank, and decided to circle the town square before heading home. She caught movement from the corner of her eye and turned her head. A squirrel darted across the street and scampered up a tree in front of the antique store.

When she faced front again, she missed her step, tripping on a half-crushed soda can perched on a rise in the sidewalk. She stumbled, trying to regain her balance, and fell on the cement. One knee skidded, peeling the skin away, while her ankle twisted under her as she collapsed.

She gasped at the jarring pain. The raw knee was bad enough, but it was her ankle that concerned her. It had already begun to swell. She pushed to her feet and limped to a nearby bench in front of the barber shop. She was out of breath and mad that she'd spooked so easily.

Karlyn debated whether she should call someone or try and walk on it. She'd suffered plenty of sprained ankles before. Sometimes getting up on it would keep the swelling and stiffness down. But she'd only had to walk a couple of blocks in the past. Logan's house was almost two miles from the town square.

"Trouble?"

She looked up to see Seth Berger approaching in street clothes, a ball cap pulled low on his brow. She knew he'd been questioned as a possible suspect in the Rainbow Murders and had taken vacation time from the department after Logan won the recent election.

Berger sneered at her. "Need help? I'm sure your fiancé would trot right down here. Oh, wait. That's right. The chief's not in town. Heard he's gallivanting off in Atlanta, chummy with those bureau guys."

Karlyn didn't like his taunting tone. She pulled out her cell.

"Guess you could call the police to come rescue you. I expect you think the force is at your disposal since you're marrying the boss. Slick city gal like you bamboozling our little country bumpkin chief."

"Considering Logan was an Academic All-American at Georgia and probably has an IQ higher than mine, I doubt he's the bumpkin type."

Berger's gaze held hers. "Then why isn't he smart enough to solve the Rainbow Killings? You solve all kinds of murders in your books. They've got pretty intricate plots. Maybe you teach real killers little tricks to keep from getting caught if they read your books. Does that make you feel guilty? Innocent people might be dead because of you. Maybe even Roy G. Biv has read your stuff and learned how to get away with murder."

Karlyn took offense at his words. "The Rainbow Killer is smarter than someone who learned something from a fictional book. He's resourceful and knows how to avoid the law, probably because he *is* in law enforcement. Like in the Ku Klux Klan days or during Freedom Summer—those kinds of men got away with a hell of a lot, abusing and killing those who were innocent."

Berger chuckled. "Oh, Little Yankee, purr away. Keep sticking your nose in enough places, and I'll bet Mr. Roy G. Biv will come for you."

The gleam in his eye caused Karlyn to go cold inside. Fear rushed through her as fast as adrenaline would. Berger was an ex-military guy who carried a deep grudge against Logan. Seth Berger could be Roy.

Suddenly, he tipped his cap to her. "I'll leave you be now, but here's some food for thought, little lady. You think you're so smart—and you think Roy is smart, too. Well, look at your own husband. He was single before you got here. Didn't date. Able to keep odd hours with his job. Went to Atlanta when he wanted or surrounding areas. A man with a badge can do just about anything.

"And he went a little crazy when his kids were killed."

Karlyn gasped in outrage.

"Oh, I knew about that. I checked him out good when he came back to the Springs, tail between his legs, all mopey and down at the mouth. Looked even

closer at him when he decided to run against me. Mr. Logan Warner. Intelligent, divorced loner with knowledge of how crime scenes work." He paused. "Don't you think it's convenient his old girlfriend who came on to him bit the dust after he got involved with you?"

Berger's smile twisted. "Then *your* ex becomes another victim of Roy's, and suddenly you and Prince Charming are engaged. Do you really know the man you're marrying, Miss High and Mighty Author? *You* could be engaged to the infamous Roy G. Biv."

He laughed. "They say the wife is the last to know. Like the BTK Killer. Usually, a wife serves as a cover." Berger studied her. "Or did you figure it out? Does death turn you on? Is that why you write about it in such detail? Hmm. Maybe you and Lover Boy have even done a vic together. Put that in your next book, Sweet Cheeks."

She sat stunned as Berger strolled off. Her ankle throbbed. Her pulse raced. She swallowed her fear as a dull ache of doubt swaddled her heart. Could Berger be right? Had she rushed too quickly into a relationship with Logan? Did she know as much about him as she thought she did?

Karlyn violently shook her head. What was she thinking? Seth Berger was a jealous prick just trying to get under her skin.

She loved Logan. Period. No ifs, ands, or buts.

Karlyn struggled to stand and limped across the street to the café. A strong shot of caffeine would clear her head.

And any doubts. Wouldn't it?

The hunger burned in him. He preferred taking his time once he located a specimen. He'd spent overnight wreaking havoc with each of them.

Except for the artist.

Much as he'd hated it, he had to rush playtime with Mario Taylor.

But the man stumbled into his pattern so beautifully, he decided to be satisfied with dallying for a short time before the kill.

It hadn't quenched his thirst. Not by a long shot.

That's why he'd come to Atlanta. He needed a larger hunting ground if he were to find the particular specimen he needed. Trolling online had given him several strong leads. And the Marriott proved to be lucky. His first stop, and he'd located the exact specimen he required.

He'd waited to see what he looked like. A buttoned-down type. Probably mid-fifties. Married, according to the gold band on his left hand. A younger man stuck to him like glue. Acted subservient. He assumed it was some underling who'd felt lucky to leave the cornfields of Iowa for a national convention in a big city.

They gathered their information packets. Slapped on the provided lanyards. He slipped a packet off the table for

later. Followed them to a downtown restaurant. Watched from a distance from the bar. The specimen knocked back several drinks. That never hurt.

He followed them down the street, keeping a comfortable distance. They stopped in front of the Marriott. Had a brief conversation before the younger man scooted off. Probably had to check in with the wifey.

The specimen entered the Marriott and headed straight for the bar.

He pulled the lanyard from his jacket pocket and placed it around his neck. Removed the packet from the briefcase he carried, full of his toys. Clutched the packet in his hand.

And casually strolled in.

He would make contact since he had the proper props. Learn where the specimen's room was through casual conversation. Make sure that the specimen got another few drinks in him—the last laced with the trusty bottle of Rohypnol in his right pocket.

And then he'd enjoy a night of unwinding in his favorite manner.

Logan poured a cup of coffee and snagged a Danish as he followed Rick Mabry into the lecture hall. He'd met some interesting cops from all over the southeastern U.S. in the bar last night, but yesterday's meetings with FBI personnel working on the Rainbow Killings had felt like a bust. He hoped today and tomorrow's sessions proved more interesting. He hated spending time away from Karlyn and that scruffy little Lucky when Roy was still on the loose.

He glanced around. "Hey, isn't that Ron Ames over there?" Logan asked. "From our Atlanta PD days?"

"Yeah. But he's put on a lot of weight." Rick thought a moment. "Didn't he have a wife that left him for another woman?"

"That's him," Logan said. "I heard last night that he's on wife number three. Had a quick, forgettable marriage right after his first divorce."

"Rebound Girl," Rick said and laughed. "I had one of those in college. I was ready to ask my girlfriend of two years to marry me when she broke up with me. I went and found the first available girl at a frat party that weekend and thought she was The One a week

into it. Fortunately, she had more emotional maturity than I did and saw what was going on."

"Did she break up with you, too?"

"Yeah. But we ran into each other a couple of years after graduation. I was visiting a buddy in Augusta for the weekend. We went to a sports bar to catch a Bulldogs game, and there was Rebound Girl." Rick smiled. "With the most beautiful girl I'd ever seen."

"Hildy?" Logan asked.

"You got it. She was Rebound Girl's cousin's roommate. I haven't looked at another woman since." Rick paused. "I'm glad you've found Karlyn, Logan. I think you'll be happy together. Of course, she'll probably pump you for crime info she can work into her plot lines."

He shook his head. "Karlyn's got a way better imagination. The Springs is small potatoes. Issuing a DUI is about as exciting as it gets. I don't think she'll be able to take any cases from the Springs and make them into a book for Matt Collins."

"Except for Roy," Rick noted.

Logan sighed. "Except Roy. She's got a notion that she should write Roy's story. I've discouraged her, but Karlyn's pretty headstrong."

"She'd have to be a strong woman to make it in the publishing business. If anyone does decide to write about Roy, I'm sure she'd do a good job of it."

"Don't tell her that," he warned. "Roy is probably the kind of guy who would love to know that a famous author has taken an interest in him. I do not want her involved in any way, shape, or form with that animal."

"Good morning, ladies and gentlemen." Bill Rutherford stood behind the podium, ready to start the day's workshop.

Logan turned to see the lecture hall had filled while they spoke. He settled back into his seat.

"I'm Bill Rutherford, a profiler for the FBI and part of the Investigative Support Unit. I work with local law enforcement throughout the southeastern United States. This seminar is devoted to the modern serial killer. There will be break-out sessions which will explore different methods recent caught and convicted killers have used, as well as how these killers implement technology into their killings. We'll also discuss patterns and how these murderers can be discovered if law enforcement can detect their repeated design when killing. And as a group, we'll review a few unsolved killings that are still active."

"How about the Roy G. Biv case?" someone near the back called out.

Rutherford looked grim. "We've planned to devote two hours after lunch today specifically on the Rainbow Killings."

"Is the FBI task force even close to solving it?" a woman on the front row asked.

"No," Rutherford said flatly and paused. "That's one of the reasons the Rainbow Killings are included in this conference. We've invited select members of the current Roy task force, as well as local law enforcement officers from every town Roy has hit in Georgia. They'll present what we know. We're hoping someone in attendance will give us that one break we need to catch this monster."

The profiler took a sip from a water glass. "In addition, we'll look at serial killings in Florida, Texas, and West Virginia. Right now, though, I'd like to introduce Fred Simpson. Fred is head of our DNA unit."

Logan's cell buzzed in his pocket. He pulled it out and saw it was a member of the Atlanta task force. He tilted the screen toward Rick to show him. The two men slipped from their row and headed out a back door.

"Warner. What's up, Bob?"

"Roy's back in Atlanta," Bob Dreyfus said. "He killed last night at a small boutique hotel in downtown. I'm notifying the heads of departments in the towns Roy's already hit."

"I've got Rick Mabry with me. We're attending the FBI regional conference at the Hilton. I'm putting you on speaker, Bob. Give us the particulars."

Logan and Rick moved toward an alcove with a few seats for privacy.

"Same M.O. This has Roy written all over it. Vic is a fifty-two-year-old financial analyst. Married. Three kids. From Des Moines but in Atlanta for a convention at the Marriott. Name of Walter Lee Buchanan, nickname Bucky."

He asked, "Do you think since small town cops haven't stopped him, he's back to challenge the big boys in Atlanta?"

"Who the hell knows with Roy?" Bob asked. "Buchanan didn't show up at an early breakfast meeting this morning. He was here with another guy from his company." Papers shuffled. "A Franklin Sommers."

"Sommers clean?" Rick asked.

"Squeaky. Married, thirty-six, deacon in his church. Doesn't drink, smoke, or swear. Had dinner with the vic last night after they registered for their conference. Said his boss had four drinks at dinner then stopped at the Marriott for a nightcap. Sommers went back to his room two blocks down to webcam a bedtime story to his two daughters. Had planned to meet up with his boss for breakfast this morning around six-thirty, back at the Marriott. That's where the financial seminar's being held."

"The vic got a drinking problem?" Logan tossed out.

"You got it. Sommers was reluctant to spill that since Buchanan is—was—his direct supervisor. He thought old Bucky had blown off breakfast due to a hangover. Seems he's done that at home in the past on several occasions. But then the boss didn't show at the first seminar that started right at eight. Sommers said Buchanan was excited to attend that session since the featured speaker was an old friend from college."

"Sommers went to Buchanan's room and found him?" Logan asked.

Dreyfus chuckled. "Warner, you should be a detective instead of a police chief. Go to the head of the class." He paused. "Yes, Sommers doubled back to their hotel and went up to knock on the door and hopefully rouse his boss. He found a pamphlet stuck in it, slightly propping the door open."

"And went in and got the fright of his life," Mabry finished.

"He's pretty shaken up. Called us from the hall on his cell. Smart enough not to touch anything in the room. His 911 call got a quick response, but dispatch knows all about the task force and routed a call to us. Based upon Sommers' brief description, we figured we had a Roy case.

"I'm here now in the hotel in the corridor. You're welcome to come look over the scene since you're only a few blocks away. Crime scene techs are in there now, but I know they'll confirm it, down to the correct color of the paint."

"Text us the address," Logan said. "We're on our

way." He ended the call and asked Rick, "When will this end?"

LOGAN FINISHED the last bite of his roast beef sandwich and washed it down with what was left in his can of Coke. He and Rick had gone back to the Hilton after spending all morning at the crime scene and with Franklin Sommers. When they returned, Rutherford gathered all Roy task force members together in a conference room during the lunch break to review the latest killing of the Des Moines financial analyst.

Rutherford asked them to share what they'd seen. Rick deferred to Logan. He walked the team through Sommers' account of the chronology of events that led to discovery of the body. He passed around copies of photos from the hotel room and early reports from the techs that Bob Dreyfus supplied them.

Discussion centered around Roy's second kill of an out-of-towner. All other victims lived in the city they'd been killed in except for Mario Taylor—and now Bucky Buchanan. Speculation as to that small difference in the killings was the only new significant fact.

Logan didn't think killing an Iowan had any significance. He left the room to clear his head before he returned to the lecture hall.

Bill Rutherford followed closely behind. "Are you heading to the classroom? I'll walk with you."

They went down the hall and up a flight of stairs from the conference room. Logan wasn't surprised to see the room at capacity with ten minutes before the session even began. Even among law enforcement officials, Roy's case tantalized people. Logan thought of it as the classic car wreck—everyone drove by slowly to eyeball the scene. He took one of the few empty seats and used the time remaining to go over some of his notes about Beth Marie's and Mario's killings, his part of the presentation.

Rutherford convened the session, introducing Felix Nixon, who took the spot behind the podium.

"No relation to Richard Nixon," Felix stated up front. "Get that some from older folks who actually remember who the hell Tricky Dick was. What you need to know about me is that I'm detail oriented. Nothing's too small. Many times, it's the tiniest item which breaks the logjam in a murder investigation, particularly when we're speaking about serial killers."

Nixon came out from behind the podium and clipped a mic onto his lapel. "I'm here to talk antisocial behaviors, so we can place Roy on the spectrum. The FBI has labeled him a psychopath."

He clicked a slide. "We believe that Roy is well-educated. Maintains a steady job. More than likely has stable relationships with people, be they work-related or with a woman."

Nixon smiled. "Psychopaths exhibit no remorse. They are risk takers and quite fearless. They compartmentalize their lives. After exquisite planning and execution of a murder, they sleep like a baby."

"What about arrogance?" asked Logan. "I see Roy as completely arrogant. Confident that he's smarter than everyone around him—including those trying to catch him."

Nixon nodded in agreement. "Assume arrogance. And cunning."

Rutherford spoke up. "As the lead profiler on this case, I believe Roy may have a military or law enforcement background. He leaves no trace of physical evidence at crime scenes. And he's a master at not being seen. Witnesses who've been with several victims minutes before claim to have never seen anyone or anything out of the ordinary."

"And yet he's killed within all genders, races, and occupations," Nixon concluded. "Bill, let's have your team present the evidence that's been collected and see what conclusions we can draw."

Logan sat through the next hour of the presentation, which went through each of Roy's victims in chronological order. Only half his mind was tuned to what was presented. He kept processing what Nixon had said, trying to draw a clear picture in his mind of what Roy could be physically, mentally, and emotionally. He reviewed the two murders in Walton Springs for the seminar's attendees and sat, waiting to see if any fresh information had been uncovered from this morning's discovered corpse.

Bob Dreyfus walked through the last Rainbow Killing, finishing with photos of the most recent murder scene.

He stared at the screen, studying the room and the positioning of Bucky Buchanan's body. Then it hit him.

"The sequence. It's wrong. Roy's gone off the reservation." He jumped to his feet and moved next to the photo of the body. Logan studied it a moment.

He turned and looked at the puzzled audience then motioned to Buchanan's naked, painted body. "Look at the color. It's violet. Roy has meticulously cycled through the colors of the rainbow. The last killing occurred in Walton Springs. The victim was spray-painted blue. The next color, what Buchanan should be, is indigo."

Logan looked back at those gathered. "He's

skipped it. Walter Buchanan is violet, like Rita Jackson. Either there's another vic we haven't discovered yet who's painted indigo, or Roy's messed with his own well-established pattern."

Rutherford cleared his throat. "This, ladies and gentlemen, may be that small break we've been looking for."

38

Karlyn sat on the sofa with her ankle propped up on two pillows. An ice bag rested on top. As a runner, she knew the drill of rest, ice, and elevation from previous mishaps. She'd begged Nelda not to tell anyone when the diner owner drove her home, but Mitchell Warner had stopped by. He'd checked over her ankle and wrapped it in an Ace bandage. He'd taken Lucky home with him, so she didn't have to worry about getting up to let the dog out.

Dr. Warner showed up again a few minutes ago, bringing a coffee cake fresh out of his wife's oven. Karlyn assured him she would keep off the ankle until tonight's dinner party. He assured her that he and Resa would swing by to pick her up so she wouldn't have to drive.

She sat with her laptop open, trying to make sense of her notes on Roy. She finally gave up and closed the file as her cell rang. Caller ID informed her that her agent was on the line.

"Hi, Alicia. Do you have a question about the outline I emailed you? I know it was shorter than usual."

Karlyn habitually stuck to a lengthy, detailed synopsis for each novel, but this time it ran less than ten pages. She assumed Alicia wanted some info filled in before she gave Karlyn her feedback.

"You are a genius, darling. I don't know who's more excited about this book, Candi or me. I love that you have even more twists than you normally do. And the pace is lightning quick. Writing that screenplay has certainly tightened up your fiction writing. This may be a first, but I don't have a single suggestion or change for you before you begin."

"Wait. You said *no* changes? Excuse me, is this Alicia Lindon, my agent, who is usually full of advice? Either someone has stolen her phone, or Alicia's had a breakdown and gone off the deep end. If word gets out that you had no editorial comments, your career will be in ruins."

"Very funny, Karlyn. I have more to talk about than this Matt proposal, but first I want to know how fast you can write it. I think the studio would be interested in this as a movie. It would translate better to screen than some of your previous work."

"I agree. I did have a movie running through my head as I wrote the outline. I don't want to sound over-confident, but I think I could have a first draft in six to eight weeks. With rewrites, maybe three months before you see it finished."

"That's exactly what I wanted to hear. The reason I asked is that Zev Bruner called. He raved about the screenplay you and Chris wrote. And he was even more excited that you found this unknown, Dakota Smith, to play Matt."

"You saw the pictures. This guy is simply gorgeous. Rugged, calm, and talented to the max."

"I agree. Zev thinks he'll be a major star. He's inked Dakota to a three-deal picture as Matt—if you agree for any more novels to be turned into movies—but he also wants him to do something different. He doesn't want him typecast as Matt. He'd like to put him in another film between Matt outings to show Dakota's depth."

"I'm not following. How does this involve me?"

"Zev wants you and Chris to come up with an original treatment for Dakota. Something totally away from action/adventure. He said the sky's the limit. Big budget or small. Your choice of genre. I've already talked to Chris's agent to see if he's willing. He said Chris couldn't wait to work with you again, especially since Scorsese has decided to put his project on the back burner for now. This would give you the opportunity to create something fresh between the two of you."

"Working with Chris on another screenplay for Dakota would be a dream come true. In fact, I'll see him and Warren tonight at my mother's dinner party. They're in town for the weekend. We'd already planned to get together and run through some ideas. Now that we'll have Dakota in mind, that will help us narrow the field. Did Zev give you any idea on the timeline?"

Alicia laughed. "It's Zev, darling. He wants it done a month before yesterday. All Hollywood producers are rush-rush. Realistically, if you had a solid screenplay in six months, the timing would be perfect. Dakota would have finished filming his first starring role as Matt. That would give him a short break while pre-production went on for the new film."

"And editing and post-production would be happening on the Matt piece. That way they could scout the locations needed, have the wardrobe meetings, and begin casting the new film. Wow. That's a lot to take in."

Karlyn paused a moment. "Oh, shit! You want me to write my new Matt book *and* this screenplay at the same time? That's insane! Not to mention Logan and I are getting married next weekend. You're still coming, I hope."

Her agent chuckled. "I wouldn't miss it. Oh, Karlyn, you're golden now. You yourself said this Matt book would move quickly. Maybe you and Chris can come up with the storyline this weekend for the screenplay. Chris could take a first pass at it while you write your novel. It's doable. I have faith in you, darling."

Her phone beeped. She glanced and saw the low battery signal flashing. Great, her phone charger was upstairs. She better wrap up their conversation before the juice ran out.

"Okay, I'll talk this over with Chris. Brainstorm. See what we come up with. I'll get back to you first thing Monday morning with what we've decided."

"That sounds lovely. Kisses to Logan. See you in person next Friday."

Karlyn hung up and set her cell back on the coffee table. She wondered what she might be getting herself into, but a part of her was thrilled to have several irons in the fire. She adored Chris. She appreciated Zev Bruner's organization and drive. She always worked best when under pressure.

A loud pounding disturbed her thoughts. She removed the ice bag from her bum ankle and hobbled to the door.

Brad waited on the porch. "I think your doorbell's still on the fritz." He handed her a cane. "I ran into Doc Warner. He said you'd sprained your ankle. I had this sitting in my closet. Thought it might come in handy."

She saw her mother's car pull up at the curb and waved.

Brad looked over his shoulder. "Looks like you'll be in good hands with Martha. Stay off the ankle. You don't want to limp at the wedding next week."

"I plan to park myself on the sofa and write all day. Then go to Mother's dinner party tonight. Would you like to come?"

He flashed a smile. "Thanks for the invite, but I've got tickets to the Braves tonight. An old friend from college came to Atlanta on business. I'm actually cutting out of work early to meet him for dinner and the game."

Martha Campbell stepped onto the porch. "Hello, Brad."

"Good morning, Martha. Sorry, I've got to run. I just dropped a cane off for Karlyn to use the next couple of days. Get better, Karlyn."

Karlyn tested the cane as her mother came through the door. She liked the support it gave her. "I've got coffee cake if you're in the mood."

"A small piece will do it for me. Nelda's promised something rich and decadent for dessert tonight."

Her mother stayed a few minutes and then made sure Karlyn was settled on the sofa with her laptop and ice bag before she left.

Karlyn thought of everything on her plate and decided the Roy book would have to go on hold indefinitely. Matt and Dakota called her muse instead. She opened her laptop up and began her new Matt Collins book.

∼

"MARTHA, IT WAS A WONDERFUL DINNER," Mitchell Warner told the group. "But I've got a six-thirty tee time in the morning. Resa and I need to head home and get some shut eye. Karlyn, are you ready to go?"

Before she could answer, Chris spoke up. "Warren and I can run Karlyn home. I want to talk shop with her for a few minutes."

Warren sighed. "I thought buying our weekend getaway place in Walton Springs would mean plenty of good food and company. With no thoughts of work." He smiled at Nelda. "You must come to Atlanta and cater something for us, love. Those chicken and dumplings were to die for."

Karlyn laughed. "And I don't think any of us had trouble finding room for the double chocolate brownies."

Chris brought her purse and cane. She hugged her mother, Nelda, Marge, and Anne goodbye, while Resa told her to call if she needed anything before Logan got back in town tomorrow night.

Karlyn got her first glimpse of the new SUV Chris purchased the week before. "I really like this. It makes me think I need to turn in my rental and buy something similar."

Especially if we have children. Thoughts of car seats and carpooling made her smile.

"If we're going to spend some weekends at our new lake house, we needed something with a lot of room," Warren explained. "My Porsche and Chris's BMW convertible aren't practical."

Chris pulled out of her mother's driveway and headed east.

"I think Anne monopolized the two of you tonight," Karlyn told the pair. "We barely had a chance to talk."

"She has some fabulous ideas on how to furnish the cottage," Warren said. "And she's gotten in some pieces at the antique store that we're looking at tomorrow."

Chris chimed in, "That's your department, Warren. Buy whatever you want for the new house. Tomorrow morning, Karlyn and I need to work up a treatment for Dakota's second film." He looked in the rearview mirror. "What are you thinking, Karlyn? Anything stand out?"

"I toyed with a few ideas this afternoon. Romantic comedy with mistaken identity seemed like a fun twist. Something like *While You Were Sleeping*."

"What about a period piece?" Warren asked. "Dakota looks like a cowboy. He's from a cowboy kind of state. Why not do something western?"

"Definitely no," Chris disagreed. "Westerns are usually action-driven. Since Dakota's turn as Matt is full of physical sequences, we need to steer clear from that if we're going to broaden Dakota's appeal." He paused. "Dystopian's hot now."

"No way," she said. "I don't know much about it. It's really not my cup of tea. And with having to turn out a new Matt book while I'm working on this screenplay, I don't have time to immerse myself in the genre and do research for it."

"Then let's stick with romantic comedy. Dakota's got a wicked sense of humor. I'd like to see that come to life on screen." Chris turned into her driveway. "Is nine too early to start?"

"Not at all," she said. "I already have a coffee cake Resa baked. I'll have the coffee on, so both of you come for breakfast."

"Great. I'm hoping we can firm up our idea and knock out a short outline." Chris looked at Warren.

"I'd also like us to hike around the lake some. See our property." He turned to Karlyn. "Marge assured me we have a dock area, so we're thinking about buying a cigarette boat."

"Sounds good." Karlyn eased from the car. Chris jumped out from the driver's seat and took her arm to help her walk up the front steps. She unlocked the door and punched in the alarm code. He kissed her cheek. She waved to Warren and watched them pull out.

She closed and locked the door and decided to gather her laptop from the den before heading upstairs. She didn't want to have some terrific idea for either Matt or Dakota and have to manage coming back down the stairs for her computer. As she crossed the foyer, she remembered she hadn't set the alarm.

Karlyn backtracked toward the front door and the alarm keypad. A knock sounded at the door. Karlyn bet Chris already had an idea and had returned to put a bug in her ear to sleep on. She put her laptop on the entryway table and eased over to the door, happy that the cane gave her some relief. She threw the deadbolt and opened the door, ready to tease Chris, and found Brad Patterson standing on the porch instead.

39

"I've been eating here since I was transferred to Atlanta," Bill Rutherford told Logan as they entered the crowded Italian eatery.

A round-faced gentlemen in his late fifties greeted them, kissing Bill on both cheeks. "Mr. Bill, we have missed you."

"Long hours with this Rainbow Killer case, Pietro. How's Carmelita?"

Pietro kissed his fingers. "My angel is gone to Savannah for a week."

"The grandbaby finally arrived?"

"Yes. She's a beauty." The *maître d'* showed the men a picture of a chubby-cheeked baby with a headful of dark hair. They raved over his good looks, and then Pietro showed them to a corner table.

"I'll bring the wine. You want the usual? And your friend?"

Logan shrugged. "I'll have whatever he's having, food and drink."

"Then I bring bread and wine first. Don't talk no business. You need to relax."

Logan eased back against the black vinyl booth. It had been a long day, crammed full of exchanging information and tossing about theories. A glass of wine would help take the edge off the tension coiled in his body.

Pietro brought an overflowing breadbasket and wine bottle to the table. He uncorked it and admonished them to let it breathe for a few minutes.

As he left, Rutherford looked at him. "What are your career goals, Logan?"

"Considering I've just run for public office and now serve as the police chief of Walton Springs, I think I've done pretty well for myself. Let me get some time in on that job, and then I'll get back to you."

"Don't you miss the challenge of the job you did in Atlanta? Homicide squad at your age? Clearance rate of over eighty percent?"

He frowned. "Why are you asking, Bill?"

"Because I think you should come to work for the bureau." He waved away Logan's protest. "You have a fine mind. You see connections others miss. You—"

"Then why can't I catch Roy?"

"Hell, we have some of the best minds working on Roy. He's eluded us all. Still, you picked up on the break in the colors. It was subtle. Not much difference between indigo and violet. But I believe you're on to something."

"That's one misstep on Roy's part, Bill. It doesn't mean that'll be his downfall. It could mean something. It could mean nothing. He might be playing us. Wanting us to go off in some wild direction. Or more likely? We haven't discovered the indigo-painted body yet." He paused and decided to come clean. "Frankly, I don't want or need to work for the FBI."

"Is it your upcoming marriage? That holding you back?"

"No," Logan said slowly, choosing his words carefully because he liked Bill Rutherford. "I like working and living in the Springs. Small town America is the backbone of this country. I want to raise a family there. With the bureau, I'd be stationed in some far-off place which would switch every couple of years if my evaluations went well. Then I'd finally work myself up to a position in a major city like Chicago or L.A. I don't want to be a nomad and drag my family around the country, much less get called away on cases and be gone for weeks at a time."

He saw the wheels turning in the profiler's head. "What if we hired you as a consultant? A freelancer. You could be based in Walton Springs."

Logan shook his head firmly. "No. That would mean nonstop travel, to wherever the next killer struck. Worse, it would include climbing into the mind of some of the worst people on the planet. That's not for me, Bill. Thanks, but no thanks."

He took the bottle of wine and poured each of them a generous glass. They talked of inconsequential things until their food arrived and then dug into their lasagna and bowls of spaghetti and meatballs with gusto.

When they finished the meal, Logan returned to his car. On the spur of the moment, he decided to drive back to the Springs. He'd viewed Saturday's agenda and didn't see anything that was worth staying another night. He thought about returning to the hotel for his overnight bag.

But that meant fifteen minutes the other direction, parking and packing, then another fifteen back. The thought of touching Karlyn was a stronger lure. If he left now from this side of town, he could be home in a little more than half an hour.

He punched in Rick's number and got his voicemail. "Hey, roomie. I'm heading back to the Springs. Would you throw my stuff in my bag and bring it with you? Nothing in there I can't live without for a day or two. Thanks, buddy."

Logan fiddled with the radio. Nothing but commercials, so he turned it off. He thought about telling Brad how someone named Nixon had run the workshop. His partner would get a kick out of that. Brad would have to come up with some new trivia that he hadn't shared. Logan already had absorbed that Tricky Dick was a cursing, poker-playing Quaker who played a mean piano. And that Nixon's daughter had married Ike's grandson.

Maybe if he could land a spot on *Who Wants to be a Millionaire* and have Brad as his lifeline, he might win enough to do a complete kitchen renovation.

As long as the category was presidents.

Presidents . . .

It hit him like a blinding light.

The pattern. Roy's pattern. His victims all shared a name with that of a United States president. So simple. So easy. And yet so hard to detect when law enforcement factored in the usual parameters—gender, ethnicity, occupation, religion.

Logan wheeled off at the next exit and pulled onto the side of the road. He grabbed his phone and Googled *Presidents*. Clicked on the Wikipedia list that came up.

"Washington, Adams, Jefferson, Madison, Mon—" He froze. "That's the pattern."

Cyndee Washington, the Asian hooker, was first. Then architect Jerry Adams. Claudia Jefferson. Jorge Madison and Clyde Monroe. Not only was Roy killing people who shared a surname with a president—but he was doing it in chronological order.

He mentally ran through the first seven victims in the Rainbow Killing spree. Number six had been Jared Quincy. The sixth president was John Quincy Adams. A clever but subtle twist.

He continued down the list. Victim Eleven had been Beth Marie Sizemore. Once again, a slight variation. No President Sizemore had ever been sworn into office.

But Beth Marie's maiden name had been Polk.

Logan stared at the list on his phone. The skip in sequence stood out. After Mario Taylor, Roy should've followed with indigo and a Pierce. Instead, he offed a painted Bucky Buchanan in violet.

Why hadn't they already found the indigo body? It wasn't like Roy to kill a victim who wouldn't be discovered within twenty-four hours. Or if Roy had deliberately skipped Pierce for a reason, what was it?

"Oh, God!"

He dropped his phone. Frantically grabbed for it. Went to his favorites and listened to the ringing. "Pick up. *Pick up!*" He waited a moment. Shit! Voicemail.

Logan let the greeting play and then let his police training kick in. It even surprised him how calm he sounded.

"Karlyn, call me when you get this. I know you were going to your mom's tonight, so I'll try you there."

He quickly scrolled and found Martha's number as his stomach twisted in knots. "Hi, Martha, it's Logan. Karlyn wasn't answering her cell. I thought I'd try her at your place to see if she's still there."

"No, Logan. She left not too long ago with Chris and Warren when your parents left. Mitchell's playing golf early tomorrow, so things broke up a little early. It's just us old ladies left, sipping wine and gossiping."

"Thanks. I'll try her on her cell again. Maybe she was in the shower and missed my call."

"Did you know she sprained her ankle while she was out jogging yesterday?"

"No. She didn't tell me." Because she wouldn't have wanted me to worry. Skip out of the conference. Come home to her.

"I think it was starting to bother her some. Poor dear, I'm sure she took some aspirin and planned to go straight to bed. She may have turned off her phone in order to get some rest. She and Chris are working on something tomorrow for Dakota Smith."

Logan's hand tightened on the phone. "Thanks anyway, Martha. See you when I get home." He hung up and redialed Karlyn's cell. Again, her voicemail came on.

All he could see was their marriage license application filled out, ready for them to submit this week. With her birth certificate as proof of identity.

Stating her name as Karlyn Pierce Campbell.

Karlyn was Roy's next victim.

And the Rainbow Killer had waited for Logan to leave town.

He jerked the car in gear and slammed his foot to the floorboard.

40

"Brad? What are you doing here? You're supposed to be in Atlanta."

"I got to feeling guilty. With Logan out of town and you with a bum ankle, I was afraid you might need something. I met my friend for dinner and headed back to the Springs. I even texted Logan and told him I'd come sleep on your couch tonight."

She lifted the cane. "You've already left me in good hands. The cane's been a lifesaver. There's no need for you to stay over."

"Don't make me beg, Karlyn. I already promised Logan I'd come play nursemaid. He seemed relieved —especially with Roy still out there. I don't want to go back on my word."

She shrugged. "Okay. Looks like the cops are ganging up on me."

Karlyn ushered him inside and locked the door, arming the alarm.

"Can I get you anything? Dr. Brad would be happy to prescribe a glass of medicinal wine for your ankle." He winked.

She laughed. "No. I've already had two tonight at

my mother's and will probably have trouble sleeping because of it."

He thought a moment. "How about I make you a cup of tea? You have any chamomile? That always helps me sleep."

"I do. But only if you'll join me in a cup. Then I think I'll hit the sack. Chris is coming over early tomorrow. We've got a lot of work to do."

"Okay. Go park yourself and elevate that ankle. I'll make the tea."

She limped back into the den and used the cane to ease onto the sofa, resting it next to her. She glanced over and saw her cell still sitting on the table. She hadn't thought to charge it when she finished talking with Alicia because she'd been distracted by the charming Matt Collins. She hoped Logan hadn't been trying to reach her on it. They hadn't bothered putting in a landline yet since they both used their cells so much.

Karlyn slipped the phone into her pocket so she'd have it when she went upstairs for the night. The charger was next to the bed. She could plug it in and call Logan to wish him sweet dreams.

And maybe talk a little dirty. The thought made her smile.

Brad joined her a few minutes later, walking slowly as he balanced two cups and saucers. "I didn't take time to find a kettle and boil the water. Hope you don't mind your teabag dropped into microwaved water." He rested both saucers on the coffee table. "Do you mind if I pick your brain for a few minutes while you drink your tea?"

"Sure." She leaned over and picked up her cup and took a sip, burning her tongue. "Whoa. Too hot. I need to let it cool some." She returned the cup to the table. "What's on your mind?"

He sat. "I was thinking about . . . well, I've actually started . . . a book. Or tried to start one."

"I'm intrigued. What's it about?"

He looked sheepish. "The presidents. What else? You know how I'm fascinated by them."

"Uh, I hadn't noticed," she deadpanned.

He laughed. "Okay. I'm obsessed. I believe they were simply ordinary men who rose to the occasion. Or at least most of them did. Fuckin' Fillmore will never earn my respect. But they were Average Joes. I want the public to relate to them as they would a friend or somebody they know.

"Think about it. How many people have gotten a speeding ticket before? Lots, right? Well, Grant got arrested for speeding while he was driving a horse and buggy in D.C. Had to pay a twenty-dollar fine, and that was plenty hefty back then. And Harding loved to play poker. Who doesn't like to do that? He once lost all the White House china when he bet it on a losing card hand." He gave her a sly look. "You do *not* want to know what Florence Harding had to say when she found out."

"You're kidding. I never knew that. It's funny you're mentioning this now because I said the same thing to Logan. That you should write a children's book about the presidents."

"I think kids would find the presidents more relatable if they knew tidbits like that. Hence, a book." He paused. "I was wondering—if I paid you for your time —would you help me out? Maybe in structuring it. Or reading it and making a few editorial suggestions?" He shook his head. "No, you're too busy. I shouldn't even ask. You've got lots of projects going, I'll bet."

"Actually, I do. I'm in the middle of writing another Matt Collins. I literally started it today. Plus, Chris and I have contracted for an original screenplay due in six months." Karlyn saw the disappointment in his eyes. "What I can do is hook you up with my agency. They have two people who represent non-fiction clients, and one has experience in children's literature. I think they'd like your angle."

"You would?" He broke out in a boyish grin. "Oh, Karlyn, that would be great." He waited a beat. "Speaking of non-fiction. You didn't mention working on your book about the Rainbow Killer."

"That's on hold. Indefinitely. You know I've done some research on killers for other books. But with all the balls I'm juggling now, those are firm contracts with deadlines. A book about Roy would be on spec. I don't have time now to pursue it. I'm hoping at least some of the research I did on serial killers and sociopaths will come in handy in some future novel, though."

He smiled. "I'm sure your Matt Collins fans will be happy that you're sticking to what you do best." He reached for his teacup. "Let's drink to that."

Karlyn picked up her cup and toasted his. "To Matt."

Brad's cell went off. He frowned as he looked at it. "Work. I've gotta take this. It's a CI. He's a little jumpy now. I'll be right back. Go ahead. Don't wait on me. Drink your tea. I won't be long."

~

LOGAN RAN his lights and siren as he raced toward home. He refused to imagine life without Karlyn. She was his world. They would build a life together.

They'd put roots down by purchasing the old Kinyon place and would raise a family.

She *had* to be okay. They *would* grow old together. He had to have faith because if he didn't, the despair he felt would swallow him whole.

He dialed the only person he trusted to keep Karlyn safe until he arrived in the Springs. Brad answered on the fourth ring.

"Where are you now?"

Brad laughed. "For once on a Friday night, I'm in the Springs. Driving home from the diner. How's the—"

"Shut up. I need a favor. I don't know who he is, but I figured out Roy's pattern."

"*What* pattern? There *is* no pattern. *That's* the pattern. That's the beauty of this monster. It's made him uncatchable."

"No, listen. It's the presidents."

"Presidents? What the hell are you talking about, Logan?"

"The presidents. Their names. Roy is killing people in the order the presidents were elected. Washington, Adams, Jeffer—"

"-son, Madison, Monroe. You're right!"

"He's coupled the chronological order with the order of the colors in the rainbow."

"Pretty damn brilliant of Roy. Sorry," Brad apologized. "Sounds like I admire the guy. I'm just pissed I didn't pick up on it. Me, of all people. It was staring us in the face. Do you know who Roy's next vic is? I heard about the Buchanan murder on the news. Wait a minute. It could be Artie Lincoln, the drama teacher. No, what about that Lincoln in dispatch they hired. Todd? Tim?"

"Karlyn. Karlyn's his next target."

"What? No. The next president would be Lincoln. Lincoln followed that asshole Buchanan. Not Campbell."

"It's her *middle* name. Pierce. Spelled like Franklin Pierce. Roy skipped from Fillmore to Buchanan."

"But . . . that doesn't make sense. Why would he break his pattern now?"

"I don't know," Logan said in frustration. All I know is that he skipped the name and the color. Bucky Buchanan's shade was violet. Not indigo."

"I still don't get it. Why Karlyn? Most of the killings have happened in Atlanta or other cities. Roy would have dozens of Pierces to choose from there. Finding out Karlyn's middle name would be a long shot."

"I don't care!" Logan yelled. "Get over there. Now. For me. For Karlyn. Keep her safe until I get there."

Brad chuckled. "Buddy, I'm pulling up in front of your house now. Believe me. I know how important she is to you."

And then Logan's gut and brain connected. No one knew presidents like Brad Patterson. A man who worked in law enforcement. Who'd be able to stage a clean crime scene that held no clues.

Brad was Roy.

41

K arlyn took a sip of the chamomile. Her tongue was still tender after scalding it a few minutes earlier. She really didn't want to drink anything this late, knowing if she did, she'd have to get up during the night to hit the bathroom. With her swollen ankle and dealing with the cane, it didn't seem worth it.

She didn't want to hurt Brad's feelings, though. He seemed proud that he was taking such good care of her for Logan. She smiled, ready to see her man again. He'd be happy to learn that she'd decided to drop the idea of working on a book about Roy G. Biv.

It did bother her that she hadn't solved the pattern of the Rainbow Killer. Not that law enforcement experts had, but she did this for a living, thinking about killers and their victims. Roy's seemingly aimless killings had to have some kind of connection. He was too clever to be that random as he killed.

Karlyn thought it sweet that Brad wanted kids to make a connection with the presidents. She thought about how he could organize his book to make it accessible to younger readers. Maybe he could group the presidents by their home states. Or by eras. Maybe sort them by their occupations. Since he was in the beginning stage, he could probably write each profile chronologically and then slide the stories into whatever slots he created as his theme.

She wondered if he could even . . .

Oh, God.

She froze. Everything became crystal clear, in the blink of an eye.

Cyndee Washington. Jerry Adams. Claudia Jefferson.

It had been staring her in the face the entire time.

Roy G. Biv selected his vics by their last names. Surnames that corresponded to the chronological order of the US presidents. She quickly ran through the list of those murdered. It all made perfect sense.

And the pit of her stomach went ice cold.

Karlyn Pierce Campbell.

She was next.

Panic flooded her, like an adrenaline rush. She knew without a doubt that the Rainbow Killer would come for her. Her mouth grew dry as sandpaper. A trembling overtook her limbs. She gripped the handle of the cane until she thought it might snap.

Then a moment of clarity cut through the maelstrom.

She'd already admitted the Rainbow Killer to her home.

Roy G. Biv had eluded capture because he knew crime scenes. Processing. Profiling. Procedures.

And presidents.

Everything she'd researched about serial killers, be they sociopaths or psychopaths, began taking form. Not as a character she'd created in a novel.

But in the form of Brad Patterson.

He had the expertise. No real attachments to anyone. Charm. Intelligence.

Karlyn had no doubt tonight he would strike here —tonight—especially with Logan out of the picture.

Immediately, her eyes focused on the teacup. She figured he'd put a sedative or possibly Rohypnol in it. She took a cleansing breath, willing herself to remain calm. Physically, she would never be able to flee with her bum ankle. She needed to mentally outsmart him.

Instinctively, she went into writer mode, playing out quick choices in her mind. She liked to plan a scene out but let the characters' dialogue and actions form organically. Tonight, in this moment, she knew the scenario—a killer stalked his supposedly clueless victim. She would have to fly by the seat of her pants and let it play out.

And hopefully survive the encounter.

She had a choice—either dump her tea and pretend to act drugged—or switch cups with him.

Karlyn heard Roy coming her way.

And made her choice.

She yawned as he entered the den. "Sorry. I'm getting a little sleepy." She watched his eyes drop to her empty cup. "The tea finally cooled off. It was delicious. Thanks for going to the effort of making it. I'm sure I'll sleep better because of it."

He sat next to her and picked up his own cup, draining it.

"Sorry that took so long. My CI needed talking off the ledge. He has a tendency to be paranoid. I give him a little TLC to boost his spirits." He laughed. "And promised him fifty bucks when I see him tomorrow."

She studied him. "You know, you'd probably be a great resource for me. Logan doesn't like to talk shop, but I'll bet you have some good stories I might be able to use. I promise I would change names and places and circumstances—if you'd talk off the record with me."

He looked pleased. "Sure. Anytime."

She twisted a lock of hair in her finger. "I'm toying with a new outline for a standalone. About a serial killer." She smiled. "Don't want to waste the background research I've already done on Roy. I'm trying to decide on his pattern."

Karlyn yawned again. "Sorry. This idea is a little rough, but at the beginning of the book, he's about to complete a cycle of murders. Maybe killing people alphabetically. Andrea, Barbara, Cathy, etc. The book would open with Zoe, the last of the women to find herself on his table. She was an investigative journalist who hunted him—only to become the hunted."

The light that sparked in his eyes gave her goose bumps. "Intriguing concept."

"Zoe plays on his ego, telling him he's too smart and will never be caught. But she knows with the end of the A-to-Z cycle that he'll need a new challenge. She begs him to spare her. She's a writer and promises to create a new challenge. If he'll let her live."

"Hmmm. What does she come up with?"

Karlyn laughed. "Who knows? It's early brainstorming floating around in my head." She paused, pretending to think. "Maybe . . . maybe he could continue the alphabet murders, but this time he cranks it up a notch. He kills a pair in each state, starting with Alabama and a couple named Albert and Alice."

He frowned. "Too simple. Besides, he wouldn't be able to hit every letter. There are no Q states. No B or Z, either."

She pretended confusion. "So? Why would that matter?"

He laughed. "Serial killers are meticulous creatures, Karlyn. Skipping letters wouldn't appeal to him."

She smiled and pointed a finger at him. "That's

what I mean. See, you can help me. If I run something by you." She stopped, letting her eyelids droop a moment. She took a deep breath and pretended to force her eyes open. "Okay, let's factor in age. Or maybe couples by anniversary. He could kill a couple married for one year, then two, then three, and so on."

She watched him consider it. "What about starting with a wedding night dual murder of the bride and groom and then progressing from there?"

The thought sickened her, knowing he was probably considering her pitch as his next crime spree, but Karlyn pushed on.

"No. I really want him to be brilliant. I need a pattern even harder to pick up on. How about Oscar winners? He could use the first or last names of Best Actor and Actress winners. Start with the first pair of winners and move forward."

He reflected on her idea a long moment. "That's clever. It might be fun to try to find a Denzel. Or a Meryl."

In that moment, watching Brad Patterson's face, he didn't even seem to be the man she'd come to know. It was as if learning he was Roy made him look completely different to her.

"Or how about the most popular birth name by year? Find the most popular boy and girl baby names of that year and kill a pair born in that year with those names." She paused. "I could take this a lot of different directions. But knowing I'd have you to brainstorm with? That would be invaluable."

Karlyn watched his eyes go glassy for a moment. He struggled to focus. He raised his brows and rotated his head around.

"I'm thinking about calling it *Illusions of Death*," she said. "You know, something that seems real—but isn't. A killer who portrays himself one way to the world. When he's actually totally different inside."

He looked at her funny, his head cocked to one side. Then she saw the dawning realization on his face.

"You know." His words slurred slightly. He closed his eyes and swallowed, sitting, not moving. Finally, he opened them. "You're right. The face we show to the world . . . is different from who we really are. The nice nurse you sit next to in church? She's a drunk. That fireman . . ." His voice trailed off, and he stared into space, his eyes unfocused.

He shook his head back and forth, trying to stay alert. "Was always good . . . guy. Take extra shift. But beat . . . wife. All the time."

He reached up and slapped himself hard, trying to stay lucid. "Seth Berger? Demons . . . run deep. Hides with . . . drugs." He gave her a sloppy grin. "I'm his . . . dealer."

He reached out and latched onto her wrist, showing unexpected strength, despite the drugged tea. Her other hand tightened on the cane. She readied herself to swing it at his head.

Suddenly, the front door burst open. The alarm screamed. Logan appeared in the foyer, his gun drawn. He raced to her and pried Brad's fingers from her wrist, shoving him away. "Don't touch her," he snarled.

Brad fell to the floor. He grunted.

A dreamy look clouded his eyes. "So smart. You . . . know. You . . . I . . . drank. Huh. I'm . . . Roy." He giggled. "Also. Cars—"

His head dropped to the side. Whatever he'd put in her tea had taken full effect. Switching their mugs had been the right move.

She shivered uncontrollably as Logan rolled Brad

over and cuffed him. He pushed aside Brad's jacket and pulled out the gun and pocketed it.

Then he came to her. Wrapped her in his arms. Safe. Safe. She was safe. She'd always be safe with him. The man she loved.

"Did he hurt you?"

Her knees went weak at the sound of his voice, husky next to her ear. Her fiancé's voice. In a week, her husband's voice. A wave of pure love washed through her, comforting her. The tremors stopped.

"Logan." Raw emotion left her speechless. But no words were necessary between them.

His mouth came down on hers. In hunger. In possession.

But most of all, in love.

EPILOGUE

Logan held the journal in his hands, ready to add it to the evidence box that would be picked up by the FBI tomorrow. Bill Rutherford insisted Logan read through it and summarize his findings. He would also testify at the trial, but that was far down the road. He stared at the thick, leather-bound volume, wondering why Brad Patterson had become a killer.

From reading it, he gleaned that Brad's parents were rarely around, using their money to travel while allowing others to raise their only child. He perfected his twisted art first in solitude, torturing animals and starting fires. In his teens, he graduated to new thrills, raping and killing hitchhikers he picked up, both male and female.

He murdered his parents on one of the rare occasions the couple returned home, covering his crime with a fire. Brad inherited their fortune in the process. He legally changed his name and with his newfound wealth pursued what he called his *specimens*.

He killed individuals before coming up with the idea of theme killings. He wrote how he believed children had a purer spirit than adults. That made their kill of greater value. The pain it caused their parents was an entertaining byproduct.

Brad, always a computer whiz, bragged in his writings about hacking into major metropolitan police departments' computers. He read files and learned how not to get caught. He created a character he named Carson Miller and committed a series of kidnappings and murders involving children of public officials.

When Logan came to this section of the journal, he had to force himself to keep reading. Even what he wrote of Alex and Ashley. Brad meticulously listed every child taken, including where their remains had been discarded. The pages written by a killer would allow the parents of two of the missing children to finally have closure after all these years.

Where Brad had gotten the idea to become a detective hadn't been recorded. With his hacking skills, he easily devised a suitable background and resume that landed him a job in Walton Springs. Whether he came to the town on purpose to partner with Logan remained unclear. He enjoyed his cover of being a small-town detective. It provided him a sense of security as he continued ramping up his kills. He was ready to allow his Carson Miller persona to claim ownership of the Rainbow Killings when the nickname Roy G. Biv came to light. He ran with it.

Logan sealed the journal in a bag and made a note regarding the chain of evidence before he placed it in the cardboard box and set it on the round table in the corner of his office. He turned out the lights and locked the door, ready to leave the ugliness behind.

As he exited the station, he saw Karlyn perched on the hood of his car. A slight breeze blew her blonde hair back from her face. He went to her and enfolded her in his arms. Warmth. Safety. Love.

He gave his wife of three days a long kiss, deep and satisfying, relishing the life they would create together. He looked down at her. "You know, I'm the luckiest guy in the world."

She beamed at him. "You are now."

Logan frowned. "Why now?"

Karlyn grinned. "Not only do you have me. And a wonderful old house. A terrific job. Fabulous friends and family."

"And a fantastic dog," he added to her list.

"That, too. But," she paused and bit her bottom lip. "You also have—*we* have—a baby on the way. I'm pregnant. We're going to be parents."

A weight he hadn't realized that was pinning him down lifted, floating away like a feather on the wind. He would be a father again. With the woman who'd brought him more joy and happiness than anyone deserved in a lifetime.

Logan kissed the mother of his child-to-be and dreamed of what the future might hold.

ALSO BY ALEXA ASTON

Discouraging the Duke
Deflecting the Duke
Disrupting the Duke
Delighting the Duke
Destiny with a Duke

DUKES OF DISTINCTION:

Duke of Renown
Duke of Charm
Duke of Disrepute
Duke of Arrogance
Duke of Honor

MEDIEVAL RUNAWAY WIVES:

Song of the Heart
A Promise of Tomorrow
Destined for Love

SOLDIERS AND SOULMATES:

To Heal an Earl
To Tame a Rogue
To Trust a Duke
To Save a Love
To Win a Widow

THE ST. CLAIRS:

Devoted to the Duke
Midnight with the Marquess
Embracing the Earl
Defending the Duke

Suddenly a St. Clair

ABOUT THE AUTHOR

A native Texan and former history teacher, award-winning and internationally bestselling author Alexa Aston lives with her husband in a Dallas suburb, where she eats her fair share of dark chocolate and plots out stories while she walks every morning. She enjoys travel, sports, and binge-watching—and never misses an episode of *Survivor*.

Alexa brings her characters to life in steamy historicals, contemporary romances, and romantic suspense novels that resonate with passion, intensity, and heart.

KEEP UP WITH ALEXA
Visit her website
Newsletter Sign-Up

MORE WAYS TO CONNECT WITH ALEXA